THE JOY OF DEPRESSION
BY
LAURA SLEEP

Chapter 1

Tess rolls over and comes to with a start. There wasn't enough bed for that roll. As she clutches the duvet and shuffles her way back in to the middle of the bed she realises that the material feels different to usual. When she's safely back in the centre she opens her eyes and is greeted by a tasteful display of beiges, browns and creams. It's like waking up in a biscuit tin. Tess groans. So all her good intentions were for nothing. The plan was to have one glass of wine, then switch to soft drinks and be home by 11, ready to get up and make the most of a Sunday rather than drifting through the day, punctuating it with naps, and then getting in a massive strop during *Dancing on Ice* because it's Monday the next day and the weekend is over. Instead (she'll need this confirming) she got shit-faced and ended up in Daisy and Simon's spare room for the umpteenth time. Still, at least the frequency of these visits means she has a toothbrush here, something which, given the taste in her mouth, she needs to use sooner rather than later.

She drags herself out of bed and puts on her skirt from the night before. She leaves the XL t-shirt she's been sleeping in (which she'll have to wash and return to Simon) on and goes to the bathroom to do some damage limitation. It's not a pretty sight. But once the eyeliner is pushed back up to where it's vaguely meant to be, her teeth are cleaned and her hair is scragged back in to a ponytail she looks almost human. A human dressed like an escapee from Bedlam. But at least the t-shirt, which is enormous on her, hides the fact that she's not wearing, and has no intention of putting on, a bra.

"Tea?"
"See this is why you don't live on your own!" Tess exclaims as she meets Simon coming out of the kitchen "Thanks, lovely. Just what I need".

She takes the tea and follows him through to the living room, where he passes a cup of tea to Daisy and settles himself back on the sofa next to her; Tess takes up residence in the armchair. Beige of course. It is some consolation that both Daisy and Simon look as rough as she feels.

"Why is it that quiet nights down the pub can descend so easily?" Simon asks.

"Debit cards and night buses", Tess replies. "Without them the evening would have ended much sooner. Why is it no matter how drunk I am I can always remember my pin number?"

"It was the shots that killed us", agrees Simon. "I would have been fine if it wasn't for them."

"Were you sick?" Tess asks.

"Nearly, there was a dicey moment, when I…" Simon breaks off and looks at Daisy who has gone a peculiar colour and is breathing in a circular way indicating she is either going to vomit or is about to play a lively number on a didgeridoo. "Perhaps we need to change the subject" he ends.

"What are you up to for the rest of the day?" Tess asks.

A small moan escapes from Daisy and she places one pyjama-clad hand over her eyes.

"We're going to my parents" Simon says. "For a full roast lunch, my brother's kids will be there and we have to go on the M25 for an hour."

This is too much for Daisy and she rushes off to the bathroom. Tess smugly sips her tea content in the knowledge that all she has to do is get herself home and die. She's already planning her diet for the day, there's nothing in the cupboards, as usual, so she'll have to stop on the way home. Salt and vinegar crisps are a must. Diet coke, obviously. And bread. Matt ate all of hers last time he stayed. What is it about boys and bread? On her own she goes through a loaf every couple of months, she has to keep it in the freezer to avoid wastage. However if she gets up 10 minutes later than Matt, he's got a slice in his mouth and two in the toaster. A crisp sandwich, she decides. That's what she needs. Just the idea of it makes her feel better.

Daisy returns. Her hair tied back and a glass of water in her hand.

"That actually helped quite a lot," she says, rubbing her stomach absent-mindedly. "Good night though wasn't it? Tilly was on good form."

"She's been on really good form lately. I think Stuart is good for her.

She's less... tense." Tess says. "It's almost like she's relaxed a bit, less anxious."

"He's not her usual type though," Simon throws this thought in to the air. This is not a new conversation. It's one they've had many times before. Never with Tilly obviously. Tilly is wonderful, she's dynamic, stunning, terrifying, exciting, slightly impulsive and, let's face it, hard work and has always dated men who match her. Male models, entrepreneurs, business men and on one occasion, a spy (not a very good one given they knew all about it). Stuart is...well Stuart is nice. They're not too sure what he does, they lost track during the explanation, something to do with shipping? Possibly moving containers around the world. Tess tried to take an interest but gave up, she can maintain a conversation with him about work, she doesn't need to care more than that. He seems to be more preoccupied than most with traffic and roads, perhaps it has something to do with that.

"Perhaps that's what she needed", Daisy adopts her usual role in the conversation. "None of those relationships worked so perhaps she needs a Stuart."

This conversation comes around approximately once a week. Normally after contact with Tilly. They are all still coming to terms with the new version of her. She's had somewhat of a Damascene conversion, from the original wild child, constantly needing bailing out and full of stories involving narcotics, celebrities and areas of London the others had only heard about to something approaching ...well... Daisy. Settled, content, enjoys a night out but overall a solid and responsible citizen. All seemingly thanks to a man called Stuart whose number she found written on her arm one morning. Tess, as ever, remains floating between the two. Enjoying both the domesticity of Daisy's life (especially as she doesn't have to do anything to maintain this) and the spontaneous, devil may care of Tilly's previous life.

Eventually Tess peels herself off the sofa and heads home. Daisy and Simon save her the walk and drop her off en route. Daisy's head hangs out of the window the whole way there. As predicted Tess achieves little. She potters, she reads, she naps, she considers ringing people, she decides she can't be bothered. Matt texts a simple question mark. She texts back a cross. They need to have a conversation, she thinks.

Their relationship is easy but he seriously needs to step it up a tad. She smiles as she flicks through her Facebook, Tilly and Daisy both suffering, some people at work have clearly had great weekends, some people have posted cryptic messages which scream both 'look at me' and 'I'm not going to actually tell you what's wrong'. She refuses to add to the myriad of 'oh Hun, what's up? Hope everything is OK" messages on their wall. Instead she makes mental notes to surreptitiously stalk their statuses for a bit. Then like a sensible and mature adult she irons a top for work the next day, quickly shoves the hoover round and is in bed with *The Big Bang Theory* lulling her to sleep by 10-30. All in all a good weekend. Unbeknownst to Tess this is the last time she will feel fully at ease with herself for quite some time.

Chapter 2

When work is going well, work is work. Sometimes it can almost be enjoyable, if you get on with the people you work with then you are essentially spending time with friends. If you don't then you are in for 8 hours of hell a day. Tess is firmly in the middle of this scale. She knows she's not saving lives or shaping the future of tomorrow. She's in PR. Keeping people in and out of the press as they so desire. As a general rule, those that can do, and those that can't want to be in the papers. She gets on best with those who have genuine talent: the actors, the presenters, those who went in to a job and got the unexpected side effect of fame and have had to take on someone to help them with it. She finds those who have done it the other way round tiresome. They wanted the fame, hired the gang and now need to find something to do. At the moment they are occupying themselves by not wearing pants.

Her team were, on the whole, lovely. Obviously there were good days and there were bad days and Tess knew exactly when these were – because she controlled Arrabella's diary. Technically, she was assistant public relations executive. Inevitably under Arrabella this had become assistant to the public relations executive. Years of working hard, making good career moves and connections had culminated in a well aimed shot to the foot and she was now effectively a well paid PA to a lunatic.

She knew that she should care more and start caring more soon. She'd come out of university and worked hard to make a mark in PR. She'd worked for free and waitressed all evening, she'd put in the overtime. When this job came up she'd campaigned to get it knowing she'd leave the comfortable job doing the PR of a small group of museums. When she heard she'd been successful Tess had been thrilled. Finally she was where she was meant to be. Her boyfriend at the time, Harry, had taken her out and blissfully they had planned their future. A year in and she had plateaued and Harry had gone as quickly as he had arrived, Tess hadn't wanted to plan her future and in particular didn't want to plan a future with Harry. So Harry had gone but she still seemed to be in the job. She rationalised it by thinking that you can live without a boyfriend but it is a lot harder to live without a job. So she had stayed put with the intention of finding something else. But she was still there. She was going to move. She knew that. Each week she bought the Guardian for the jobs pages and one day soon she was going to actually look at them. But she was fine. She earned enough, the people were nice. Dealing with Arrabella took up more of her day than she would like, but her job, her actual job rather than the one Arrabella made her do, was interesting. She just didn't get a chance to do it very often. To be frank it was a relief to go home and not have to worry about the phone ringing. Or to hear someone in the office report a "crisis" and know full well that she wouldn't have to be the one to deal with it. She got all the vicarious thrill out of there being a drama and none of the responsibility. She was sure that one day it would begin to bother her but for now it was nice not caring. She was a member of the masses. One of the 90% who went to work for the cash rather than for any higher calling. Tess was beginning to look at this as her paid version of a gap year. She kept setting herself deadlines as to when she would start to look for new work but this deadline had moved four times already and she had stopped setting new targets.

Tilly had told her that she was "too comfortable". But what was wrong with that? Surely an aim in everyone's life is to be 'comfortable'. Why is it only in the world of work that it is seen as a bad thing? Tess often thought about suggesting to people in happy and comfortable marriages that they really should leave and be in a relationship that is more difficult and challenging. She'd suggested this theory to Will one night in the pub. With his usual annoying logic, he'd pointed out that it wasn't that she shouldn't be comfortable it was that she was capable of more and wasn't fulfilling her potential. She admitted that he had a point but still didn't quite get round to applying for the account manager job at a rival firm that he had told her about.

Sometimes a night out with Will was a bit like a night out with her school report. Annoyingly though she did care what he thought about her and his comments were beginning to make her feel a bit uneasy. Nina, her other ally at work, was rapidly shooting up the ranks too and her every success made Tess question what exactly she was doing. She felt that the job had already served its purpose by bringing Will and Nina in to her life. Although *Harrison, Richardson and Taylor* liked to pride itself on being an informal company where everyone was one big happily family, in reality it was much like any other company. You made friends with the people you liked and tolerated the rest. She'd instantly clicked with Will and Nina and was happy to rub along with the rest. On her first day Uta, who had shown her around, had introduced everyone according to the company style. Therefore Tess only got everyone's first names and a bizarre in-joke at which she smiled politely. Whilst this was appreciated and helped put her at ease she couldn't help thinking that a chart with everyone's job titles and position would have been slightly more useful. Especially after she asked the head of corporate mergers to grab her a coffee whilst she was out.

Luckily this had in a strange way worked in her favour. A couple of weeks after the coffee incident, Uta (who had made it her business to know everything about everyone and make sure everyone knew she knew) perched on the corner of Tess' desk and asked if Tess knew that the man she had been bantering back and forth with was actually Will Hastings. Rising star and head of *Harrison, Richardson and Taylor*'s European operations.

Her stuttered attempt at an apology and explanation to Will had caused him untold amusement. In truth he had found Tess' attitude refreshing. He was slightly sick of being seen as the wunderkind and the arse licking that went with it. It also got a rise out of Arrabella which pleased him enormously. However he did point out to Tess that whilst it was fine to mess with Uta's head (which Tess did in the form of an entirely fictional domestic and social life which played to Uta's love of gossip, the fact that Tess couldn't keep track of the lies she told merely added to the fun) it probably wasn't a good idea to piss Arrabella off.

Sadly this warning was too little too late. Arrabella found Tess flippant, irreverent and too clever by half. She disliked the way she had a joke for everyone yet dealt with Arrabella with little more than a raised eyebrow. Something Arrabella, who had spent years in the mirror trying to perfect that move, couldn't do. She bitterly resented Tess' easy friendship with Will and her kinship with Nina. She also knew that Tess was more than capable of doing her job.

Tess' opinion of Arrabella was more succinct: Arrabella was a bitch.

Still, Tess wanted a quiet life. So she toned down some of her behaviour or at least didn't tell Will about it. It didn't serve any purpose for him to know what every time Arrabella annoyed her Tess shredded a random page of her filofax and had secretly been filling Arrabella's special tin of herbal, Chinese tea with a combination of Tesco value loose tea and All Bran for about six months. She also made more of an effort to be nice. So every morning when she got off the bus she headed to Starbucks and ordered her own coffee (venti black Americano) and picked up one for Arrabella (a mocha choca extra whipped cream filth). A coffee that she wouldn't be reimbursed for on the fiction that they took it in turns to buy coffee. Tess had stopped keeping track a long time ago. As predicted, this morning, the coffee is greeted with no more than a grunt and a request for sugar. Tess fishes the sachets she picked up out of her pocket and hands them to Arrabella, who snatches them, making Tess wobble and throw scalding hot coffee over her hand. Clearly Arrabella didn't have a good weekend and now the office is going to suffer for it.

The upside of the strop was that Tess was able to get a lot done without interruptions. This week is all about working towards the arrival of THE AMERICANS (capitals very much needed). Tess had lost count of how many emails she had received about this visit. She'd only been cc'd of course but the entire company was on red alert. It was the PR equivalent of a papal visit. She fully expected the American boss to drive through the corridors in a pope-mobile whilst they all stood and received his blessing. Tess' role in their arrival is minimal but her part in ensuring that Arrabella doesn't go bananas is enormous.

It leads to a tense working atmosphere. The preparations also mean that Will isn't in the office very much and he is generally the only person who can control Arrabella. By the time Wednesday rolls around the tension is such that cigarette breaks with Nina (Nina smokes, Tess watches and enjoys the time away from her desk) are not enough. She calls Matt and arranges to meet him that night.

Matt and Tess have a simple relationship, They are friends. Friends who spend a lot of time together and occasionally, when neither is in a couple or actively pursuing someone, extend their friendship in to dubious territory. They are not, they are both keen to stress, in a "relationship". Tilly has a hunch which will forever remain unconfirmed. Daisy, bless her, would be utterly unable to grasp it and would have a breakdown so she is left to futilely comment on what a lovely couple they would make if only Tess would give Matt a chance.

Tess will not give Matt a chance. Matt doesn't want a chance. Tess doesn't want Matt. Matt doesn't want Tess. They do however both very much enjoy the arrangement. Best mates with benefits. It's lasted about 4 years now. Waxing and waning depending on the relationship status of them both.

However a stressful week at work, Americans arriving in a matter of days and Tess needs to get rid of some tension. Matt is happy to oblige and the rest of the week passes far more pleasantly.

Chapter 3

There's something up. Tess can feel it. Tilly never normally bothers to organise any kind of social event. Tess or Daisy does it. Well to be perfectly honest Daisy does it and occasionally Tess feels guilty and sends an email. So the very fact that Tilly has sent an invitation asking people round for dinner means there's something in the air. The fact that Tess has woken up to three texts messages from Tilly reminding her about tonight and asking her if she has remembered confirms that this is no ordinary dinner. To be on the safe side Tess actually uses sponges and brushes to put on her make up, rather than her usual 'smearing' technique. She also goes to the trouble of wearing jeans and a fancy top when usually for a night in with the couples she'll wear some horrendous combination of jogging bottoms and freebie work t-shirts. She has a feeling there are going to be photos taken tonight and she doesn't want to be preserved for eternity toasting the happy couple in a 'Hott!' (the latest boy band they are trying to promote) t-shirt.

Tilly has also refused to meet for lunch, claiming she needs to prep for the dinner party. This definitely means there is an announcement. And hopefully a sizeable dinner. It's quite sweet really. Tess has no illusions that people are in the slightest bit interested in what she gets up to and also has no ability to keep secrets therefore everything is told in real time to whoever she happens to be speaking to. If it is of interest she assumes it will be passed on to anyone who cares saving her the job. Daisy meanwhile got all her news out of the way within about six months when she was twenty-one and hasn't made any changes since.

Given that she's gone to the effort of actually wearing outside clothes and she's not needed at Tilly's till seven she meets Will for a late afternoon drink. The pub is like a reverse Tardis. Empty on the inside and spilling out on to the pavement. Londoners are desperately trying to lap up the final rays of the September sunshine. Will and Tess sit on the same side of the pub table so they are both in full glare of the diluted sun.

"It's not been a bad summer, has it", Will says. Taking a mouthful of his beer.

"Compared to the last couple of years I think we could mark it down as a heat wave", replies Tess, "ooh this is nice, try a bit. "

She offers her fruits of the forest cider to Will and he obliging takes a gulp.

"Oh that is nice. I might have one of those next."

"I need to swap to soft after this. Bit rude to turn up to a dinner party half pissed."

"Dinner party", Will laughs. "Do people still have dinner parties?"

"Civilised people do. What do you want me to say? I'm going to my friends for tea? We're a bit past fish fingers and mash potato."

"Dinner party makes you sound like Margo from the Good Life." Will says.

"I always felt sorry for her. No sense of humour. She never quite got what was going on. And Jerry fancied Barbara. Sad thing in life to be merely tolerated and not quite sure what you're doing wrong." Tess replies.

"You are aware it was a sitcom not a documentary?" Will asked, looking longingly at a man lighting up a cigarette, he'd only recently given up and sometimes these wandering conversations with Tess required artificial stimulants. Thankfully Tess was as hypnotised by the cigarette (or rather the man holding it) and the sunshine and was temporarily distracted from the role of Penelope Keith in a forty year old sitcom.

"Would you like me to get you an ice cube? You could dribble it down your front." Will asked

"Eh?"

"The way you're staring at that guy and pushing your chest out; you're about five minutes away from being in a Robert Palmer video."

"Led Zeppelin?"

Will groans. "Addicted to Love. The girls with the guitars and red lipstick"

"Oh piss off. Anyway he's not interested. Look he's gone inside." This is as close to Tess will come to an admission of letching. "Shame, I was enjoying the view. Probably got a girlfriend"

"He probably thinks you're with me."

"Hmmmmm", Tess murmurs, then lets Will's comment hover between them for a while before she changes the subject. Will and Tess' relationship is the great unspoken topic. Will fancies Tess. A lot. Whilst fully aware of this fact Tess refuses to acknowledge it, working on the principal that if it is ignored it will go away. Will knows that Tess knows but isn't quite ready to be rejected to his face so they continue the slightly painful (for those around them) dance of Will living in constant hope and Tess living in constant denial.

Not that Will is a monster. Far from it. As he is fond of reminding Tess someone once mistook him for Ryan Reynolds when they were in a nightclub in Shoreditch. Tess is equally fond of reminding Will that that was the same night that she failed to recognise herself in a mirror. Perhaps once upon a time they could have got together. It's just that the window of opportunity has been missed. When Tess met Will it was at the interview for her job. Although he is now not technically her boss it was sometime before the subject could be raised and by then they had (for Tess) moved in to friends territory. For Will the fire and hope still burn. He tried to point out to Tess that no would think anything of an office romance between the two of them as no one would assume she got anything out of it. As soon as the words 'No one's going to think you slept your way to the middle are they?' left his mouth he knew it was a mistake but it was too late to take it back. Mainly because Tess had got out of the cab whilst it was temporarily stopped in traffic and headed off down High Holborn. Numerous Starbucks and wispa bars later he was forgiven and the topic had never come up again.

"So I'm guessing engagement." Tess says. Steering the conversation back to Tilly and the dinner party.
"They're buying a house," counters Will.
"In this market? In London? They're not secret millionaires. Besides look at the evidence. Intimate dinner party to announce it to those closest. Tilly's been on lock down to avoid a news leakage. Oh and I bet she's asked you what you're up to Friday or Saturday."
Will begrudgingly admitted he had.
"Point proven, next weekend there will be engagement drinks. Drinks you will be buying, my friend, as you are going to lose."

It was a pointless argument. Not only did it not matter, it was also circular. Until Tilly told them, if indeed there was anything to tell, it all remained a work of fiction. But it kept them chattering and happily bickering away until it turned chilly in the dying sun and Tess accepted Will's offered jacket to wear as he walked her to Tilly's and then carried on to his evening.

At 1am that morning Tess sent Will a text.

"I was right. Act surprised".

Chapter 4

From the minute Tilly had opened the door Tess knew it was a night like no other. Tilly was practically glowing. She had a quality which was almost ethereal. The last time Tess had seen such a glow was on her sister minutes after she had given birth. A look that seemed to say 'I have fulfilled my purpose in life'. Tess was greeted with a glass of wine and she went through to the living room where Daisy and Simon sat with crudités, drinks and looks of expectation.

As always with Tilly the story was told in real time with excessive detail. She had had an awful day at work and had been venting to Stuart, all she wanted to do was go home and slump in front of the telly with packet of digestives and a gin and tonic. Instead she had been greeted by Stuart in a Tuxedo. A line of rose petals led the way to the bathroom where she was greeted by candles, a bottle of champagne and a bubble bath. There by a dimly lit avocado bathroom suite (they rented) Stuart asked her to be his wife. After the announcement Daisy practically came in her pants and flung herself on Tilly, Simon shook Stuart's hand and Tess waited for someone to be free so she could offer her congratulations and silently wondered what had possessed Stuart to propose in such a bloody awful and clichéd way. Still she supposed it had worked. When she prised Daisy off her and finally got to hug Tilly, Tess had never seen her friend so happy.

The rest of the evening was taken up by wedding talk. Dates were flung around, plans were made. Eyebrows were raised, mainly by Simon and Tess. As Daisy pointed out on the way home every one gets a little carried away when they first get engaged and sooner rather than later Stuart and Tilly would realise that getting married in the woods on Christmas Eve was not the most practical of plans.

As Tess took her make up off that night she suddenly realised that she and Daisy had just assumed they were going to be bridesmaids and hadn't actually been asked. They'd both been Daisy's and Tess hadn't even questioned that they might be passed over in favour of a younger female relative or childhood friend. Tess didn't really care either way. It would be nice to be involved and obviously she'd want to support Tilly but she didn't need a fancy dress to do it. She was happy to be a plain clothed bridesmaid. She doubted that Daisy would feel the same way though and was just spending some time having fictional conversations in her head where she broke the news to Daisy that she might not be getting a free dress, when her phone bleeped and she saw that Tilly had text both her and Daisy asking them for lunch the next day. Clearly this was to be the Bridesmaid announcement. 'How dull', thought Tess, 'such a missed opportunity for an America's Next Top Model style contest'.

However a whole new style of competition was launched at lunch the next day. That of "World's Most Ridiculous Wedding". Offers of bridesmaid-ship were proffered and accepted and after the screeches and squeals of excitement died down Tilly outlined her plans. It wasn't so much that she was hitting the ground running, it was more that hitting the ground would slow down the juggernaut that was Tilly's wedding and would simply lose valuable time. The wedding was to be this year.

Daisy's mouth dropped open. Hers had been basic and even that had taken nearly a year of planning. Before she could stop herself she gasped "Are you pregnant?"

As Tess said to Nina the following day in the kitchen at work, that comment meant she was instantly elevated to best bridesmaid. It was quickly established that this was not a shotgun wedding but was a way of making sure it wouldn't become one. Stuart and Tilly were broody and they were traditional. Well Stuart was and as Tilly said, so was she now. Not known for conservative approach to life pre-Stuart she was now a signed up member of the old fashioned club.

"I'm even going to change my name!" Tilly exclaimed. "Me! I never thought I'd do that. If my nineteen year old self could see me now she'd be disgusted. But I don't care! Stuart wants to do it all traditionally . He's old fashioned like that."
Tess swallows the drink that she's been threatening to spit all over the table. "Not that old fashioned. You already live together and you slept together the first night you met, when if I remember rightly you

weren't sure of his name as you were off your face on coke."

"Ecstasy" Tilly murmurs her correction. "He doesn't know that by the way; don't mention it in your speech."

"I have to give a speech? I thought my role was purely decorative?"

"I'd like one of you two to give one."

Tess and Daisy point at each other and then fall silent. Hoping that this idea would go the same way as many of the others Tilly has had and never materialise. If Tilly went through with all the things she'd thought were a good idea over the years then they'd be friends with a vegan marathon runner who guerrilla gardened at the weekends instead of a person they actually wanted to be around.

When it came to weddings Tess had always been pleased that she got to do the girl side of things. Mainly because it involved a lot of drinking and mucking around in spas. The boys had to do all the dull things like organise cars and if you were an usher you had to give your outfit back. Girls got to keep theirs on the fiction that they would wear it again. The excitement of Tilly's announcement doesn't wear off and emails are pinged back and forth all week (with Daisy joining in belatedly in the evenings) and plans are made for a dress shopping expedition.

Although the emails concentrate on big pouffy dresses and fairytale romances they actually ground Tess during the week. The Americans arrive and the whole company loses the plot. Even Will snaps at her when she asks why he is excited when he is the 'Head of European Markets'. Her geography is shit but even she can work out he won't be part of the discussions. Arrabella meanwhile has lost it. Although she is a pain in the arse Arrabella is also aware of her shortcomings. She knows she's not up to these meetings but that she will be expected to attend them and contribute. So Tess and Nina spend the week coaching her. It is utterly unappreciated but they both hope it will make their lives easier. Tess because she won't have to deal with the fall out and Nina because she needs this deal to go well and doesn't want Arrabella mucking it up.

"She's quite thick isn't she?" Nina says, when they let Arrabella take a toilet break and duck out of their coaching.

"Not so much thick as 'differently abled'." Tess corrects. "She's actually quite good at percentages. Too much time in designer clothing sales I think."

"She'd better not screw this up."

"Why do you care so much?"

"Do you know how much business this is going to bring in? The second their plane lands tomorrow the clock is ticking. We need this deal. And I am not going to let some highly strung Sloane ranger screw it up."

"Easy tiger. You're like one of those odd bods on *'The Apprentice'*. Are you going to start holding your phone at a right angle to your face when you make calls? "

"I think the stress is getting to me. It's like a pressure cooker in our office. Gordon had a meeting yesterday to coach us all. Three people cried."

"Oh is that what was up with Arrabella? I thought she'd locked herself out of her blackberry again."

Eventually the great day arrives and the office empties out as everyone heads to board room A. Tess, who's not invited, occupies herself by putting all of Arrabella's files back on the shelf. In a difficult moment Arrabella had melodramatically thrown them on the floor. Tess then settles down and ploughs through all of the work that she hadn't been able to do the rest of the week. Both work for Arrabella and work of her own involving her own clients. She also emails Tilly to finalise plans for the weekend. Drinks tonight and dresses tomorrow. Or as Tess chooses to look at it – free flowing champagne.

She's heavily involved in the life of Shannon Jackson, page three girl turned anti-sunbed campaigner, when her phone rings. Having worked in near silence for most of the morning she is startled. Even more so when it's Arrabella on the other end of the phone.

"Tess we need you up here. Can you come up to the boardroom?"

Tess is surprised. Perhaps Will and Nina have put a word in for her. Perhaps those coaching sessions with Arrabella have paid off and she's going to get a chance to shine. She straightens her skirt, reapplies her lipstick and takes her notebook and pen up to the boardroom.

She's back five minutes later. They had wanted coffee. Her notebook had come in handy as all the Americans had wanted insanely complicated combinations of caffeine involving 'half and half' and 'equal'. She makes the lot with sugar and watered down whole milk and then returns to her desk.

"Bring on the weekend.," she types to Tilly.

Chapter 5

The last time Tess had seen so many net petticoats she'd been seven and in a badly dressed production of *Oliver!* starring as a woman who had her purse snatched. The sight of so much synthetic material had gone some way to distract the parents from the sight of a nine year old Bill Sykes being hanged from the P.E ropes but it wasn't an experience she was keen to repeat.

"What is it," she hissed to Tilly from the corner of her mouth "about getting married that makes women want to dress up as shepherdesses?"

"Shhhhh, they'll hear you," Tilly whispered, shooting a look at the matronly figures behind the counter who had so far referred to their stock as 'gowns', suggested Tilly wear 'structured' 'under things' and had made them put on white cotton gloves before they touch anything.

"What kind of thing do you want me to look for?" Tess asked loudly, which had the unfortunate effect of summoning over a Matron who could have benefited from a bit of 'structuring herself'.

"What we have to remember is that they look so different on than they do on the hanger." Matron said.

"Which is why you should try on as many as you can!" exclaimed Daisy, who bustled over, her left arm already sagging under the weight of dresses which she had chosen. Tilly flinched and threw a pained glance at Tess who studiously avoided her gaze. Tilly could deal with this one on her own.

"What did we say on the way here Daisy?" Tilly asked in a manner normally used when talking a child down from a tree. "No bling, no shiny things and no dress that weighs more than I do."

"You'll find that the heavier the dress then the more embellishment it will be able to take." This could have been either the Matron or Daisy. Neither was listening. Tess decided to accept that she was out of her depth here and instead accepted a glass of sparkling elderflower, drinks of colour being unwelcome in the ethnically cleansed shop, and sat back to enjoy Tilly's impromptu fashion show. She was looking forward to seeing someone who prides themselves on being put together and fashionable at all times wearing dresses that Barbara Cartland would have thought of as too froo froo.

But, to Tess and Tilly's surprise, it didn't happen. Everything looked good. Which made two dilemmas. Tilly was unable to choose a wedding dress and Tess began to rethink her wardrobe so that everything she wore involved white lace and a veil. Daisy meanwhile looked in paradise. She was wearing a veil and looking through a rail of dresses that were her size and not Tilly's.

"Wishing you could do it all again Dais?" Tess asked

"Hmmmm?" Daisy was in a world of her own. "Oh yeah, I mean, it would certainly be different. For one thing I wouldn't do my own hair".
Tess didn't look at her. They hadn't spoken about Daisy's wedding hair for the last seven years and she had no intention of starting now.
"It was just so different. I mean we'd only been out of university six weeks. Ridiculous now you think about it"
"Worked out OK in the end though didn't it?" Tess prompted, she knew her role in the what I would have changed about my wedding day conversation, they'd started the day Daisy had got back from honeymoon.
"Yeah" Daisy said half-heartedly then pulled herself together "Yes, yes of course it did but it makes you think. What were we thinking getting married at twenty-one? Why didn't anyone stop us?"
"Why would we have stopped you? You were, are, love's young dream. We were thrilled and it made us feel grown up without the commitment. Everything OK? I mean you and Simon...."

Tess trailed off she wasn't sure where the conversation was going and was certain that this wasn't the place to have it, it was like planning a bar mitzvah at a hog roast. Luckily she wasn't too hungover. The engagement drinks the night before had been relatively tame. There'd been a few toasts, tasteful crudités going round on trays and had all been over by 10-30. They must be growing up. When Daisy and Simon got engaged they'd had drinks in the Union and Tess had fallen asleep in a nightclub. She tried to remember how Simon and Daisy seemed last night. She couldn't really recall. She'd been preoccupied as Matt had been at the drinks and Tess had tried to adopt a style of behaviour which would suggest there was nothing between them. She hadn't been successful but it was fun to watch her try. Will had also been there. Tess had wanted him to settle his bet by keeping her in drinks but, in another move that signposted them getting older, the drinks were free, all paid for by the happy couple. It was a sure sign they were growing up. Especially as none of them had taken advantage and over indulged.

Daisy still hadn't responded to Tess' ineffectual questioning but thankfully, just as she was about to try again, the curtain of a changing room was flung back and there stood Tilly in a Tudor style dress encompassing Queen Anne sleeves which grazed the floor. She bowed at the girls then did a courtly-style dance to where they stood.

"My lieges" she said, then turned to Tess and whispered "I look like a dick, can we get away from Hinge and Bracket and shop somewhere normal?"
"As soon as you get changed"

Tilly danced back to the changing room revealing a row of bulldog clips holding the excess material of the wedding dress up and down her back. She fought off a matron who was alarmingly keen to help her undress and instead beckoned to Tess and Daisy. Daisy sprinted off towards the dressing room, desperate to touch the wedding dresses and equally as keen to cut her conversation with Tess short.

Three wedding shops later and the girls sank gratefully into the sofas at the café. Daisy eyed the menu whilst Tilly ordered a mint tea (pre-wedding cleanse) and Tess, with her head on the table, asked for an Americano with two extra shots (will to live left somewhere in "You're Special Day")
"I mean it's not even a pun, they just can't use bloody apostrophes. Do we honestly expect them to be able to order a dress, get it made in the Far East and shipped over here without screwing it up? I mean what if they mistake London for Lagos? Eh? No Daisy I'm fine. What? If you want a cake then have a cake, you don't need my permission."

Daisy didn't order cake. She wasn't going to sit there like a big cow.

Munching away on cake like a big, fat, housefrau whilst the others complained about how they looked in bikinis. The last time Daisy had worn a bikini it had been on her honeymoon. She'd stood outside Boots four days after they'd got back and flipped eagerly through the packets of recently developed photographs. She'd burnt all the swimwear pictures in the barbecue they'd been given by Great Uncle Horace as a wedding present and then denied any knowledge of their existence to Simon. She didn't think she'd bother to screen photos now. She didn't worry what she looked like in front of Simon. She got more dressed up to go to work than she did for Simon. Still, at least at work it was appreciated.

"The problem is" Tilly was saying, "is that I don't know what kind of bride I am."
"Bride bride", mumbled Tess looking around for sugar, she unwrapped a sugar cube and put it in her mouth whole, the intense sweetness bringing her a welcome reprieve from the coma she was beginning to sink in to. "You're a woman not Barbie, you don't dress to a theme. You're a bride, you wear a wedding dress. What else would you be? Cowboy bride? Flamenco bride? I'm not coming if you're burlesque bride."
"No," Tilly continued. "Am I sophisticated bride, am I timeless bride? Am I fashionable bride? Am I demure bride?"
Daisy spluttered in to her latte and Tess looked studiously at the wall.
"What kind of bride were you Dais?" Tilly asked and both she and Tess turn to look at her.
"Child bride."
Oh. Now both Tess and Tilly find the wall equally fascinating. The conversation hangs in the air for a second before it too dies of embarrassment and Tess is left to come to the rescue.
"What are you ladies up to tonight?" She asked
"Dinner with some of Stuart's friends, hopefully won't be a late one, I'm knackered. God I'm old. All I want to do is get a takeaway, put my pyjamas on and watch something utterly mindless." Tilly groans, throwing her arms out in an exaggerated yawn.
"Mwahahaha," this is Tess' approximation of an evil laugh "that's exactly what I am doing. Well, substitute takeaway for toast as I don't get paid till next week and replace 'utterly mindless' with the first series of Community and you've got my night."

"Do you need to borrow some money?"

"You can come to ours if you're on your own."

The two comments fly at her simultaneously and both come with concerned looks.

"Erm thanks guys. No, I'm fine for cash thanks Tilly, it's just the last few days before payday, you know how it is."

They stare at her.

"Or not. And it wasn't a hint Daisy. You and Stuart don't need me hanging around."

"We want you to come!"

Tess is torn. How to say you don't want to go when you have just freely admitted that you have no other plans. What weirdo would turn down company and a night out over sitting on their own in an empty flat eating toast?

"Can I let you know how I feel later? Tilly's right it has been a long day" And it's so much easier to blow you out via text that it is to do it to your face.

"Of course you can, but don't sit on your own all night," Daisy's concern is slightly offset by the enormous brown milk moustache she's currently wearing. Tess licks her own top lip and motions to Daisy to do the same. The cups jump as Tilly heaves a pile of wedding magazines, the only actual purchase of the day, on to the table.

"Let's at least try and narrow it down." She says, "Fold the corner over on any page you see something you like. No colour, no glitter and no cut-outs. Go!"

Daisy and Tess mouth 'cut-outs?' at each other and set to their task.

By the time Tess arrives home all the good feelings about her evening have disappeared. What this morning had seemed indulgent and relaxing now seems sad and empty. She plonks the loaf of sourdough (her treat) on the worktop and flicks on the kettle. Whilst waiting for it to boil she taps out a text to Daisy, turning down her invitation and takes her shoes off in her usual slovenly manner. The manner her mother refers to as 'breaking the backs down'. As Tess kicks them under the kitchen table she remembers that Daisy has a shoe cupboard under the stairs and all the shoes live in a rack. Tess has an old bucket that she keeps in a cupboard and it's so overflowing with shoes that she inevitably only wears the two pairs that are on top. It's this thought that makes Tess pick the shoes up from their resting place and chuck them in the cupboard. The thought that Tilly has shoe trees that all her footwear is crucified on nightly mollifies her somewhat. There's always someone worse off than you, and in this situation, that person is Stuart.

By half past eight Tess has eaten, attempted to have a long soak in the bath and discovered that she had a twenty minute dip maximum and is now in her pyjamas watching Ant and Dec encourage Jonathan Wilkes in some impossible challenge (a career?). The night she was looking forward to all week is in fact monumentally dull. She refuses to accept that Daisy may have been right and invite herself round, so instead reads for a bit and stares at the clock until she deems it acceptable to go to bed. What is annoying is that come Monday afternoon she'll be longing for a weekend like this.

Chapter 6

"So how was the wedding dress shopping?"

It's Monday morning and Tess is watching Nina smoke, Tess will go back to the office stinking so she assumes she has achieved as much as Nina.

"Yeah it was quite fun. It's difficult to know where to start, I mean on TV they walk out in a dress, everyone wets their pants with joy and then they talk about 'the one'. Tilly either looked lovely in everything or bloody awful, there were probably about five that would look great. Up to her really. How did you know?"

"The dress? First one I tried on. Loved it. Tried on some more to get some other ideas but kept coming back to that one. Loved that dress. Loved it. Still got it actually. Picked the wrong husband but I really got the dress right."

"Wear it next time."

"I would you know. Great dress. What about you. Did you try any on?"

"No, we weren't doing bridesmaids' dresses on this trip, going to get Tilly sorted first then we'll fit in with a theme."

"No, I meant didn't you try on any wedding dresses?"

"Er no, wasn't really about me. Besides what's the point on trying on dresses that cost more than I could possibly afford for a fictional occasion? Hardly an investment buy."

"You must have thought about what you'd have though. You must have an idea in mind."

"Not really, no. I've always just assumed the nursing home will lay something on. Give me a fresh catheter and rouge my cheeks."

"Tess….."

"Nina… shall we go back in? Arrabella times me you know."

They head back up, Nina spraying herself with perfume in the mistaken belief that it masks the smell of the already stale smoke. Tess doesn't bother, using the smell of smoke on her as a reason for her being out of the office. She's going to start being more secretive with her weekend plans, she thinks, everyone in the office (with the exclusion of Arrabella) has asked her about her weekend shopping trip. She's been forced to use words like 'tulle' and 'sweetheart neckline' more times in an hour than she has in her life. All other trips will be conducted in secret she vows, Tilly must be climbing the walls, it must be all anyone is talking to her about. However it is a welcome diversion from talking about the Americans. Now the meeting is over it is dissected at every opportunity. Tess hopes they make a decision soon and put them out of their misery.

"I'm loving it!" Tilly's voice bellows down the handset so loudly that Tess flinches

"Shhhhhh, you've got a phone, you don't need to shout"

"Seriously, it's great. What's not to love? Everyone loves a bride! Anyway, that's not why I'm calling. At dinner Saturday…."

"Oh yeah, how was it? Where did you go?" Tess interrupts.

"Yeah, yeah it was good, went to some Italian in Clapham, anyway"

"Clapham! That's a bit of a schlepp!"

"No, it's fine, few stops on the Northern line, ANYWAY, there was this friend of Stuarts there, Dev?"

"Oh, was he.." Tess tries to interject but Tilly tired of not being able to make her point carries on talking over her.

"And he bought with him his friend Ralph, they were at Uni in Durham together and now Ralph's moved to London."

"Ralph?"

"Ralph"

"Like the penis in Forever?" Tess asks

Tilly laughs "He can't help his name!"

"Remember page 106?"

"You always were a filthy cow. Anyway what do you think?"

"About what?"

"Tess, about Ralph."

"What about him?"

"God you're annoying sometimes. Do you want me to set you up?"

"Er no."

"Why not?"

"Well all I know about him is that he's a friend of Stuart's friend Dev and he went to university in Durham. I'm not going to go for a drink with someone based on that. Especially when I'll be chanting 'penis, penis, penis' in my head."

"Look, he's nice, he's single, he's our age, what have you got to lose?" Tilly's not going to let this one drop.

"A pleasant evening doing something I actually want to do?"
"Sitting round Daisy's house eating pizza? You can do that any time. You're never going to meet anyone if you don't put yourself out there."
"So I don't meet anyone. Is that the worst thing in the world?"
"No, but I don't understand why you're actively avoiding it." Tilly wants this to happen.
"Are we really going to argue over this? Look if I happen to meet someone and it all works out then wonderful. But I'm not going to go on some arranged date when we both know why we're there and we've got you and Stuart encouraging us like we're two backwards children having to play together because we've got no social skills."
"That was weirdly specific. Did that happen to you?"
"Yes. Ask Daisy, it's how she arranged for me to meet you."

Tess decides to grasp the nettle. She knows something is going on with Daisy. She arranges to meet her for coffee and after a few introductory conversations she goes for it.
"So, tell me if I'm way off beam here but is there something going on with you. I felt you didn't want to say anything in front of Tilly but there's something up isn't there? You can tell me. You know I'm not going to judge."

The problem with being free and easy, and (on the whole) non-judgemental, is that people seem to take it as a challenge. Sat in front of Daisy and listening to her elucidate on what she'd been doing was pushing Tess to her non-judging limits. She was partly judging Daisy for her actions but mainly she was judging her for being an idiot.

His name was Kyle ("is he a cowboy?" asked Tess and then immediately shut up as she caught the annoyed and hurt look that flashed across Daisy's face). He was the new year 6 teacher at Daisy's school and they were working together on the school play. He was funny, he was charming, he was complimentary and more importantly... he got her (Tess had to work so hard at not rolling her eyes. There were only so many times you could get away with saying you had to look at the ceiling quickly). Their relationship was developing via email. Daisy said they were exchanging nearly 10 a day.
"You never check your emails — you said that you're in the classroom all the time!" Tess knew she shouldn't interrupt but Daisy never, ever

responded to emails.

"It's the 20th century Tess. We're allowed laptops. I just set the kids some maths."

Tess didn't think now was the time to remind Daisy of her claim that teachers worked harder than anyone else in the world, trumped only by Somalian child soldiers. Tess still had the flow chart somewhere that she and Tilly had created when they were drunk. So instead she simply said:

"It's the 21st century. Just add one to the 20 of 2014 . It doesn't matter how or when you are emailing him. It's why you are emailing him."

Apparently it was because he made her feel valued. He was married too and so he knew exactly what she was going through.

"What are you going through?"

"Just marriage stuff. You wouldn't understand."

"Try me."

"There's no way you could get it."

"Fine." Tess sat back in her chair and picked up her cup. She knew that Daisy would crack first.

She was right.

"I know you think everything is perfect and Simon and I are great. But just because Simon is your friend it doesn't mean that it's a barrel of laughs being married to him. You're just used to us being together and so is he. We're together because we're together and nothing more than that." Daisy pulled a face and avoided Tess' eyes.

"That's not true?"

"It's how I feel. Doesn't that make it true? He takes me for granted, we were too young when we got together and now it's just accepted that we are. It's the same old stuff day in day out, relentless monotony. And I'm bored. So bored. Kyle makes me realise that there's more to life. He's in the same situation and for the first time in a long time I am excited about something, I've got something to look forward to. I swear when I see I've got an email from him my heart speeds up."

"OK." Tess was going to shut this down. Daisy was too far gone with all the Mills and Boon romance and she wasn't sure how much more she could take. "I'm not going to ask you any more, but think about this Daisy and I mean this with the best will in the world. Isn't this just a crush? That you might be reading a bit too much in to it? I know it's fun and exciting but it's not real is it? It's a couple of emails with a coworker. What you and Simon have is real."

"I knew you wouldn't understand."

"I don't know what she wanted me to do." Tess complains to Nina. "Ask details, gasp and giggle at every ridiculous (and imaginary) detail. She's married and she's married to one of my friends. What was she expecting?"

"What does he look like?"

"Well he's either tall and blond or he's blond with a beard. I found his profile on Facebook but he's got his security settings right up so I can only see the two photos he alternates as his profile pictures. One is him and a mate and I don't know which one is him and the other photo is a sunset."

"A sunset, wow he must be really well travelled and like, deep." Nina is pretty scathing of Facebook and the images people project of themselves on it. "Least he's worked out how to limit what people can see. He must get some credit for that."

Both Tess and Nina were single enough to have perfected the art of Facebook stalking. Tess reckoned she could track anyone down, no matter how obscure in under twenty minutes. North Koreans and those over seventy excluded.

"I wouldn't worry about it." Nina declares. "When I was married, towards the end, I was so unhappy I wouldn't have looked at another man. The thought of voluntarily hooking up with anyone ever again." She shudders then brightens, "I soon got over that!"

"But Daisy's not like you. She's never been on her own. She wouldn't leave Simon unless she had a back up. But honestly, I don't think there is anything in it. She's just creating drama out of nothing. The novelty of being a young married has worn off. You know now that we're not actually young any more." They both grimace. "And she sees Tilly all excited and the attention she is getting and she's jealous and fancies a bit of it."

"Then why is she telling you?"

"It's not drama if nobody else knows. And swearing me to secrecy makes it more of a thing. Actually her telling me makes me more convinced there's nothing going on. If there was surely you'd keep quiet about it in case Simon found out about it."

"Unless she wants him to know."

"I don't think there's anything for him to find out. Least that's what I'm hoping."

"Are you following any of this?"

"That's what I'm saying. I'm not sure there is anything to follow."

"Not Daisy, this." Nina nods at the TV. They are watching the latest BBC4 Swedish/ Norwegian /generic Scandinavian crime drama. All office conversations were revolving around it so they were trying to upgrade their viewing habits from scripted reality TV series on ITV2. There was only so much they needed to know about Peter Andre, although now they were on series three they were fairly certain that he loved his kids.

"Not a clue. Possibly the one with the jumper has a master plan so the man who looks a bit like a black Andy Crane is suspicious or possibly in on it. Bad Hair there is simply frowning a lot. Therefore he is either deeply committed to cracking this crime or he's got piles."

Nina has picked up the remote control. "The Crystal Maze is on Challenge."

"Do it."

"So enough about Daisy's imaginary love life. What's going on with yours? Fuck me, those jumpsuits aren't flattering to the fuller thigh are they?"

"I have no love life."

"Oh that's not true. Doesn't Tilly want to set you up with someone? Plus the whole Matt situation."

"I'm not going on that date."

"Why not?"

"I don't want to. I'm fine as I am. I'm not interested in meeting someone. And Matt's fine, it's nice and easy. It is what it is. No more, no less."

"Don't you think it's stopping you from finding someone else?"

"I don't want someone. And there is no else as Matt isn't a someone."

"Oh come on."

"Why is it so hard to believe? You're single!"

"And I'd love it if someone else came along. If anyone wants to set me up then they can go for it. I know I'm fine on my own but long term I want a partner. Everyone does."

"I don't."

"You're only saying that because you think you have to. Deep down no one wants to be on their own. There's no shame in admitting you want to be with someone. Pretending you don't is merely slowing up the process of meeting someone."

"That's crap. That's just your opinion, it's like me not liking someone's boyfriend and saying that them being with them is meaning they're not going to meet someone else so should keep dating on the side. They've made a decision to be with someone and we have to accept that that is it for them. I don't want someone so people have to accept that's it for me. It's a choice, not a resignation."

The easy back and forth of a few minutes ago has passed. They turn their attention to a woman with a bubble perm trying to swing across a small channel of water on a rope. As the silence grows Nina chances it.

"There's always Will."

"No!"

"OK."

"Nina, I'm going to give you the benefit of the doubt and assume this is coming from a place of caring rather than a place of being annoying. But I'm fine. I'm not emotional stunted. I like my own company and I have great friends. Leave me be."

The subject is dropped.

Nina has never questioned her like that before. She's always been fine with the way things are. Tess is in a slight mood on the way home. She's almost tempted to call Matt but she doesn't want to prove Nina right. She doesn't need anyone. She'll deal with this on her own. Her resolve is set. See she can manage her own life. Her resolve lasts about a day and then she cracks and calls the one person she knows will tell it to her straight.

"The animals went in two by two, by two, by two."

"That's lovely Finn, can you put Mummy back on the phone... You're hilarious you know?"

Her sister is laughing as she comes back on the phone. "Oh you've got to admit that's funny. And how sweet is it? I swear I was almost in tears when he got up in Sunday school and sang it to us all."

"Ahhhh. Bless. You're just a little sap."

"Oh you'll understand when it's your turn."

"Which brings me back to my original question. Do you think I need to start dating more?"

"More would imply you're dating at all."

"Oh for fucks sake, I do alright."

"Language," Hannah corrects mildly.

"Are Finn and Jake swearing? Aren't they a bit young for the F word?" Tess flinches at slipping in to Hannah speak and saying things like the 'F word'.

"Don't be stupid. That's how I speak to Garry."

Tess is mildly surprised. Not at Hannah correcting her husband but at Garry actually having enough personality to swear.

"Well why don't you go out with this Ralph guy?" Hannah asks. "I mean you're not twenty one any more. You probably should think about the long term."

Plenty of arguments swim in to Tess' head but she knows better than to raise them with Hannah. She lives a completely different life to Tess and their relationship works better when Tess is very much in a support role to her sister.

"Did you get the text from Mum?" Tess asks.

"Yes", replied Hannah. "Who taught her text speak?"

"Well going by the text, someone who learnt it as a foreign language. It barely makes sense. "She means the 14th doesn't she?"

"Yes, I rang Dad to clarify. We'll be driving down if you want a lift. "

"Thanks, but by the time I've got all the way out to you it'll probably be quicker on the train."

"And you won't have to listen to Mr Tumble on repeat."

"You know the thought had never crossed my mind." Tess lies. "Right well, I guess I'll see you then. I don't think I am realistically going to see you before then."

"Wait, wait before you go … what do you know about excel?"

"Eh? What do you need to know?"

"Formulas and inputting and I don't know. Opening documents."

"It's fairly self explanatory, ask the dog in the corner if you get stuck. Aren't you married to an accountant?"

"Yes, well there's a bit of a difference of opinion."

"About excel? What could.. you know what, I don't think I want to know."

"I'll bore you when I see you."

"Look forward to it."

Tess knew she shouldn't time conversations with her sister merely to fill in the gap whilst she was walking to see someone else but it was always good to have an excuse to get off the phone. There was a limit to how many times she could claim that she was desperate for the loo without starting rumours about her having an irritable bowel. She waved at Matt as she hung up. He held out a coffee to her and she took it and they wandered through the park as he filled her in on his life. Here was someone who was happy in his own skin. What she thinks she likes most about him is his ability to see the bigger picture. To not get caught up in the petty stuff. She also likes that they can have incredibly in depth conversations about *Mad Men* and not judge the other.

Do relationships need defining? Tess is of the opinion that sometimes definitions do more harm than good. Of course, some are basic. Mother, Father, Sister, Brother. The slightly murkier – step-brother, half-sister, second cousin once removed. As with all language the descriptions are subjective. If you say "I went shopping with my Mother" someone may conjure up an image of a cosy day swanning around Westfield punctuated by coffee and chat. To someone else it may provoke an image of hell – recollections of teenage years spent screaming at each other through a flimsy changing room curtain in C&A. Yet the word is the same. Not that she is suggesting that the relational names are abolished. It would be ridiculous. You may as well suggest that all adjectives are banned on the grounds that they too are subjective – that the word 'very' has varying different levels of intensity for different people. Then why not do away with colours. We can never be sure of what another person is seeing when you see 'green'. But if we can accept all these differences and understand that people have different interpretations of words why when it comes to love are the fields of definitions so narrow? Sometimes Tess' wondered if too much Sex and the City had affected her brain.

Therefore Tess is fine to live in a world without definitions. To have 'friends' and to accept that not all friends are equal. Some provide comfort, some provide humour, some support. Some times you strike gold and have a friends who provides all facets in the relationship. Tess counts herself lucky that she has four or five of these. The fact that she sleeps with Matt does not change his definition as friend any more than her jogging with Nina changes her definition. Friends are friends. She's not five. She doesn't need to grade her relationships. None are better than others. They are what they are and she is lucky to have them all. They're all learning curves and she's happy to see where they lead.

She stretches out and kisses the learning curve asleep next to her. Inevitably the pleasant and friendly walk in the park descended to this. First they walked, then they walked to the pub, then they walked back to hers. She's drunk and so her thoughts aren't clear but right now this all makes perfect sense.

"Do you ever think we should go out?" she asks Matt.
Matt's head leaps off the pillow and he desperately looks around for his trousers.
"Calm down", Tess continues. "I don't want to go out with you."
"Then why would you say such things?"
Matt lies back down and melodramatically places his hand over his wildly beating heart. Tess rolls on to her side and props her head up on her hand.
"People think we're weird."
"Oh really?" He gasps. "Oh hang on, I don't care."
"Nina thinks it's really strange."
"We're not strange. We're the future."
"Are we?"
"OK." Matt can see he's not going to get any rest until this dealt with.
" Answer yes or no as quick as you can to the following questions."
"This could end badly."
"Just do it."
"Fine."
"Right, we'll start slow." Matt sits up, prepared for his quiz. Tess lies on her back and shuts her eyes. Totally prepared for the task ahead of her.
"Fine. I'm ready."
"Is your full name Tess Elizabeth Acraman?" Matt asks.
Tess' eyes instantly reopen. "No."
"Isn't it?"
"No. I'm TessA Rose Acraman." Tess clarifies.
"Well I never knew that. That's nice. Rose, I like it. And Tess is short for something. I thought you were just Tess. Anyway. Are you twenty eight years old?"
"Yes."
"Do you enjoy sleeping with me?"

Tess laughs "Yes!"

"No laughter please this is a serious business. Do you in anyway feel used, degraded or vulnerable?"

"No."

"Do I make you feel like a prostitute?"

"No."

"Do you feel you get as much from this arrangement as I do?"

"Yes."

"Do you feel like you are using me?"

"No."

"Would you like me to be your boyfriend?"

Tess shudders. "No."

"Do you want us to stop?"

"No."

"Well then I declare us fine. Apart from the slightly hurtful shudder. Oh yes I saw you Tessa. I know I look like a Greek God but I am actually human."

"I apologise."

"Thank you. Now stop worrying."

Matt lies back down and mashes his head in to the pillow, making himself comfortable. He gives Tess' hand a reassuring squeeze then gives himself up to sleep. She is mollified. It's nice to be affirmed. Lately it seems as though everyone is trying to upgrade her. She closes her eyes. Still, she thinks, it might be nice to be with someone who knows her middle name.

Chapter 7

Tess packs Arrabella off to a meeting and sighs with relief. How does someone get to a position of power and still be so helpless? Tess and Nina once concocted an elaborate scenario to explain how Arrabella keeps her job. It involved the managing director, an affair and Arrabella blackmailing him. It was all a drunken fantasy but the more time Tess spends with her the more she thinks she and Nina could be on to something. Today Arrabella had panicked that she wasn't prepared for the meeting she had with a prospective client. Tess had provided her with a biography of the 'star', examples of their work with former clients with similar backgrounds and a disgustingly sweet coffee and two muffins. Arrabella had called her an idiot because the muffin was regular blueberry not 'skinny'. Rather than argue the point that the coffee alone had over five hundred calories in it before she had added three sugars she had simply put her coat back on and gone to Starbucks to exchange them. Whilst waiting in the queue she had noticed that the skinny muffin was a mere thirty calories lighter than the normal. On her return Arrabella had grabbed the muffin and inhaled it, Tess had then escorted her to the lift coaching her on the task ahead of her. As she leant in to the lift and pressed the down button for her Tess said goodbye:

"Now remember you have lunch at two at Albertos. The table is in your name and John will meet you there. Natasha's school play is at four so we'll just see you tomorrow. Hope it all goes well."

The lift doors shut and Tess walked back to the office. Now the babysitting was over, she could actually do some work. She had clients of her own. A few low grade ones who she placed in magazines such as 'Smash!" and "Like it!" where they would tell horror stories of their cosmetic surgeries and tangled love lives.

Will grinned at her as she came back in the office.

"All OK?" he asked.

"She's on her own now for the rest of the day, if she doesn't make it in tomorrow I'll alert the police. How are you?"

"Yeah good, so did you apply?"

Tess has no idea what he is talking about.

"Apply for what? Oh that job you sent me, I didn't get round to it and I think it's closed now."

"No the closing date is tomorrow."

"I can't write an application by tomorrow. Not one good enough to get me a job anyway."

"I'll help you. We can easily get it done between us. Besides, even if you don't get it, it's still good experience."

"Of being rejected?"

Will shakes his head and smiles. "Of writing an application, of going to an interview," he lists. "You can't be Arrabella's assistant forever."

"Well technically I'm not her assistant at the moment. "

They pause, considering the child care Tess has done already today.

"OK", she admits. "I need to get away from her but it's not too bad."

"This is a great opportunity", Will insists. "Don't let it pass you by. We'll do it tonight. We can get a pizza and a bottle of wine in and do it after everyone's gone. It'll be fun."

Fun? Hardly but Tess knows when she's beaten. Besides she has nothing to lose. Even if she gets it she doesn't have to take it. She's simply keeping her options open.

"OK. Thanks Will. I appreciate it." She says, hoping he'll pay for the pizza.

"Now back to your desk. At the moment you still work here." Will replies, knowing full well he'll end up paying for the pizza.

He's probably right, Tess thinks as she heads back to her desk. She can do more, and that evening as Will carefully ekes information out of her and skilfully arranges it in answer to the application questions she realises she is capable of doing this job. The time spent running around after a lunatic has made her forget that she actually is quite talented at what she does. It's a shame that it takes some one talking her through it to remind her that she is able to do more than get coffee and babysitting a peri-menopausal harridan with childcare issues. As she presses send on the application form and gives Will a celebratory hug she realises that she is actually excited about where this could go.

Chapter 8

Despite not having lived at home for nearly ten years, there is something about going to her parents' house which makes Tess regress. Made even odder by the fact that she has never lived in the house they are in now. When Hannah was "settled" as her parents put it and when they eventually realised that Tess was never going to "settle" they upped sticks from the Surrey commuter belt and moved to her mother's native Bath. Her mother is now back in her family fold and her dad has a shed. He claims to have taken up woodwork although nothing has ever been produced to verify this. The pack of cards, radio and many, many books stored in there demonstrates that the shed mainly operates as a refuge, whilst his wife and her sister analyse every member of the women's institute at volume. More often than not he is joined by the dog. However Tess still feels enough at home to always leave room in her bag to bring back food, forgotten childhood relics and anything else she feels is missing from her flat. She's hoping for a few towels this time round.

The train journey is uneventful, she bats texts back and forward with Tilly and Daisy until she can't speak about weddings or crushes any more. Tess doesn't know what is going on with Daisy, in fact she's fairly convinced that whatever is happening is only really happening in Daisy's head but she still feels like she is being complicit in something she wants no part of. It seems that for years Daisy has loved the fact that Simon and Tess are friends. But now she is going through this she automatically assumes that Tess will be on her side. Tess is unsure why this is. Is it because they are both girls? Technically Tess is closer to Daisy but being close to her doesn't mean she automatically supports her every move and in this case she is moving closer and closer to Simon. She wants to protect him from something he is unaware of. Plus, if your wife is going to behave like this he's going to want to know that her friends aren't supporting her in it. Having never really thought of herself as having a moral compass Tess is firmly set on where she lies with this. Now she just needs to tell Daisy. Not replying to a text might not be the strongest way of getting her point across but it's a start.

As soon as the door of her parents house is opened she is set upon by a whirlwind of small arms and legs. A child hangs from each arm and the dog does excited laps around her. She abandons her bag and drags the boys through to the kitchen to greet the rest of her family. The excitement of her arrival soon wanes for her nephews and they head back out to the garden. There is of course a pot of tea on the go and she props herself up against the Aga and fills her mother in on what she's been up to. An edited, PG version of what she's been up to. Hannah and Garry sit on the battered old sofa in the corner. Garry is on particularly nauseating form and keeps asking Hannah if she is OK. "Of course she's OK", thinks Tess. "She's sat on a sofa drinking tea whilst her children terrorize my dad in the garden. It's not like she's in any danger." Eventually Garry disappears and the women are left to catch up. Hannah is surprisingly reticent to talk about her life, Tess is unsure if she actually has no news or if she is being kindly in front of the spinster sister. Thankfully their mother has never let a conversational gap go unfilled so they are soon up to date on their cousins, their aunts and uncles, their parents' neighbours, all of Bath's women's institute and her mother's friends' children who they have never met. Every so often Tess will try and catch Hannah's eye. There are some things only a sibling will understand. But Hannah sits. Perfectly still. Looking either in to her cup of tea or studying her nails with an air that suggests she's never seen them before. Tess shrugs and collapses back in to the comfortable sofa and listens to a strange story about a prolapse. Halfway through the sorry tale she begins to do her pelvic floor exercises.

When their dad staggers in looking absolutely shattered Tess is amazed to realise that she has already been there nearly an hour. The two boys bundle in behind him. Tess always feels guilty about grouping them together as the "boys" when they are so different but thanks to a small age gap, and Hannah's odd habit of dressing them alike, there is the tendency to think of them as a unit. They hurtle in to the kitchen and Garry, who is hot on their heels, cuddles them both and practically arranges them in front of Hannah and Tess who are still slumped on the sofa.
"Yes Garry," thinks Tess. "Children. Very nice." This time Hannah does catch Tess' eye but rather than a shared sisterly moment bonding over the children and the circle of life, it is a look that seems to convey annoyance. Tess is a bit thrown. Not that she doesn't agree that Garry

is a dick but it seems a bit harsh for his wife to be in on it.

Weekends have a tendency to pass quickly. Everybody knows that there are varying degrees of time. Eight hours on a plane does not pass at the same speed as eight hours on holiday. Two small boys also tend to speed up the space-time continuum. Whereas Nina and Tess can pass an entire day with no more activity planned than a trip to a coffee shop, with Finn and Jake there seems to be a constant need to do 'something'. And tipping them unsupervised in to the garden doesn't seem to be an option. So she finger paints, she reads, she is a horse, she is a human swing and eventually she is just Tess catching up with her family on a walk across the fields with the two boys running ahead yet still in sight.

Hannah remains in a strop. This is annoying for many reasons. The first being that since her parents moved West they are rarely all together as a family and it would be nice to make the most of it rather than have it slightly tainted by a grown woman acting like a teenager. Tess wished Hannah would either say what is wrong or get over it. Slumping around and insisting you're fine is just plain irritating and invites people to constantly ask if you're OK. Which triggers Hannah being annoyed because she is constantly being asked if she is OK however this doesn't prompt her to change her behaviour so people don't have to ask. It is what their mother would refer to as attention seeking. However the move seems to have triggered a personality change in their mother and she is loving the drama. Which leads to the second annoying thing. Tess' mother constantly grabbing Tess' arm and asking if she knows what is wrong with Hannah.

"No. I don't." Tess eventually responds "I spoke to her a couple of weeks ago and she was fine then."

"A couple of weeks?" Her mother is horrified "Anything could have happened. I can't believe you left it that long."

"She didn't call me either."

"She's got the boys. She can't be on the phone day and night. She needs support. Maybe she and Garry have fallen out."

"They seem fine."

"Well there's something."

"Why don't you ask her?"

"Oh I can't ask her. It's not my place to interfere."

"No, nor mine."

"Oh you could ask her. "

Tess looks at her mother. She is smiling and waving at her grandsons. She looks like a devoted grandmother. Little would anyone know that under than sensible quilted jacket beats the heart of a gossip mastermind. Fortunately Tess knows what to do. They catch Hannah up where she is walking alone and she starts a conversation about Fiona Bruce. Her mother's kryptonite. Soon Hannah is bought out of her shell and is agreeing emphatically with their mother's analysis of Fiona's hair. Their father is still sadly lost to Garry but you can't win them all.

They are halfway through pudding when Garry lays down his spoon and stage whispers to Finn and Jake "do you want to know a secret?" They cheer their agreement, they are after all five and under. Garry is encouraged by this reaction and hams up his part by continuing "shall we tell Grandma and Grandpa too?"

"Yesssss!" the boys cheer, bouncing around in their seats.

"And Auntie Tess too?"

'Oh for goodness sake Garry', thinks Tess, 'put us all out of our misery before you get the next door neighbours involved.' Thankfully it would seem that relational telepathy has skipped a generation and Jake and Finn put her thoughts in to words for her.

"Tell us, tell us." They shout.

Hannah is suspiciously quiet during all this and keeps shooting daggers at Garry. Possibly aware that he is monopolising what was a pleasant dinner by acting like a dick.

"Tell us." Oh Lord, the parents have joined in now. Perhaps it's time to start looking at care homes.

Garry looks around, ensuring he has everyone's full attention, then announces with absolute glee. "Mummy's having a baby"

"Oooooh!" the shriek of joy from their mother shatters eardrums and also acts as a diversion from everyone else's reactions. Their Father is equally as delighted but expresses it through shaking Garry's hand until it could come off. Jake is bouncing around in his chair with excitement whilst Finn clearly couldn't give a shit and isn't even attempting to hide it, such social niceties being beyond a four year old. He was probably hoping for a dog. Tess puts her arms out and he crawls on to her lap.

Hannah looks at Tess and Tess is surprised to see the start of tears in sister's eyes. Tess smiles at her and mouths 'well done'. Hannah merely shrugs and motions for Finn to come to her. He slides off Tess' lap obediently and Hannah pulls him close. Tess gets to her feet and congratulates Garry who is clearly thrilled. He has a triumphant look on his face and accepts the congratulations that are flying around with ease.

Inevitably the rest of the evening is taken up by talk of names and colours of blankets. Hannah's only a few weeks along. About a month and Tess thinks that Hannah was hoping to keep it under wraps for a wee bit longer. She hadn't announced her previous pregnancies until the three month mark. She assumes it is this that is making Hannah shoot daggers at Garry who in turn has perfected the art of not quite meeting his wife's gaze. He is also alarmingly keen that Tess travel back with them tomorrow, something which Tess is determined is not going to happen. She waves her return ticket around like a shield. The more Hannah ignores him the more persistent Garry becomes. He's a few short steps away from suggesting that Tess join them in bed that night. Tess wouldn't blame him, there's no way she would want to be in his shoes at the moment.

An uncomfortable bath time follows. Tess stays downstairs and tidies away the dinner things. She's never really seen why children's baths are seen as a spectator event. Conversely her parents can't keep away from seeing their grandsons splashing around in the warm water, playing with Tess and Hannah's old bath toys. It appears that all conversations are being conducted through the boys as Hannah is still refusing to talk to Garry and Garry is scared of Hannah. Her parents have picked up on the atmosphere and they too now address all comments either to the boys or to each other.

There is a slight shock ahead though. When two damp boys is tiny dressing gowns barrel towards her to say goodnight Tess is surprised to see Hannah behind them in the hall putting her coat on.
"Where are you off to?" Tess asks
"Just popping out for a bit. Garry's going to stay here, I've told mum and dad, I'll be back in a bit." This is the most Hannah has said in four hours.

"Where are you going? Tess asks.

There's no reply, Hannah simply turns on her heel and walks out the front door.

"Where's Mummy gone?" Jake asks, looking at Tess.

"I have absolutely no idea." Tess replies.

"Tess". Hisses Garry, who has suddenly appeared on the stairs. He looks like he has been hosing down a hippo. His shirt is see through in places and he has a towel slung over one shoulder. "Don't scare them, she'll be back soon."

Tess looks at the boys who are selecting a bedtime story from the low shelf of the bookcase and wonders how, with Garry for a father and a mother who has had just wandered off, she is getting blamed for the future emotional scarring of her nephews.

After the children are safely in bed and asleep (seemingly unscarred by their aunts actions) a pot of tea is made and the world's most pointless conversation is held. That is a discussion on where Hannah has gone and when she might be back. Apparently she told Garry and her parents that she had arranged to meet up with 'friends'. They are all politely ignoring the fact that Hannah doesn't know anyone in Bath. Or, Tess notes, has any friends. Garry calls her mobile a few times which isn't answered and then is eventually found in Hannah and Garry's bedroom. At a loss for what to do her Dad suggests they play Trivial Pursuit and they break in to (for once) equal teams. Girls vs boys. There's no way Tess is going to be on a team with Garry.

Several hours later Hannah reappears during a particularly difficult question about Phar Lap. The wedge is gratefully abandoned and all attention is fixed upon the returnee. Who doesn't want the attention and is utterly disgusted by the concern lavished upon her, merely saying

"I left a note." She then takes herself off to bed with Garry following dejectedly behind. Tess and her parents stay in the living room and keep attempting to have a conversation to cover the argument that is starting above them. Eventually they give up the pretence and simply listen. Tess is even shushed by her father at one point. Tess has a strong suspicion that if she hadn't been there then her Aunt Susan would be on speaker phone.

Not that there is much to listen to. It mainly consists of Garry hissing

"What do you want me to do?" and Hannah insisting that she doesn't want to talk about it. They eventually go quiet and the others go to bed.

On her arrival in the kitchen the next day Tess is greeted as the prodigal son. The atmosphere hangs heavy in the air and it would appear that everyone else has been up since 6-30 and is now desperate for conversation. Hannah isn't talking to anyone but the boys. Garry is over compensating by talking to everyone. But no one is talking to him for fear of upsetting Hannah. The only neutral territory is the boys and even they look slightly startled by the level of attention they are getting. Unusually her parents don't suggest Hannah and the boys going with them to their church. Possibly because it's considered bad form in the Church of England to turn up with Satan.

As soon as she possibly can Tess moots the possibility of her leaving, under the pretence that it is of the utmost importance that she get back to London as soon as possible, after all, she has to be at work in a mere twenty three hours.. No one argues with her and instead the idea is seized upon and everyone battles to be the one to give her a lift to the station. Hannah wins by virtue of being utterly terrifying and the minute she puts herself forward everyone fully supports her and thinks that it's a marvellous idea. Everyone that is except Tess who actually has to get in a car with her. Tess puts her things together (offers of food and towels are sadly not forth coming, no one is going to put this weekend down as a success) and she says her goodbyes. There are sweet hugs and soft kisses from the boys, a hug of quiet desperation from Garry (who would probably pay good money to make his escape with her), her Dad checks that she is OK for money and her mother pulls her close and whispers in her ear "see if you can get to the bottom of what's up with her."

The drive to the station is in silence. Thankfully it's not a long trip. Tess stares out the window and admires the regency architecture. If she gets the 10-20 back to Paddington she could call Nina and Will and see if they fancy doing something this afternoon. After this weekend she could do with a drink. She's slightly irritated that the weekend was ruined, these opportunities for them to be together come around so rarely. She rests her head on the window and is daydreaming when

Hannah startles her by saying:

"We should go for a drink soon."

Tess jumps then responds "Yeah, I'll need to look at my diary tomorrow at work but I should be able to get out to you one night this week or next."

"No, Garry can babysit. I'll come in to town, we'll go somewhere decent."

Tess is surprised. This never happens. She tries to see as much of Hannah as she can and can cope with but visits are always at Hannah's house, the last time they went out together was shortly before Jake was born. It's not that Hannah is being selfish; it's simply easier for Tess to come to her. No need to organise babysitters or make arrangements. Plus by the time it gets to seven pm Hannah can barely put one foot in front of the other such is her tiredness, let alone get dressed up and make it in to London. It makes far more sense for Tess to hop on a train after work. It occasionally bothers Tess but even she can see the logic in saving babysitting for occasions more exciting than seeing your sister.

"Great." She says. She's fairly certain this will never happen so she doesn't give it a lot of thought. Instead she concentrates on keeping her breakfast down. Hannah is not a natural driver and some of her manoeuvres are particularly aggressive this morning.

At the station Tess awkwardly tries to hug Hannah and she half-heartedly reciprocates. The result is more of a wrestling hold than anything close to affection. Tess slides out of the 4x4, never having worked out how to dismount gracefully from enormous cars. She hefts her bag out of the boot and walks towards the station entrance. She turns and waves as she heads up the stairs. When she gets to the platform she can still see Hannah parked in the drop off zone so she waves again. She doesn't move. She is still there as Tess' train pulls out of Bath ten minutes later.

"Hv u askd Hnh wot ws wrng?"

"Lt us no whn your bck and whn wee cn rng u"

Tess' mother has never really mastered texting. Her style is somewhere between hoodie and technophobe. Aunt Susan had mentioned 'textspeak' to her and they have now both adopted the method of removing all vowels whilst occasionally confusing things by throwing in a number. Tess finds texts asking after her m8s and if she had a gr8 time quite endearing and so doesn't want to correct her. At some point she'll introduce her parents to the concept of predictive text and blow their minds. Perhaps that will be a treat for Christmas; she thinks it will take a good few days' hot housing. Nina and Will (who are both capable of texting properly) accept the offer of an afternoon drink and Will offers to meet her from the station. Tess thinks how nice it will be to be with people who won't be in random moods. To not have to engage in complicated games of conversational chess, where she has to be three moves ahead. This thought and the gentle rhythm of the train lulls her to sleep and she wakes up as the train is pulling in to Paddington.

Chapter 9

Despite meaning to bring her lunch with her to work Tess has failed again. She starts each week with good intentions and then forgets them as she is running out of the door trying to catch her bus. Therefore she does the next best thing and accompanies Nina to Tesco. This way she can tell herself that it is just like bringing her lunch from home as she is getting it from the same place that she does her food shopping.

Tess rummages through the sandwiches on the shelf hoping that someone has put an avocado and bacon in amongst the tuna sweetcorn. She admits defeat and settles for a chicken salad and wanders over to where Nina is reading the nutritional information on the back of a pack of sushi. Tess puts the packet of salt and vinegar McCoys she is holding back on the shelf.

"Have you ever been to New York?" Nina asks.

Tess is not thrown by the non-sequitur; Nina has a tendency to leap around in conversations.

"Yeah, once. It was great. Of course I spent most of it lost. I can't work cities built on a grid. Why?"

"I might be going." Nina replies.

"Oh cool. When?"

"Not sure yet. It's all up in the air at the moment. But I want to talk to someone who knows the city. I've only been to California and I'm not sure Disneyland is a fair representation of the States."

"I'm not sure New York is either. Who are you going with? Dylan?"

Dylan is the uber-rich banker Nina was seeing. He was a wanker but he was also the only person Tess could think of that could stump up the cash for a mini break to New York.

"Oh God no. I showed you his last 'gift' didn't I?" Nina asks.

"Mmmmm." Gold plated handcuffs aren't for everyone.

"Anyway, no. It's a work thing. But keep it under your hat, Michael doesn't know."

Michael is the company's CEO. He doesn't know Tess' name so it's unlikely they would indulge in a secret trading session.

"It's not through us then?" Tess asks.

"No, look it's all very hush hush, which is why I haven't said anything. Remember when the Americans came over for that meeting about Whysfirth?"

Please, that was like asking if someone remembered childbirth.

"Yeah." Tess grunts.

"Well they liked what I had to say and they told me to keep in touch, so I did, then Brick called, don't smirk he can't help his name, and he might have something for me."

"What are they offering you?"

"Executive of Far East Operations."

"Fucking hell."

A woman with a toddler in a pushchair glares at her. Tess smiles an apology. Nina can tell Tess hasn't grasped the whole truth.

"Based in New York." Nina clarifies.

"You're moving to New York!" Tess shouts. She is grasped firmly by the arm by Nina and marched to the freezer section.

"For fuck's sake Tess, what part of keep it quiet didn't you get? It's all up in the air at the moment anyway. I'm going to fly out, talk to them and see if I like the city. I might not want to move there."

"Yeah, because no one likes New York."

Nina laughs "Well I might be the exception. Look, just keep your mouth shut until I know what I am doing. It's an amazing opportunity. We can't stay here forever."

"Why not?" Tess didn't mean to say it aloud but it's a valid question so she let's it stand.

"Well *Harrison, Richardson and Taylor* is a great launch pad and had given me some amazing opportunities but it's time to spread my wings."

"Sounds like you're reading me your resignation letter." Tess grumbles.

"I've always wanted to work abroad." she shrugs. "It was always in my career plan. You know."

No. Tess doesn't know. She's only ever campaigned to get one job and that's the one she's in. A move which didn't really work in her favour. Her career has been on ice since she started at *Harrison, Richardson and Taylor*. But the bills are paid, she's fine, she's got friends at work. Well one less now. Bollocks. Who's she going to play with now?

Nina has to rush back to the office for a meeting. Tess has no such demands on her time and so takes a slow wander back. She is totally preoccupied. Yes she'll miss Nina but she's sure they'll stay in touch and now she can go and play in New York. But she's not too keen on the light it shines on her own career. Why does everyone keep doing things? It really draws attention to the fact that Tess isn't doing anything.

Chapter 10

"It is a truth universally acknowledged that a girl (woman) who is not married and does not have a family is that way because she has thrown her all in to her career." types Matt. Instant messaging is a mixed blessing in offices everywhere. Simultaneously letting people know you are at your desk and online (if not replying to the email they have sent you) and also allowing people unlimited wittering with their friends.

"You have neither", he continues "and therefore you make people uncomfortable."

"Well." Tess replies. "Firstly, I am merely on a career break before I return to my previous greatness. Secondly, you have neither either."

"Ah yes. But I am a man. My lack of career makes me free spirited and my lack of marriage makes me a lovable rogue that women think they can change." Matt answers. Slightly smugly.

"Can't I be a charming, lovable, free spirit?" she asks.

"No. You're an under achieving, unweddable mess. Just the way it is. Sorry"

Tess laughs. This has the unfortunate affect of reminding Arrabella that she hasn't demanded something in the last ten minutes and her status might be in question.

"I'm glad you have time on your hands for fun Tess." she says loudly. "Have you confirmed my appointments for tomorrow?"

Oh Arrabella sometimes you make your own traps.

"Yep," replies Tess equally loudly. "Nails at 11 and hair at 2."

A few senior heads pop up. Tess smiles winningly at Arrabella.

"Right time for coffee then I think. Tess, would you mind?"

Bum. Tess grabs her bag and heads out the office and in to the rain.

She can only blame Nina's bombshell and the resulting career assessment for what she does next. As she carefully carries a tray of coffees along the street like the world's oldest work experience, she works her phone out of her pocket with her free hand and texts Tilly.

"Go on then. Set me up with Ralph the Penis."

Well it's easier than changing jobs.

Chapter 11

Tess had thought a Sunday night quite a strange night for a first date when Peni.. sorry, Ralph, suggested it. But she'd gone along with it as according to Tilly men want to be in control and make decisions. . Except Stuart. He does what he's told and he likes it.

They are going for cocktails followed by dinner. The incredibly awkward conversation they had had on the phone had sorted out dates, times and a meeting location. So here she is. Unusually overdressed for a Sunday night in skin-tight black jeans, strappy top with a transparent patterned shirt over the top. She's wearing heels, as despite being 5ft 8, skinny jeans and flat shoes make her feel like a golf club. So a pair of black wedges finish the look, extending her already slim legs quite nicely.

Tess stands outside the tube and subtly adjusts her top. She had found this bra at the back of the drawer and wondered why she didn't wear it more often. She could remember why now. Her boobs took this bra as a personal challenge and they devoted their time to getting free. Glancing down she notices that she has four boobs so she subtly tries to shake herself back down. Turning sideways and pulling the cups of the bra away from her she gives a little jump hoping that would rearrange her. A man waiting near-by eyes her efforts so Tess glares at him. She bets he wouldn't think twice about rearranging his bits in public. In fact he's doing it right now.

"Tess?" A voice asks.

"Yes? Hi. Ralph?" Tess replies.

"That's me!"

'I'm not sure I'd admit that' is Tess' immediate thought. 'I'm going to kill Tilly' is her second. Then the doubt kicks in. Clearly this is what people view as a result for her. This is the best she can do.

Standing in front of her was a jockey. A whipperty thin man of about 5 ft 2. A height Tilly and Stuart had described as 'average'. Tess was touching on 6ft in her heels. She looked like his carer. He also appeared to be on his way to the Sports Personality of the Year awards as he was wearing a tuxedo complete with a bow tie. Tess was beginning to panic that she was seriously under-dressed for the night ahead.

"I thought All Bar One." Ralph says.

Tess looked at him in disbelief then took the offered ladylike hand of the tiny man dressed as a magician and escorted him carefully across the road and in to the empty bar.

Matt is doubled up laughing. Tess rips the duvet from him and buries herself in it.

"Is that what I attract?" she asks. "Do people really think that is what I should be dating? Everyone else can have people they fancy but I've missed the boat so I can have 'someone'."

She had called Matt from the taxi home. Ralph, she now assumed he was called that because he was the same height as an average penis, had talked about himself in the bar. And there was a lot to say. And he said it all in the third person. Ralph was amazing at everything apparently. Had been everywhere and done everything and done it better than anyone else. Tess had stopped contributing comments after a while, Ralph clearly thought her interjections slowed down the wonderful story of Ralph and his works. So she took the sensible route and sat in silence and drank. Then later over dinner Ralph had turned his attention to her and gave her the benefit of his advice.

She drank too much.

She wasn't interested in him so clearly she had something wrong with her.

She was too tall.

She was too old to have long hair.

She shouldn't have offered to buy him a drink. It was unladylike.

Tess immediately changed her order to steak now it was clear that they weren't going dutch. Why she didn't get up and walk away was beyond her. Perhaps it was manners, perhaps it was shock. Perhaps it was being torn apart by an absolute prick that made her feel inadequate and want to stick the date out to prove him wrong. So she sat politely, thanked him for a nice evening then cried in the cab home and texted Matt asking him if he wanted to come over.

Every women's magazine in the world would tell her that validating herself through sex with Matt was the wrong thing to do but she wanted to be with someone who actually liked her.

"Aww come here." says Matt, he can see Tess' bottom lip start to wobble and she begins to rub her neck, a sure sign that tears were on the horizon. He pulls her in to a hug and kisses the top of her head as he says "He's a dick. Anyone can see that."

"I didn't even want to go!" Tess is enraged with the injustice of it all.

"I know, I know you didn't." Matt placates her. "Still it got Tilly off your back and now you can get back to normal."

"I've said I'm sorry." Tilly isn't really that contrite.

"Oh it's going to take more than that Matilda." Tess wants a full apology.

"We've all had bad dates." protests Tilly.

"Yes. But there's bad dates and then there's the real problem: Your friend thinking that a pernickety, mean little man is a good match for her friend who she actually likes."

"I'm sorry, OK?" Tilly tries to explain. "He's single and he's friends with Dev, who's lovely. I just thought, you know, you're both unattached and on the market, so what's the harm? There's not that many single guys of our age out there."

"I know! That's what I was saying." Tess exclaims.

"No, you said you were fine." Tilly spots the flaw in Tess' argument.

"But if it's lack of availability then there is an answer. We need to go online."

"NO." Tess shouts.

"YES!" Daisy claps her hands with glee.

"Oh you're joining us now are you?" Tess asks.

"Back in the land of the living?" questions Tilly.

Daisy wipes the back of her hand across her mouth, the black stains from the red wine remain lodged in her lip lines. What was meant to be a sensible night planning a hen do and helping with other wedding plans descended in to chaos when both Daisy and Tess bought two bottles of wine each with them. Daisy is now flat on her back with her legs propped against a wall claiming it's the only way to stop the room spinning and ensuring she's not sick. Tess and Tilly are slightly hardier drinkers but they are definitely worse for wear. Stuart came home an hour ago, saw the state they were in and immediately repaired to the bedroom, leaving them to it.

"Do it, do it. "Daisy chants. Delighted at the opportunity to set Tess up. This really annoys Tess for some reason and being drunk means she speaks too quickly.

"Oooh what about that guy you work with Daisy? Kyle is it? I could go out with him." Her face is the picture of innocence but her voice is knowing.

"Kyle?" Tilly perks up at the possibility of a man for Tess.

"He's married," snaps Daisy.

"Oh is he?" Tess plays dumb. "From the way you talk about him, I assumed he was single. He does flirt a lot for someone who's taken."

"Who is he? Why haven't I heard of him?" Tilly is curious.

"He's someone I work with. He's nobody." Daisy says. "Sorry. Not an option"

Tilly is oblivious to the tension and gets back to the matter in hand.

"Then online dating it is!"

"No." says Tess.

"Yes!" they both roar back at her. Daisy reaches under the sofa for the laptop whilst Tilly rummages in her bag before emerging victoriously with her credit card.

"I'll get you the first six months," she says. "A present."

"You don't have to do that," says Tess. "Don't be silly."

"I'm about to spunk twenty grand on a wedding," Tilly rationalises. "I don't think an extra ten pounds a month is really here or there."

Before Tess knows what is happening, she has a user name (the disappointingly bland Tess123) and a password. A photo of her has gone up (a decent one that Tilly has on her computer rather than one they have taken tonight) and the whole process is really out of her hands. She only has to chip in occasionally as Tilly and Daisy are content to answer most of the questions for her.

"Age range – 25 to 40?" Tilly ponders.

"30 to 45," Daisy corrects. "She likes them old."

"I do," Tess agrees. She empties the last of the wine in to her glass.

"Pets. No. Smoker. She'd prefer non-smoker, wouldn't she?"

"She'd probably take social."

Tess nods her agreement and shuts her eyes. The next thing she knows it's morning and Daisy is rammed in next to her on the sofa and Tilly has disappeared.

Chapter 12

It would seem that two days are now required to get over a hangover. Tess isn't irresponsible. She hadn't planned to get absolutely destroyed on wine the weekend before a job interview but even though she had, she had done it on a Saturday night and even through a storming hangover on the Sunday she had prepared for the interview which was scheduled for first thing Monday morning. Will had been thrilled when she'd got the interview and had offered to come over on Sunday and help her prepare but she had turned him down as she felt he had done enough and didn't want to take up any more of his time. As she sat in the all glass reception area of the fancy offices and adjusted her one and only suit (worn only for interviews) she wished she had taken him up on the offer. She wasn't ready for this. She accepted the glass of water she was offered by the helpful receptionist and immediately spilt it on her trousers. When she was called in she was confronted by six people sitting across the table from her. All of whom were better dressed, better groomed and in three cases younger than her.

"You don't know you fucked it up," Nina consoled.
"Mhamamamaahdn," Tess replies, her voice masked and garbled by the fact she is sobbing and blowing her nose at the same time.
"Do you want me to call my contact there?" Will offers.
"No," she hiccups. "I just want to forget it happened and go home and wait for the rejection letter."
All three of them are crammed in to the disabled loo on their floor. Tess is sat in the sink, Will is on the loo (lid down) and Nina is balancing precariously on one of the rails. They feel no guilt for occupying the toilet in this way. There are no disabled people on their floor and the toilet is used pretty much exclusively by Martin from accounts for his afternoon dumping sessions. It's only mid morning so they have escaped the bowel induced fog he creates daily.
"You don't know how it went." Will tries to be helpful.
"They asked me for an example of me using my initiative and I panicked and told them about replacing the file I lost that time without anyone finding out. And I'd practised that question, I had a great answer all lined up and it just went out of my head."

"Well that's not great but I'm sure there were other questions you answered well," Nina soothes.

"Oh yes, there was when they asked me what I liked doing in my spare time and I claimed I could ski. They asked me what my favourite slope was and I said the snow dome at Milton Keynes. I've never been skiing in my life. And I've never been to Milton Keynes!" her voice breaks and she starts to sob again.

"Well, that's a good thing." Will rubs her back. "There's too many roundabouts in Milton Keynes. You wouldn't like it."

Eventually Tess' sobbing slows and she is able to consider leaving the toilet. Nina nips off to get her make up bag so she can attempt to repair Tess' face. They all know what is important here. Arrabella must never ever realise that Tess has been crying.

Will and Tess look at each other.

"I'm sorry I let you down," Tess says.

"You haven't let me down," Will replies.

"I have. You helped me so much with this and I wasted the whole opportunity. I panicked and I was unprepared and …."

Will can see that she is working her way up to another crying explosion so comes over and lifts her off the sink and hugs her.

"You haven't let me down. You've just had a bad morning. You don't know how it went. You don't know what the other candidates were like. They might have killed someone."

Tess laughs in to his chest and he kisses the top of his head. When Nina returns she does a wonderful job of not reacting.

Tess pulls away from Will and accepts the proffered make up bag.

"So you think you can put up with me here for a bit longer?"

"Of course!" Will says. Nina just catches her eye in the age spotted mirror and smiles.

The inevitable rejection letter arrives on Friday. Long enough, as she says to Will, to pretend that they've considered it, but if you think about it; not long enough to have seriously considered her, let someone else know they got the job, have them accept and then write to the runners up to say they haven't got it. They must have decided instantly she wasn't worth even being a back up and posted the letter almost immediately after she left the interview.

"You think too much," is Will's only reply. He refuses to talk about the interview anymore and stops suggesting jobs that Tess could go for but occasionally she looks at his screen and can see job websites. Rather than take this as a supportive gesture Tess automatically assumes he wants her gone.

Tess can't help thinking that it's worrying that she has spent more time preparing for an internet date than she did for a job interview. Nina helps her to get ready in the toilets at the office and she heads out immediately after work. She straightens her skirt and heads to the lifts. "You look nice." Will turns the corner just as she presses the button to summons the lift.
"Thanks Will, you're working late for a Friday."
"Just wanted to wrap something up so I don't have to come back to it on Monday. You off out with Nina, I could come for a quick one." Will looks hopeful.
Tess squirms. "Actually, err, I've got a sort of date. Thing." She mumbles. Will tries and fails to hide his disappointment. "Oh OK, didn't know you were, er dating. Me too! So er, oh, wouldn't you know it I've left my coat in the office. I'll see you Monday. Have fun on your date."
He turns on his heel and walks back to the office. His coat over his arm. The lift bings and it's doors open. Tess turns towards it.
"And where were you thirty seconds ago?" She asks.

The date is 'nice'. Nice man, nice conversation, nice meal. Not amazing. Not awful enough to get an amusing anecdote out of it. They go to a nice Italian and order a nice bottle of wine. The evening is perfectly pleasant and she has a good time. However whilst Dan, for that is his nice name, is recounting a fairly humorous story about the time he got trapped in a pair of trousers at the gym, Tess can't help but think that she is looking forward more to tomorrow evening when she is having dinner with Tilly and Stuart and Daisy and Simon. She lets her mind wander and considers what it would be like to add him in to the mix of her friends. He would get on with them all she is sure. He seems like a sociable, funny guy with no obvious social issues. But would she be happy for him to be associated with her. For him to be linked to her. For his every move to be a reflection on her. To put her stamp on him and say 'hands off ladies he's mine'. To like him so much she wants him to be permanently associated with her. No. In a word. She can't think how he would enhance her life. The fictional dinner party is not improved by his presence. But if she imagines him not being there she is immediately lighter hearted and more free and easy. Not being responsible for anyone else and not having to worry about anyone else makes her instantly happier.

The story comes to an end and Tess pulls herself out of her daydream and laughs at his anecdote. He's a nice guy, she'd like to see him again but only as friends. Is it rude to suggest that? Although to her it's a compliment it could be seen as a rejection. She will compromise, she decides, and add him on Facebook. He walks her home and they have a snog on her doorstep. She's not going to ask him to come in. It's not really her style and at the back of her mind she is aware that inviting someone you met online in to your house isn't a good idea. One pleasant meal in an Italian doesn't really guarantee that someone isn't an axe murderer.

They say goodnight and Tess finds it strange that someone can come in to your life and only be in it for one night. There's no point in pretending that they'll be more to it than that, she's already composing the 'thanks but no thanks' text in her head.

Chapter 13

It should be a great day. After a leisurely brunch with Matt in a local cafe, Tilly is picking her and Daisy up and they are heading to Westfield to look at, and possibly buy, bridesmaid's dresses. Then after some celebratory champagne in a bar the boys will join them for dinner. Perfect. It's a bank holiday weekend and Tess doesn't plan on wasting a second of it.

It starts so well. Brunch is great. After the date is dissected (and most importantly of all Matt agrees with her on all of her points and makes her feel less of a freak) they read the Saturday papers in companionable silence and make a good headway in to the crossword. Tilly and Daisy pop in to join them for a quick coffee before they head to the shops and they catch up with Matt. It's shaping up to be a good Saturday and then they get to Westfield and the problems start. Daisy has a severe case of Kyle-mentionitis but despite Tilly's obvious interest she refuses to expand because (as she whispers to Tess later in the toilets) she doesn't want to shatter Tilly's illusions of love with the wedding being so close. She has, however, helpfully printed off some emails for Tess to read. Tess trawls them desperately looking for subtext but as far as she can see they are just emails about the school play.
"Are they in code?" she asks Daisy.
Daisy snatches the emails back and then the day rapidly goes down hill.

"Things always come up small in this shop," Tilly says.
Daisy is standing in the lavish changing room in a dress that matches Tess'. But whereas Tess' is done up and she's forced her feet in to some ridiculously high heels, Daisy's hangs open from the waist as the zip refused to go any further up and she's left her boots on.
"What about that halter neck one?" Tess asks.
"You hated that," snaps Daisy.
"I didn't hate, hate it. I just wasn't that keen. Perhaps we should try it on so we've got an idea of what we're looking for. It's like when we were looking for Tilly's dress, things that didn't look that great on the hanger looked brilliant on. Didn't they Tilly?"

"Absolutely Tess. Shall I go and get them?" For some reason Tilly and Tess have started talking like Blue Peter presenters in order to chivvy Daisy along.

It doesn't work "No, don't bother." She snaps. " Whatever I try on, I'm going to look like a fat cow. Let's just go to Evans."

She stomps back off to the changing rooms. The others widen their eyes at each other and Tess heads back in to the cubicles to take off the dress they won't be buying.

They decide to do the only sensible thing. Bring the drinking forward. Tilly, considering she is a bride only a few months away from her wedding is surprisingly laid back about the whole thing.

"Why don't you wear different things?" she suggests. "You don't have to wear the same, it doesn't matter."

"Yeah," Daisy says sarcastically. "Then Tess can wear something nice and I can be the fat bridesmaid who has to wear something different."

"You're not fat." Tilly protests.

"Yes I am." Daisy retorts.

"No you're not."

"Yes I am."

Tess loses patience and joins in. "No you're not. You just have massive, flipping tits and there's nothing we can do about it so will you please get over yourself?"

Daisy slams her drink down and storms off.

"Thanks Tess, thanks a lot, that's really helpful," Tilly says standing up and following Daisy.

Left on her own at the table, Tess ignores the curious stares of the other patrons who have witnessed the raised voices and walk outs. She uses the opportunity to text Dan and officially thank him for a nice evening. She also texts Will telling him about the dress shopping and her unfortunate outburst. Unlike usual he doesn't instantly reply.

When Daisy and Tilly return it's clear that Daisy has been crying and is still struggling to control her tears.

"Sorry Daisy," Tess says. "I didn't mean to upset you."

"Daisy's still a bit upset, aren't you Daisy?" Tilly says, looking at Daisy who nods her agreement. "We're going to finish our drinks and then we thought we'd go back to Debenhams and perhaps you could both try some different styles of dresses."

"Good idea." Tess agrees. "And I am very sorry."

The atmosphere is deeply uncomfortable and then Tilly does the unthinkable and goes to the bar leaving Daisy and Tess alone.

"You're upset with me because of Kyle aren't you?" Daisy says

"I'm worried about you. Kyle, this whole dress thing, you've never had any body hang ups. What's up?" Tess is genuinely concerned about Daisy.

"Nothing. I'm fine. I know you can't get on board with this Kyle thing but you may need to accept him."

"Why, what's happened?" Tess asks.

"Well, you've seen the emails" This is Daisy's final word on the matter as Tilly comes back carrying more drinks.

'How much is Daisy reading in to this?' Tess wonders. 'It's not that she's reading a sub text that isn't there; she's imagining an entire relationship that isn't there.' Poor Simon, poor Daisy.

The next round of dress shopping is marginally more successful. It's possible that being half cut makes things a lot easier. No purchases are made but it is established that Tess and Daisy can wear different things in styles that flatter their individual body shapes. Tilly and Tess are looking forward to the arrival of the boys as they hope that this will ease some of the tension. But when they arrive at the restaurant Tess is immediately put out. Despite their being five of them the table is a table for four with a place stuck on the end and there is no question of who takes it. The couples immediately take the proper places leaving Tess to sit on the end and be constantly bumped by waiters and people on their way to the toilet.

It has never bothered Tess to be the spare wheel but tonight the couples are particularly couply. Tilly and Stuart can be forgiven, they are newly engaged. But Simon and Daisy? Especially given what Daisy is telling her. Tess is very confused and spends a lot of her time watching Daisy and how she acts around Simon. There are no outward signs that she is in a 'dead' marriage. The night passes very slowly. Tess feels like she is on a French exchange. They are fine and polite to her, they include her in conversations but she has the feeling they are going to go home and laugh at her trainers. For the first time with her friends she feels that she's not enough. The weekend is soured.

On Sunday, for the first time in a long time Tess doesn't revel in the emptiness and cleanliness of her flat. Instead she is bored. She doesn't want to be on her own but Tilly has plans, she suspects Daisy is still in a mood with her, Nina has thrown her completely, Hannah will be busy being pregnant (she really ought to ring her, if only to get her mother off her back), she can't be bothered with Matt. She realises the person she wants to see is Will He's been a bit strange since the whole date thing, but when she texts and invites him over, surprisingly, he accepts.

He appears with a bottle of wine and the Chinese delivery man standing behind him.
"I guess I'll have to abandon the lie that I cooked," Tess says.
He leans forward and kisses her on the cheek.
He takes his shoes off as he comes in and hangs his coat in the exact spot that Tess would have placed it herself. He then follows her through to the kitchen and uncorks the wine whilst Tess gets plates out of cupboards and arranges the food on the table.

Tess wonders if she dreamed Will being in a mood with her. He's being absolutely fine with her tonight. Back to normal, not a strop in sight. Perhaps she was confused by Daisy's odd behaviour of late and was now unable to decide what was normal and what was not. Perhaps she's turned in to Daisy and is now completely unable to distinguish between imagination and reality.

"I just think a lot has changed over the last few months or so and I've not really appreciated it. You know?" Tess says, once dinner is over (plates rinsed and stacked in the dishwasher and the rubbish in a bag outside the front door ready for Will to take with him when he goes so the whole house doesn't get stunk out). They have moved in to the living room with another bottle of wine, they are both fully taking advantage of the fact that there is no work tomorrow. They are at either end of the sofa with Tess' feet in Will's lap.

"You mean like Tilly and Simon?" Will asks.
"Yeah, I think so. I mean it's not like it's a massive shock, it was pretty obvious it was headed that way and they're great with one another. I'm happy for them. But Daisy's lost the plot, that whole Kyle thing is weird.

Ni... people making changes at work." Tess winces, although she's corrected herself she's doesn't want to give out information she's not sure is common knowledge.

"I know about Nina, she resigned the other day." Will says "We'll miss her but it's a great opportunity."

"Oh OK, didn't know she'd told you." Tess says "But yeah, like she's making changes. Everyone seems to have a plan or have exciting things happen to them and I don't. And I used to be fine with that. I used to love that. But now I think maybe it's not that great? Perhaps I'd like something happen to me. But I don't know what. If I look at my life I'm happy, yet I feel really unsettled at the same time. I've never felt like this and I don't like it."

"I didn't know you were dating." Will says. It's a complete non-sequitur but it somehow works in this free wheeling conversation. "I thought all that kind of thing wasn't for you?"

"It's not. I mean I didn't think it was. But whenever I said that to people they made me feel like a complete weirdo. I mean who doesn't want somebody to love them? So I thought perhaps I should date, maybe people have got a point. Maybe I would be better paired off."

"And?" Will asks.

"I still don't think it's for me." Tess light-heartedly recounts some of the dates she has been on. But when she finishes and looks over at Will he isn't laughing. "So maybe I am one of those people who's fundamentally single. Other people can have relationships but they're not for the likes of me."

"Maybe you've just not met the right person yet," he says.

"Isn't that the ultimate get out clause? The battle cry for the people who want you to be in a relationship?" Tess argues. "Don't you think it's a myth that everything will fall in to place if you meet the fictional 'one'? Do you think one person is capable of making you change everything about yourself?"

"The right person wouldn't want you to change. And you would want to work through the hard stuff because you want to be with them." Will replies.

"That makes more sense but this person is still mythical. Where would you meet them? Online? It's hardly the slow build up. It's all based on instantly liking someone and having them feel the same. And the first date has to be amazing or there's no second date. There's no try it and see. You cut someone off after one date. It's brutal." Tess can see all the flaws in the system but no answers.

"Perhaps someone you already know?" Will suggests.

"Perhaps." Oh shit. Tess knows where this is leading. She needs to shut it down.

But does she? She has sort of accepted, as society and her friends hammer it home, that she needs a partner. Could she do better than Will? He's good looking, he's successful, he's funny, he gets on with her friends. She's not sure if she fancies him but perhaps that's merely a case of mind over matter. Something to power through. Because more importantly he is one of her best friends and she knows that he loves her. He won't hurt her, he won't do anything that's not in her best interests. As a re-introduction to relationships he couldn't be a better choice. If she's going to give it a try there is no better candidate. And in that moment she makes up her mind.

She puts her glass of wine down, takes her feet out of Will's lap and moves slightly closer to him.

"Perhaps." She says again.

Will is sure he's reading all the signs right but he's not going to lie, he's been wrong in the past. So he keeps quiet and studies his glass of wine. Suddenly there is a hand on his thigh. He looks up and in to Tess' eyes. Sod it. He puts his wine down.

"Perhaps me," he says and kisses her.

Both Will and Tess are surprised that she eagerly kisses him back.

Chapter 14

The advice that Tess read in Just 17 nearly twenty years ago may be horrible dated but she's pretty sure that it still stands. Sadly like most of the advice she chose to ignore it. Which is why she is in the situation now. The second the laugh leaves her mouth she regrets it. She immediately slaps her hand across her mouth but only makes her look smug.

"OK. Not the reaction I was hoping for," says Will.

As nice as the kiss had been it had been mainly driven by idle curiosity and a desire not to be seen as frigid (in many ways Just 17 spoke directly to Tess). It was only when her brain caught up with her mouth that she had come to her senses and pulled away. Both of them were in shock, Will shocked that an event he dreamt of for so many years had finally happened and been successful and Tess shocked that it had happened at all, they fell in to silence.

Luckily for Tess Will decides to fill the gap in conversation and she is given a bit more thinking time.

"Sorry." He says. "No actually I'm not sorry. I like you Tess. Really like you. I have done for years. Since the moment I met you actually. I love being your friend. But I want more. What do you think?"

Tess doesn't know what she thinks and so remains silent and staring at Will. She's suddenly feeling quite drunk and is pretty sure she doesn't want to make a life changing decision with this much alcohol in her.

Luckily Will knows the way to Tess' heart and goes in to the kitchen to put the kettle on. Tess falls back on the sofa. This is not how she thought the evening would turn out. She's not sure what to do next. Whilst she really wants a cup of tea she hopes Will takes his time making it so she can have some thinking time. Her main thought is one she didn't expect to have... that was actually very enjoyable. More than enjoyable in fact. She touches the skin around her mouth, it's slightly sore from Will's stubble and she smiles as she remembers the feeling of his mouth on hers. There's a noise as Will appears in the doorway.

"So". Will hands her a cup of coffee then goes and sits in the armchair in the opposite corner of the room and sits and looks at Tess.

"So" Tess echoes.

Silence falls.

"I'm not falling for that again," Will says. "Your turn. You know where I stand. It's your turn to speak. I can sit here all day if I have to. But at the end of the day you kissed me so the ball's in your court."

"Why do you sound like a stroppy geography teacher?" Tess asks.

"Tess." Will's not in the mood for games.

"OK. Ermm. I don't know. I mean, thank you. But I don't know what you want me to say. I mean I know what you want me to say but I don't know if I'm there yet but I, I don't know," Tess ends weakly.

"Then it's a no isn't it." Will says.

"Why is it a no?" Tess asks.

"If you don't know if you want to be with me then it's a no." Will is fairly certain where he stands.

"No, hang on." Tess argues "You've had what .. four years to process this information, to know where you stand and decide what to do. I've had what four minutes? I went in for a snog, not to sign away the next sixty years of my life. A kiss that's what I went for. A kiss. And it was very nice."

"Nice," Will mutters.

"More than nice", Tess corrects. "Would I like to do it again... yes? But what does that mean? Are we in a relationship? Are we dating? It's you Will, it's not a snog in a club with a random. Kissing you comes with consequences and it's not a reflection on you that thinking about them isn't an easy thing. Plus I'm drunk and I'm tired and I'm really aware that I've started something that I don't know where's it going and I'm sorry for that."

"You want to do it again?" Will asks.

For once Tess doesn't go for the quick retort and instead decides to grasp the nettle.

"Yes."

This time, if anything, it's better. But eventually Tess draws it to a halt. She's still not sure about it. Dating Will isn't just dating Will. It's dating Will, all their friends and family and diving in to a fully blown relationship. They'll bypass all the fun getting to know you stuff and go straight in to the grind. She can't pretend to be well read and more interesting than she is. He knows her. He's seen every side of her. There are those who would say that is a good thing, an honest thing. Tess calls those people hippies. She wants the fun stuff first and that's not going to happen. Her and Will can claim all they like it's going to be casual but they both know it's never going to be. Plus work is an added complication.

There's the toot of a car horn outside.

"That's my cab," says Will.
"When did you call that?" Tess wonders.
"Pre-booked, it's a Saturday night, and I wasn't expecting, well, all this."
Tess smiles. It's such a sensible thing to do, such a Will thing to do. Tess spends hours sitting at people's houses aware that she is keeping them from going to bed and desperately willing the non pre-booked mini cab to arrive. She's suddenly filled with fondness for sensible Will. She leans forward and gives him a hug.
"We'll talk soon yeah?" Will says.
"Mmmmm"
"And no pressure. I mean that. If tonight's all there is then well, that's fine."
"Is it?" she asks.
"Well no. But ....no pressure," he repeats.
The car outside hoots again and Tess releases Will and stands back.
"It'll sort itself out, " are her final words to him as he leaves.
Tess stands by the door and watches him as he heads down the stairs.

It'll sort itself out. Hardly words of encouragement he thinks. He gives the cab driver his address and then settles back into the air freshener fug of the back seat. He has hope and for now that is enough. When he gets home he opens the front door and everything is just as he left it, every room is spotless. He almost wishes he had left a cup out or something just to make his house looked lived in. He kicks his shoes off and leaves them where they land, just so the place seems like it has a bit of life in it.

Tess opens the window to let the fresh evening air in. Then she pads around picking up wine glasses and mugs and returning them to the kitchen where she rinses them before placing them in the dishwasher. Once the cushions are plumped and she's rubbed away the ring from wine glass that Will placed on the floor she shuts the window and turns the lights out. She knows that the bed has fresh covers on and that gives Tess real contentment. There's now not a thing out of place and nothing will be out of place unless she moves it. Perfect. She smiles at the showroom perfect living room. "Goodnight house," she breathes.

"Bloody hell. I'm drunk," Tess and Will say at the same time and head to bed.

Chapter 15

"Daisy calm down." Tess is already regretting this. When they had all been at university and lived together for three years it had been second nature to get in from a night out or a date and instantly sit up with the others and dissect the night. Modern technology meant that Tess was able to carry this tradition on. She had sat in bed last night and sent a couple of drunken misspelled texts to Tilly and Daisy and then, much like university, had fallen in to a deep sleep, fully dressed on top of the covers. When she woke up she had discovered that the others were over-excited and had arranged a get together to fully investigate what was going on.

Unfortunately as Tess had had no input in organising this meeting it was arranged around Daisy and Tilly's social diaries and so at 9am on a Bank Holiday Monday morning they were sat around in a near empty cafe just around the corner from Tilly's house. Daisy had taken pity on Tess and had picked her up. However Daisy's hope of getting the inside track on Tess' news was scuppered when Tess spent the whole journey silent with sunglasses on. Twenty minutes in to breakfast and they had ordered, watched Tess drink two cups of coffee and they still hadn't found out what was going on. Daisy was approaching breaking point.

"Tell me and I'll calm down," she reasons. "I don't want the breakfasts to arrive and then you've got another excuse not to say anything."

"It's not a deliberate plan," Tess tries to defend herself. "I under estimated how much I drunk last night and I feel rough. You're meant to have a lie in on a Bank Holiday you know. Not get up earlier than you do normally. Also I'm not sure I have more to add to what I told you. Will and I went out, well stayed in, we had a nice time, it was like every other night and then out of nowhere we kiss."

"Out of nowhere?" Tilly questions. "He's fancied you for ages."

"Well yes, but he's never done anything about it so it was out of the blue."

"You must have been giving him signals, that's what it'll be. Subconsciously you wanted it to happen and so your body language gave you away and that's why he made his move." Daisy sits back in her chair, contented that she has cracked the mystery. Tilly and Tess stare at her.

"Well I was presenting. You know, Baboon style. Had my big purple bottom right in his face"

"You can mock but why did he suddenly decide now was the time? What was different about last night? What were you wearing?" Daisy asks.

Tilly laughs, "Yeah, what were you wearing? What was it you had on that finally pushed him in to overdrive? Was it that PVC nurses outfit again? We've warned you about that."

Daisy goes to defend herself but Tess jumps in. She hates to admit it but this is actually fun. If she could forget that she's hungover and that she has to deal with the Will problem then she could really enjoy this. It's quite exciting having the gossip and drama be about her for once. She's normally always cast in the supporting role.

"Look it doesn't matter how it happened or," she shoots a look at Daisy, "what I was wearing. What I need to know is what the hell do I do now? I have to go to work with him tomorrow and I have no idea what I am going to say."

"How did you leave it?" Tilly asks.

"Ball's in my court. He said I need time to think about it. Totally up to me."

"Well that's nice." Daisy says.

"No it's not!" Tess disagrees. "He's totally fucked me over. He snogs me because he wants to and now I have to make all the decisions."

"Whereas it would have been much kinder to force you in to a relationship with no choice." Tilly says.

Breakfast arrives and Tess lands on the toast like a woman possessed. The problem may be a bit overwhelming but carbohydrates are going to help enormously. Tilly looks at the toast with envy then pushes her fruit salad around the bowl. Daisy meanwhile is letting her bacon sandwich grow cold and has plonked a note pad on the table.

"You need a list of pros and cons," she uncaps her pen and looks at Tess expectantly.

"It's not about pros and cons. Will's perfect on paper, I love him, he's great, last night was...," she peters out and blushes, she hopes this makes her look demure and modest. It actually makes her look like the biggest whore in Christendom. "The problem is do I want to be in a relationship with him? We work together, he's one of my best friends, we're so close."

"That's what makes it so perfect!" Daisy exclaims.

"That what makes it so complicated," Tess corrects. "I've got so much to lose. Say we go out, then we split up, in one go I've lost a friend, work is horrendous and I'm worse off than when I started. This isn't going to be a casual, see how you go thing. If it happens it's going to be full blown serious bonanza. It can't not be."

"Why are you splitting up?" Daisy again.

"It would be nice to have the option." Tess says. "Until last night I've never thought of Will that way. I'm playing catch up and the option of feeling my way in isn't there. I have to go for it and if it doesn't work out then our friendship is ruined and I really don't want that."

"This may not be particularly helpful", Tilly says. "But I reckon your friendship is fucked either way."

All three of them let this settle in. It is actually the most helpful thing any one has said all morning. For Daisy it proves her right – Tess should go for it, she has nothing to lose. For Tilly it proves her right – it gives Tess options. For Tess it proves her right – she's screwed whatever she does.

"Can we talk about something else? "Tess asks
"Look. " Daisy says "You want to go out with someone, it's difficult to meet someone. A gorgeous man who you already really like has put himself out there for you. We're not young any more you owe it to yourself to try this or you'll be 35 and single."
Tess is about to ask if that is the worst thing in the world. Then she looks at Daisy's and Tilly's faces and realises that, yes, in their eyes it would be the worst thing in the world. She's not really enjoying this any more and really wants the spotlight off her. She asks Tilly about the wedding plans and chews on a bit of toast as the topic is, thankfully, changed.

Does she want to be 35 and single? Well she never thought she'd be 28 and single but here she is. If anything it seems to be getting easier as she gets older. However the rest of the world certainly seems to think she should pair off. It would be easier to give it a try. She's tired. She can be as successful and happy as she likes but people won't believe she's happy unless she's with someone. She's tired of arguing her case. It sounds like a poor defence. It's like people who declare how much they love being fat and wouldn't be any other way. It sounds like they are protesting too much, they say how happy they are but you can't help thinking that if given the opportunity to be a size 10 they would, ahem, bite your hand off. Although she is fine and she's happy, to the outside world she is failing and she is bored of feeling like a failure. Least this way she could say that she tried. She wants to be accepted. Besides, surely people want the best for her; they must know that being with someone is better than being on your own. She should do this. She needs to grow up. It's not just someone anyway; it's Will. She stands to lose so much if she says no and this could be amazing.

"...doesn't eat lamb and so many people don't eat beef and chicken is just a bit..." Tilly is explaining the latest menu issues when Tess interrupts her.

"I'm going to do it." She says.

"Really?" Daisy squeals. Even Tilly looks happy at being interrupted.

"Yeah, I think this is right. I think I need to give it a shot. Do you think it's too early to go round there? I need to do this now before I bottle it."

"Don't go yet." Daisy and Tilly say at the same time.

"You don't think I'm doing the right thing?"

"No," Tilly lays her hand on Tess' arm. "We think you look like shit."

Chapter 16

It had seemed to escape Daisy's notice that Will and Tess saw each other pretty much every day. Therefore she lay on Tess' bed and critiqued every outfit Tess put on. She was willing to admit that she had slightly lost perspective when she tried to talk Tess in to wearing a tailored suit with nothing underneath.

"It's 11 o clock on a Monday Daisy." Tess says "Do you not think he's going to think it's a bit odd that I turn up in a suit I only wear to interviews and I've forgotten to wear a shirt? Besides didn't that look go out with the Spice Girls? He made his move last night after I'd scragged my hair back and was wearing one of his hoodies."

"OK maybe not the suit." Daisy concedes. "I just get a bit jealous that you don't have to wear a bra. There's so many things that I can't wear and it's not that I'm fat, I'm not, it's just.."

"Daisy". It's not that Tess is unsympathetic to Daisy's enormous breasts it's just that it's a conversation they have had before and although Tess got a great set of knives in the Habitat closing down sale she's not fully confident of her ability to perform a breast reduction. Besides, she has a monumental day ahead of her. Although hopefully not too monumental; if she could be home by mid-afternoon then that would be great, she'd like to put the hoover round and phone her Mum before Homeland starts at 9.

Daisy puts down one of the bras she is holding and looks up.

"You bounce back well from a hangover."

"I thank you. Now wish me luck. Want to walk with me to Will's? Or you can stay here if you like. You've got your keys haven't you?" Tess asks.

"I'll walk with you to Clemence Street. Simon's going to finish work soon, I'll go and meet him, try and convince him to take me for lunch."

"Hmmmm." Tess murmurs.

Daisy gives up. It's clear Tess isn't listening. Why would she?
She doesn't care why Simon has been working on a Bank
Holiday. She's not asked Daisy one thing about herself. Breakfast
was dedicated to Tess' news and then the wedding. Daisy wasn't
asked anything. She's still convinced that Tess is being strange
with her because of Kyle. She wants to text him but she's heard
so many stories of affairs being discovered through the spouse
reading text messages. Although she knew Simon wouldn't read
her phone, he wouldn't notice if she conducted a rampant
session of phone sex with Kyle on the landline whilst Simon sat
beside her but she couldn't say the same for Kyle's wife.

She thinks of the afternoon Tess has ahead of her and sighs.
She needs to do some marking and convince Simon that he
needs to sort the recycling out. It's threatening to take over the
kitchen. He won't do it. He'll argue that he's been at work all
morning, probably getting a dig in there somewhere that not
every job comes with sixteen weeks holiday. His failure to grasp
that she has to work during the school holidays hasn't changed
over the seven years she's been teaching. She can't face the
argument so knows that come 9pm tonight she'll be on her
hands and knees in the kitchen pulling the plastic inner bag out
of the cardboard cereal box.
"You good?" Tess interrupts Daisy's train of thought.
"Yup. Let's go get him" Daisy says.

Once she's said goodbye to a suddenly quiet and subdued Daisy,
Tess decides to calm her nerves by giving Hannah a call. A bit of
familial chaos would take her mind off what she was about to
do. Besides, after the weekend of hell at their parents house
and Hannah's strange behaviour at the station she had
promised herself that she would stay in better touch with her
sister (and not report back to their Mother). However life had

got away from her and she simply hadn't had a second. Not that she'd say this to either Hannah or her Mother as she knew it would provoke a competition of 'Who is busier'. A competition she knew she wouldn't win. The phone at Hannah's rang unanswered so Tess gave up and vowed to try when she got home.

Will liked living in Central London, he felt part of things and had a ridiculously short commute to work. However lately he was thinking about moving. When he'd bought this place he had been 25 and had just been bought over from Dublin as the new big thing. He'd taken one look at the concierge desk, the lifts and the huge white space and signed his life away. He hadn't realised that living in the square mile meant that there were no supermarkets, he had to spend a fortune to park his car and at the weekends the place became like the scene of an apocalyptic horror film. It just emptied, there was no one around. But it was the supermarkets that grated on him today. The only open corner shop had furnished him with milk and bread but he had a real craving for an omelette and he wasn't sure he had it in him to go foraging further afield for eggs. He felt pathetic. A fully grown man nearly destroyed by a lack of eggs.

If he could be bothered to walk to Liverpool Street there would be a Starbucks open. If the thought of it didn't make him want to top himself he could go to the McDonalds at the station. He shook his head; this is why he had turned his back on suburbia. Sitting under fluorescent lighting in a chain restaurant was not for him. He sighed and opened the fridge again desperately hoping that it had self produced food. The internal phone rang.
"Hello?" he said.
"We have a Tess in reception. Can we send her up?" The concierge asked.
"Aaa yeah."

Yeah! No! He runs to the mirror and plays with his hair. The artfully dishevelled look is only achieved by a good ten minutes hard work with a variety of products. Left to its own devices his hair is more 'bouf'. He swaps his t-shirt for a slightly cleaner one (and he knows that green brings out his eyes) and by the time the lift bings he is stood with studied nonchalance at the door to the flat. Tess emerges looking amazing, hair shining, jeans, heels and oh shit a loose green t-shirt type top.

Why is Will dressed like her? Tess had spent the walk and the trip up in the lift thinking about what to say but she can see Will and can see herself reflected in the mirror behind him. They look like Topsy and Tim and it throws her. The pre-planned speech written by her and Daisy (with a little help from Richard Curtis) goes out of the window and she laughs.
"Hello." She says.
"Hello." Will replies.
She slowly approaches him and then cautiously puts her arms around him. He hugs her back and she can feel his kiss on the top of her head.
"Yes," she says. "Let's try this."

Chapter 17

Tess had always imagined the beginning of a relationship to be like a film. Perhaps Will would leap out a doorway with an enormous bunch of flowers and Tess would throw her hands up to her face and laugh and laugh. They would cook together and force one another to taste the food, whilst laughing. Perhaps they'd amusingly smear the food on one another's faces. They would go on bicycle rides but for some reason only hire one bicycle and Tess would sit on the handlebars or in the basket and they'd wobble amusingly through a park.

Of course she would have to buy a whole new wardrobe which would include a lot of kooky hats.

Shockingly none of this happens. They are just them but together. They go to the cinema, they go to work, they go out to eat, they stay in to eat. Their trial period passes quickly and Tess is amazed to find that weeks go past and they are still together and she is surprised to find she likes it. She particularly likes that Will loves a bit of gossip. Not in a malicious way (although he was quite scathing about Lindsay Lohan's latest make up look) but in a 'let's talk about our friends' way.

She is also greatly relieved to find that Will has friends. She knew this of course and had met many of them as he had hers over the years, but as she becomes more involved in Will's life she is pleased to find that his friends are as important to him as hers are to her.

She is surprised at how easy it is. How relaxed it is. She has never found being in a relationship easy, she's only really ever felt at easy when she's alone, but with Will it's ....not too shit.

That may be damming it with faint praise but it's a novelty to Tess. As the time goes past she fully expects it to get worse but it stays the same. She is waiting for something to happen. Something bad. Tess isn't by nature a 'glass half full' type. She's not even a 'glass half empty' sort. More 'glass is half empty and the glass is going to break and kill us all.' But with Will she gets some perspective. The feeling that it's all going to fall apart lifts a little. But on the other hand Tess always quite liked that life could turn on a dime. That she had no ties. That she could, if needs be, suddenly move to Nicaragua. Not that she would have done, but she liked to have the choice. Now she feels a bit more tied. A bit more weighted down.

So this is a relationship. It's... nice. It seems to be a bit like a gigantic pair of scales.
She loses a bit of independence. She gains support.
She loses time on her own. She gains someone to share a random thought with at 3am (this is not always appreciated). She loses something of herself. She gains being part of something bigger than herself.

It's early days and it's too soon to see if the gamble has paid off but so far so good. She's pleased that she's going through all this with Will. She thinks it would be a bit rubbish with someone else. For all she feels she is losing, whenever she feels panicked she looks at Will and decides to try again for another day. Time passes and soon they have begun to become a 'we'. People talk to them as a singular unit and Tess begins to loose sight of who she was.

The being in a relationship meant of course that there were things that had to be done. Well to be more accurate, things that can't be done anymore. She decided to nip this in the bud early on and so, as was their wont, Tess and Matt went to feed the ducks.

"I'm happy for you T." Matt says.

"Thanks, and obviously we'll still be friends, we just won't, well you know." Tess clarifies.

"Absolutely. So Will eh? I always knew he liked you. Didn't think you were interested."

"Well there you go. Life is full of surprises. What about you? Any one on the scene?"

"Oh god you've turned in to one of them." Matt says.

"What?" Tess turns to him affronted. She slops some of her coffee on to him, it splatters on to his upper thigh, Tess goes to wipe it away and then realises that it might not be the best idea and so withdraws her hand. "What do you mean, one of them?" She asks.

"You're paired up so now you want everyone else to be."

"Oh shut up, I was just making conversation. Being polite." Tess says.

"How many years have I known you?" Matt asks.

"Oh I don't know. Five? Six? You had a deeply unpleasant pair of glasses."

"Six years and I liked those glasses.. Anyway, in all that time I have never, ever, known you to be polite, in fact it was you who referred to those glasses as 'paedo goggles' a mere twenty minutes after I'd met you. And also you have never had to 'make' conversation. We have talked about everything under the sun, travel, kids TV, animals, food poisoning, the benefits of an open door immigration policy. You have never had to search around for conversation and come up with my relationship status. Now you're in one you want everyone else to be in one to. You want to reaffirm your choices by making everyone else do the same." Matt rants.

"You're making far too much out of one innocent comment. I think I've touched a nerve." Tess argues.

"That is the most offensive thing you have ever said to me. A few weeks in a couple and you've already learnt the script." He leans over and kisses her on the cheek, then stands up and brushes down his trousers. "Say hi to Will for me, I'll see you when I see you."

And with that he walks off and out of the park. Tess continues to text him over the next few days and gets no response. It's not lost on her that she had worried that being in a relationship would wreck a friendship. It would appear she was right, she'd just been worried about the wrong friendship.

"He obviously fancies you and is upset you don't want to take it further." Nina is reapplying her make up in the mirror whilst Tess sits on the bank of sinks, rummaging through Nina's make up bag (Nina has Elizabeth Arden and grown up cosmetics. Tess tends to buy whatever is cheapest) and filling her in on her altercation with Matt. She gives her the bare bones but avoids mentioning that the reason she ended her arrangement with Matt was because of Will.
"Well we've been sleeping together on and off for nearly six years. I had sort of assumed he liked me but he never wanted to take things further. That was our thing. We didn't want to be in a relationship." Tess explains.
"But now you are in a relationship and he regrets not getting in there sooner." Nina is sure she's right.
"No, that's not it. It's not how we were and if he had wanted that then he had plenty of time to do it and never did. We didn't want to be in a relationship." Tess has said this to Nina many times but it's never really sunk in.
"Well with out wishing to sound like my Mother 'why would he buy the cow when he's getting the milk for free?'"
"Nina!" Tess stares at Nina laughing at her audacity. Nina smiles back.

"I don't know Tess. What do you want me to say?" Nina's laughing too. "You didn't want to go out with him, now you're not. Ta da."

"Ta da. Brilliant. Thanks." Tess says. "Oh I don't know. Maybe he'll get over it. I've been out with people before, and there was Harry - that was practically a relationship, and he's never got arsey. I didn't go demented when he dated that child 'Chanelle'. Anyway. What are you getting all tarted up for?"

"Just something I'm trying." Nina replies. "Ever noticed that American women are very 'groomed'? Thought I'd try and make it a habit before I get there so I don't spend the first few weeks experimenting and looking like Bobo the clown."

"Not long now." Tess says.

It was now common knowledge that Nina was leaving and heading to the States. It had provoked a mixture of jealousy and admiration. It also meant that Nina was spending an astonishing amount of time at work as she had to recruit someone for her role and hand over to them before she left. She had recommended Tess apply for her job. Tess had considered it for about thirty seconds and then disregarded it out of hand. She couldn't do it, she didn't want it, she would be applying because it was 'the next step' and it was expected. There was also the fear that she might actually get the job and be dreadful at it. Also she worried that if she got it and then it got out about her and Will it would be assumed it would be nepotism rather than a bit of gross miscasting. She had decided that the best thing to do was nothing. It couldn't go wrong if she didn't try. As usual Tess managed to underestimate herself and come up with problems that weren't even in existence yet in one fell swoop.

"So who's the new you?" Tess asks Nina.

"Barry."

"Barry? That's not a new you. That's crap."

"He was the best person for the job, we weren't recruiting for your new best friend." Nina explains.

"You're so corporate."

Nina leans over and draws a giant red clowns mouth on Tess with her expensive new lipstick.

"Professional to the core." She says. "Back to work Bobo".

"And the annoying thing is that I do actually have work to do." Tess complains to Daisy on the phone later that night.

"Welcome to the real world Tess, nice of you to join us." Daisy is not sympathetic to Tess' plight.

"Work, work. Not tasks to be completed but 'projects'."

"Isn't that what you wanted? Anyway that wasn't why I was calling." Daisy says.

'Don't let it be Kyle, don't let it be Kyle, don't let it be Kyle' Tess thinks.

"Simon." Daisy says.

"Oh!" Tess is surprised.

"My husband," Daisy clarifies sarcastically.

"My friend," Tess rallies pointedly.

"His birthday."

"His thirtieth. Terrifying."

"So I was thinking we should do something big." Daisy suggests.

"I've already had an invite from him? Aren't we going for dinner at Jago's?" Tess asks.

"Yes, yes I know that. But he's thinking that's it. An intimate dinner party with his closest friends. What I was thinking was after dinner we suggest going for a drink and then we go to the Lord Louis, they've got that room upstairs, and there's a whole secondary surprise party for him, with everyone there."

Tess is surprised, and a little relieved. Daisy doing something nice for Simon makes Tess happy.

"That sounds really, really lovely Daisy. Great idea. Let me know what I can do to help." She says.

Chapter 18

Although Will and Tess talk about most things. Will loves to talk and in Tess' mind talking kills time before she can go to sleep again. But the one thing they haven't spoken about is how they conduct themselves at work. Tess doesn't want to talk about it with Will because she knows his opinion. He thinks they should do what they want and people will have to respect it and go along with it. It's a lot easier to do what you want and behave how you like when you are the boss. Whatever gossip or snidey remarks reach Will's ears won't affect him. He is untouchable, oh yes he'll be angry on Tess' behalf but ultimately he will rise above it. No one is going to go out of their way to offend him; he's in an ivory tower, protected by his job title and the fact that so many are dependent on him for their jobs. Tess meanwhile is in the trenches and will have to deal with all the flak their relationship might generate. Although she hasn't taken on any more roles and isn't being favoured in anyway people ill think that there is a chance she might be as she has the boss's ear (amongst other body parts). Her co-workers will feel she has an unfair advantage and also that she isn't one of them anymore. Therefore Tess makes the decision to say nothing at work. To barely acknowledge Will and to entrench herself even more deeply with Arrabella.

Tess has made some crap decisions in her time but this one really ranks up there with the some of the worst. But unlike the time Tess decided to go vegan this time she can't admit that she has made a mistake. She also can't ask anyone at work for help. As to ask someone means she also has to divulge that she is in a relationship with Will and she's just not 'there' yet. She also refuses to discuss it with Will and so she lets it build and fester. Whole imaginary scenes take place in her head before breakfast.

She has, in short, turned in to Daisy. Living half in a fictional world and creating drama out of situations which haven't happened yet.

Nina would be the obvious person to tell. She knows the business inside out, knows all the characters and their relationships, knows all the power games and the rivalries and she's leaving. She can say whatever she wants safe in the knowledge that Nina will be several thousand miles away working for a rival company and if she suddenly loses her mind and says anything it could be written off as the ramblings of a jealous competitor. But Nina is, rightly, all consumed with the move and is working all hours of the day and night. Tess doesn't want to throw this on her.

There is a chance that Tess has fallen in to the trap of many new couples and is assuming that the rest of the world is actually interested in her relationship and that it is now the most important thing in the whole universe and occupies everyone's waking moments. She is too far gone now to take a step back and realise that no one really gives a shit and they are all much too concerned with their own lives.

Arrabella meanwhile is shocked to suddenly have an assistant. Tess and Arrabella have never really seen eye to eye on this. Tess' dogged insistence on doing the job she actually applied for rather than slavishly serve and cater to Arrabella's every whim does not sit well with Arrabella. She is in a slightly difficult situation as Tess does do her actual job and so Arrabella cannot report her to Human Resources or pull her in to disciplinary boards, but at the same time there is a constant push pull of roles. Tess is also very good at her job and would be very good at Arrabella's job but Arrabella is not one to nurture new talent. She's more of a 'seek and destroy' anyone who is a threat kind of girl. This is because Arrabella is thick. So when Tess suddenly starts offering to get coffees, picking up dry cleaning and actually doing Arrabella's expenses rather than simply printing off the companies expenses policy and how- to guide off the intranet and leaving it on Arrabella's desk she doesn't think that there is something afoot. That this could be the biggest clue to an uprising ever, but instead Arrabella thinks she's finally broken Tess and she finally has the assistant she always wanted and is free to dream up even more ways of off loading her job, household affairs and day to day running of her life on to her. Arrabella is proud that she has shaped Tess in to an uber assistant.

Attempting to do her own job and run Arrabella's life means that she is spending a lot more time at work, something that does not please her or Will. Add to this trying to be a bridesmaid, support Daisy through whatever the hell this is and help Nina with the move and Tess is stretched. The 'me time' which she relied heavily upon is getting smaller and smaller. She vastly underestimated how much time being a girlfriend took up. Whatever 'me' time there was is now 'we' time. With no time to herself she constantly feels like she is forgetting something.

It is a phone call from her mother which makes her realise what that is.

"Have you spoken to Hannah?" her mother asks.
"No, I've not really had a chance."
"Well could you?"
"Yeah, why has something happened?" Tess thought perhaps she'd missed something. Her parents were the only people in the world (except cold callers) who used her landline, there could well be a message on there from them. The first thing they did when they walked in to the house was dial 1471, it didn't cross their minds that Tess may not have picked up the receiver for a couple of months.

Her Mother let out a sigh, whether this was directed at Tess' laxness or Hannah in general it was impossible to tell.
"No, it's just... you know she can be difficult. If you could just reach out and make contact it would be helpful. She's so busy with the boys and I think she'd appreciate a phone call every now and then."

Tess had stopped asking why all the effort and the impetus in her relationship with Hannah had to come from her a long time ago. She also didn't ask why she had to act as a go between and informant for her parents. It was generally accepted that Hannah was difficult and Tess was not, therefore Hannah could behave how she liked and be awful and Tess had to give in and accommodate her or be accused of being awkward (something no one would ever accuse Hannah of in case she knifed them). Hannah provided the moods and the storms and it was Tess' job to provide the calm.

Tess had once tried to rebel against this status quo. When Tess had been twelve and Hannah had just turned fourteen. There had been a family barbecue at her Uncle and Aunt's. Not her Aunt Susan but her father's brother, a side of the family they didn't see so often. It was her Uncle's fiftieth or a wedding anniversary or something, Tess couldn't remember the details. What she could remember was that as they all began to sort themselves out and get ready Hannah decided that she wasn't going to go.

Tess has been ready earlier than everyone else. Being pre-teen she had yet to discover make up and had simply put on the only dressy outfit she owned, purchased with great excitement at C&A some time earlier. She was lying on the living room floor watching the Brookside omnibus (quietly, her mother didn't really approve of the goings on in the Close) and half-heartedly flicking through that day's *Independent* that her Father had left on the sofa when she became aware of raised voices above her.

"Hannah! I am not going to argue about this," she could hear her Mother saying. Tess carefully turned the TV down a few notches. Not just so she could hear what was happening but also because Hannah had a 'take no prisoners' approach to arguing and so Tess had to be on red alert in case Hannah decided to start bringing Tess in to the argument and Tess had to spring in to action, run upstairs and defend her honour.

"Just do as I ask. Please Hannah. Just this once," she heard her Mother continue, a weary note to her voice. "We need to go in ten minutes. Just co-operate for once. It's important to your father."

"I don't see why I have to go anyway. We never see them, they don't give a shit about me anyway."

"Language," she heard her Father interject. "Hannah. We're going in ten minutes. Change. Now please."
Tess heard the bedroom door slam and heavy footsteps make their way across the landing. Feeling reassured that she wasn't going to be bought in to this particular row she relaxed slightly and turned the television back up. Suddenly her father appeared in the doorway.
"You set?" he said, tossing the car keys up and down in his hand.
Tess and her father made their way out of the house and headed to the car.
"We're getting in the car! Come on! Mary!" Her Dad shouted as they headed out and he left the front door open behind them.
Her Dad got in the driver's seat and Tess sat behind him.
Hannah always sat behind her mother in the passenger's seat as she wanted more leg room. Tess was told to go along with it "because it wasn't worth the argument." Even though she was

two years younger than Hannah Tess was already taller than her. Hannah had peaked at five foot three. Tess had powered on way past her. Whenever Tess bought up the car unfairness in later life Hannah always responded with 'well it obviously didn't stunt your growth'.

As they sat in the car, time sped by, she and her dad flicked through the radio stations before settling on an old Elvis Costello song, both knowing full well that when Hannah got in the car she would insist they all listen to her music (currently the Wonder Stuff album 'Hup', Tess had professed her preference for 'Never Loved Elvis' and been told it was 'too commercial') or on the radio being turned down so she could listen to her walkman without being distracted by the background noise of the radio. After fifteen minutes and after her Dad bibbing the horn a few times and muttering 'this is ridiculous what are they doing in there?' her Mum came out of the front door visibly upset and shut the front door behind her. She got in the car.
"She's not coming."

Her Dad went to get out of the car but her Mother put her hand on his arm.
"The mood she's in it's best she doesn't come. She was vile."
Her Mum started to cry softly and her Dad, although clearly angry, put the car in reverse and eased the car off the drive. Normally Tess would try and break the tension. She would ignore her Mother's tears and try and change the subject. But this time Tess couldn't be bothered. She was sick of being the "good" child.

So that day, as she sat in a car that was full of anger and resentment and knowing that whatever happened at her Uncle's the day was pretty much ruined regardless, Tess decided that she had had enough. So she decided to channel Hannah.

Even sixteen years later it embarrassed her to think of how she had behaved that day. She was horrible. A textbook vile teen. She was sullen, she was rude, she bickered, she picked holes in anything anyone said. She declared every activity or suggestion 'boring'. She responded to all requests with a sigh and grunt. She made her younger cousins cry. She was used to the raised eyebrows of her relatives and her parents' embarrassed and upset looks but this time they were aimed at her and not Hannah. And she hated it. She hated the drive home with the heavy silence and she hated that she didn't know how to say sorry and explain.

As she had stomped off to bed that night she was unsure of how to change things. She had responded to the telling off she had got with a shrug but really she had wanted to cry. As she lay in bed she had two thoughts. One: she would never behave like that again and Two: she felt sorry for Hannah. To be that far gone, to be that unhappy and to be so labelled by everyone around you that you weren't sure how to come back from it and turn things around. She vowed there and then to accept the label of the 'easy' child and to carry on accommodating Hannah and they were now their roles. Of course now they were adults things had changed. Hannah had mellowed somewhat and to a certain extent Hannah was now responsible for her own behaviour and Garry picked up the slack. Tess had also stopped the secrecy with Hannah. If Hannah was going to be an odd bod then Tess wasn't going to pretend that her behaviour was normal. So after a phone call with her Mother, Tess would simply pick the phone up and say to Hannah 'Mum's on alert again – call her' or 'Mum thinks you're in a mood. Give her a ring'. Hannah would whinge and complain but the animosity had gone, not everything was a personal attack. The teenager who was so convinced that the world was against her was gone.

But lately Hannah had changed yet again. There was an element of self pity. A refusal to let any one in. And once again Tess was expected to ease Hannah's path. So she listened to her Mother, vowed to talk to Hannah and report back. Then as the phone call came to an end she reassured her Mother that she was fine and everything was good. Now was not the time to tell her about Will. She would save that for another day. As she put the phone down she immediately rang Hannah whilst it was on her mind. There was no answer and so she left a message and then instantly forgot all about it.

Chapter 19

Will was at her house, again. Tess didn't really mind but it seemed a bit non-stop. They seemed to have by-passed the dating part of the relationship and replaced it with Will simply being there all the time. Tess wasn't sure how to handle it. It seemed a bit rude to simply carry on as if he wasn't there but equally things needed to be done. She hadn't done any washing in weeks as she didn't have a tumble drier and she didn't want Will to see her pants drying on radiators and over the bath. She needed some time on her own, but she was unsure of how to suggest it without somehow implying that she didn't want him around.

There also always seemed to be something. Obviously she knew Will had friends. She had met many of them, liked some of them (there was the token exception of his friend Amanda who seemed to be determined to be the most important woman in his life – despite being married to his mate Michael – and obviously Tess' elevation to girlfriend status had improved things enormously). But now it would seem there was a whole other group of people she had never met before but now they were 'a couple' they could socialise with. Tess was unsure what any of them had in common, she wasn't even sure they liked each other but they seemed to get a lot of pleasure from sitting around and talking about how similar their lives were and how 'crazy' it was that they had all this and were still so young. Tess once pointed out that they were all knocking on thirty so weren't that young and that by their age her parents had popped out a couple of kids so if anything they were living some sort of extended adolescence. A polite silence and a squeeze on her knee from Will had ensured she was quiet (and drunk) for the rest of the evening whilst they talked mortgages, kids (fictional, only two of them were pregnant) and interior decorating.

She resented her life being taken up like this. Not that she begrudged Will his friends. She wanted him to spend time with them. But she wanted him to spend time with his actual friends. Not this bunch of self-congratulatory smugs. His friends who liked him when he was single, friends who were there for him when his lifestyle didn't match theirs. He deserved that. She wanted that for him. It would also get her out of talking to people who assumed she wanted the same as them.

Kids.

Tess was not maternal. She saw no reason to explain her decision. People were allowed to bring life in to the world for no more reason than they "wanted" children. Tess didn't want children but had to provide a long list of reasons why not. 'Because I don't' was apparently not valid. But that was all they were going to get. Even the dreaded words 'you'll change your mind' couldn't set her off. She merely replied 'So might you' then they wrote her off as an aggressive lunatic and she could carry on.

Not that this was so easy with Will. He wanted children. And he wanted them with Tess. He was firmly of the opinion that because his was the 'right' opinion she would come round. Depriving someone of children was far crueller than forcing someone to have them and raise them. She wasn't too worried. She refused to believe this was something they needed to decide months in to going out. But it was annoying to go around the supermarket with Will.
"Look, you're pulling faces at that baby, you like kids. You're so good with them." Will said encouragingly.
"I believe there's more to it than pulling faces at them in

supermarkets."

"You love Finn and Jake."

"I like kids. I don't want my own. I like pancakes. I don't want to dedicate my life to them" Tess attempted to explain.

"That's a crap analogy and it makes no sense." Will said.

"It was the best I could come up with at short notice and we're in the baking aisle."

But it had to be said, being with Will was nice. Perhaps not better than being on her own but different and she wanted a change.

Chapter 20

After approaching three women, Will was arousing the suspicions of the WHSmith's security guard. All the women had refused to do what he asked. He was going to have to bite the bullet. He nodded to the guard and then marched with determination towards the magazine section. Barely stopping, he picked up *Cosmopolitan*, *Company* and *Glamour* and put them all under a copy of Top Gear magazine. He then went straight to the cash tills, paid and walked out. The guard smiled at him as he walked past. Will merely held his head higher.

That night he sat on his sofa agog. He turned the pages of the magazine slowly, what age group were these aimed at? The level of detail was astonishing. And the pictures! The articles themselves were no help whatsoever for his problem. It would appear that whatever Tess wanted was normal. And if he questioned her then he was evil. According to these the only unusual thing about women and sex was that they ever got anything else done. Sex was apparently mandatory for the first date and if anyone questioned that then they were right wing judgemental prudes. Unless of course the woman didn't want to have sex on the first date, in which case, if a man suggested it he was a chauvinistic rapist. Are rapists chauvinists by definition Will wondered? Then he shook his head and got himself back to the matter in hand. He and Tess had been going out for a while now and their relationship could have been in *High School Musical*. He'd try to raise the subject but she had said she wanted to take it slow and, of course, he respected that. If she wanted to wait for three years that would be fine but he needed to have an end date. He'd kissed Tess goodnight at her door and then headed home alone again. Now it was just him and the magazines. Actually these magazines might come in handy after all....

Tess sighed as her phone lit up. She knew that despite saying goodbye to him half an hour ago this would be her goodnight text from Will. She had loads of them. One for every night they had been together. She might have to start staying the night at his if only to stop the flipping text messages. Although maybe he'd text her while she was in the bathroom. She stopped herself, she knew she was being unreasonable. Most women would kill for what she had. Will was attentive, caring and devoted. Work wasn't as awkward as she had thought it would be. She had decreed that no one at the office knew about them and Will was fine for no one to know about his private life. In fact most people thought that they had had a row as Tess had slightly over reacted and barely acknowledged Will at all. The rest was fine. It was nice to be wined and dined. She actively enjoyed kissing Will and really wanted to take it further, it's just she knew that the moment she did she would be very much committed. At the moment there was still a chance she could get out of this relationship and Tess wasn't quite sure she was ready to lose her escape route. She wasn't used to having to spend so much time with another person and being expected to enjoy it. She had always had friends and people to do something with. Now she had someone to do nothing with. And nothing didn't seem to have an end point.

On the bright side, she kept telling herself, if she had to be constantly supervised, be forced to talk all the time, not be able to walk from one room to another without being expected to have a conversation about it, constantly have to tell someone what she was doing and not be able to make a decision about her own life (meeting someone for a drink, organising weekend plans) without first checking that other plans hadn't already made plans for her or without checking if he wanted to tag along with her plans; then she was glad that it was Will. She could spend more time with him than most people.

Truth was she wanted to sleep with Will. In fact it was taking all her self control not to. She suddenly, after years of not viewing him that way at all, couldn't stop thinking about him that way. It's just that she knew that that would lead to her or him having to stay over and then spending all the next day together and the next night and the next until they were living together and she would have to get an allotment or a shed or something.

However she wasn't sure how much longer she could hold out. She usually had Matt for, er, *needs* like this and now she had a good looking guy, who was mad about her, and had a sexy accent, at her disposal and he wouldn't put any pressure on her whatsoever. So it was really up to her to make the next move .

Tess had no body hang ups. She knew she wasn't a supermodel but she also knew she wasn't Bella Emberg. She wouldn't strut around in her underwear and had the usual bikini issues that every woman had but she was sensible enough to know that Will wasn't going to vomit at the sight of her. Still it wasn't every day that you had to take your clothes off in front of your friend and boss and see them without theirs on. Therefore she had a plan.

"Hello, it's me." Tess said.
"Hello, you." Will replied.
"Did we make any plans for tonight? I've had a thought."
"We said we would do something but we didn't say what. What have you got in mind?" Will wandered outside the pub so he could hear Tess better. He could hear the taunts from his friends about him being under the thumb and laughingly gave them the middle finger as he pushed open the pub door.
"There's a film festival on at the Electric. It starts at six and they are showing two art house films tonight and two tomorrow."
Tess tried to sound casual and spontaneous.

"Which ones?"

" Some French things which I've never heard of but there's a bar at the Electric so if it's awful we can drink our way through it."
The drinking was Tess' real plan. But she wanted to look like she had some form of cultural identity and had ideas above just constantly going to the pub.

"OK." Will was hesitant but he too wanted to appear cultural. "French films. I can do that. Meet you outside at ten to?"

"Perfect. See you then."

They hang up. Tess is quite smug. Drink in the dark whilst watching a fancy pants arts film then when just drunk enough go back to Will's house (then she could leave in the morning and not write off the next day) and move this thing to the next level.

Chapter 21

Oh. Good. Grief.

Will can barely stand he is laughing so much. He is doubled over and hanging on to a trustafarians wheelie bin for support.

Tess meanwhile is indignant. "18! That is not an 18. That's an x. Surely. Do they still have an X rating. 18?" She grabs her phone out of her bag and starts to google film classifications.

Will can't speak. Tess isn't normally such a prude but her well laid plans have been slightly destroyed. Turns out she'd been trying to subtly romance and woo Will by accidentally taking him to see porn. Unsimulated, closely shot porn. Shot in an arty fashion but undeniably live footage of two actors having noisy, not entirely attractive, sex.

Throughout the first film Will and Tess had wrestled the armrest up and Tess had snuggled in to him. It had been a beautiful shot story of love and loss had touched them both and they had snogged their way through the interval. Will had mentally planned a romantic trip to Paris. Tess planned to buy a stripy jumper. Then the second film had started, it was clear that this was a different kettle of fish. The second the underpants hit the floor and they were treated to a full frontal they leapt apart as if they had been shot. At first Tess had tried to pretend that she was fine with it. To look as though she was a sophisticated girl about town who saw this solely as a piece of art work. Then she looked at Will who had tears of mirth running down his face and she cracked up as well. After being hushed by people who were much more mature and sophisticated, Tess simply turned her back on Will and died of embarrassment.

There was no way she could carry out the rest of her plans for the evening now. They were wrecked and it looked like Will had pulled a stomach muscle from laughing so hard. She was suddenly and irrationally angry and frustrated.

"Right. Well that was fun. Hope you enjoyed it. I'm going to make a move." Tess flung her bag over her shoulder and stormed off.

She set off down the street and quite a pace. Will had to jog to catch up with her.

"What's up with you?" he asked.

"Nothing. I'm fine. It was an honest mistake you know. Glad it's amused you so much." Tess snapped.

"Oh come on, you can't be in a strop about this."

"I'm not in a strop." She was in a strop.

"It was a mistake Tess, a funny mistake. You were laughing too." Will reasoned.

"Yeah and then I stopped." Tess said. "90 minutes later and you're still going. Nothing is that funny." Oh sod it thought Tess I already sound mental and I've clearly screwed up the rest of the night. I might as well go for it. "So you're basically laughing at me. I made mistake and it's the funniest thing ever. Let's all laugh at Tess. Well I'm sorry I'm not as clever as you Will. I'm sorry I'm not as sophisticated as you. I'm sorry I've ruined the evening. Let's just call it quits and I'll see you on Monday."

She storms off again and this time Will lets her go.

The journey home had not helped to dim Tess' mood. Loved up couples were everywhere and tourists with enormous wheely suitcases had blocked every tube escalator and doorway. She had swerved around them all muttering under her breath. One couple was particularly startled when they stopped for a quick snog at the top of an escalator and a pale woman barked 'When you've finished making love' at them.

She stopped at the corner shop and bought a bottle of wine and as she rounded the corner she saw a figure in the doorway. Oh bloody hell the tramp was back. Then the tramp stood up and walked towards her.

"Have you calmed down?" asked tramp/Will

"Not really, no." Tess replied.

"Want to tell me what it was about."

"Not really, no." She doesn't open the door and hopes that will act as a hint to Will to leave.

"Tough." He takes the bottle of wine from her and removes the foil top. Then balancing on one foot he takes his shoe off and places the bottle in the shoe and starts smacking it against the wall. The cork pops out a little way and will pulls it out with his teeth. He takes a swig and then hands the bottle to Tess. She has a swig.

"Impressive. Where did you learn to do that." She asks.

"Don't change the subject. Speak."

"Fine. Don't look at me."

He respects her request and they sit back to back on the doorstep. Passing the wine between them whilst Tess haltingly stutters out what she had planned for that evening.

"...and then I thought we'd go back to yours and you know.... because I want to and I know you wouldn't.... so I thought maybe... and then that, fucking PORN comes on and now...Oh I don't know, I'm stroppy, you're annoyed. Let's just write it off and we'll do it another day OK."

To his eternal credit Will doesn't laugh. He doesn't even speak, he holds his hand out for the bottle and Tess passes it to him. He places it on the floor then turns and grabs Tess' face between his hands. He kisses her with more passion than he ever has before. Tess eagerly responds and soon their hands are grabbing at one another. They are on their feet and Will is pushing her against the brick wall. Tess elongates her body against his.

"Will, Will..." she murmurs

"Erghthgh" is his response.

"I know we're not sticking to the plans this evening but I never ever wanted us to take this next step on the street against a wall." She says.

He pulls her unbuttoned (how the hell had that happened?) shirt around her and stamps impatiently as Tess fumbles for her keys and opens the door. They grope and kiss their way along the communal stairs and corridor and finally arrive at Tess' flat. Tess opens the door and is glad that her bedroom will be spotless as usual. Turns out she needn't have worried. Will kicks the door shut behind him and they get no further than the hallway.

Chapter 22

Will braces his leg against Tess. It forces her to stand up right. Whilst she's on the back foot he replaces her glass of wine with a pint of water.

"Drink it." He orders.

In the corner Stuart is doing something similar for Tilly although she is slumped in a chair with her head between her legs. He exchanges rueful looks with Will. Will sympathises with him. In his professional opinion Tilly is about five minutes away from lavishly vomiting. Tess is in a slightly better state but this makes her more dangerous.

"I can't believe she's done this. I'm gunna say something." Tess slurs. How the hell did she get her hands on her glass of wine again? She can barely speak but she can perform sleight of hand magic tricks. Will swaps her drinks again and tries to reason with her.

"You're not going to say anything. Not here and not now." He says.

"She's out of order." Tess' voice is dangerously loud.

"She is, but Simon's not. It's his birthday and he doesn't need or deserve you fighting with his wife. This may seem like a great idea now but it's a dreadful idea and I am not going to let you do it."

"Let me?" Tess questions.

"Not a discussion for now dear."

"Look at her." Tess gestures by flinging her arm wide. Will dodges the swinging limb and catches Tess before she topples over.

"Please Tess, for Simon." He pleads.

This has some effect on Tess and she gulps back some of the water. She then follows Tilly as she makes a dash to the toilets.

For all her closeness issues Tess is surprisingly good at holding back people's hair whilst they vomit.

Will goes over to Stuart and they sit and chat about their respective partners, the party and Stuart's stag. As Stuart speaks Will takes the opportunity to look at Daisy and the source of Tess' rage.

Daisy had taken it upon herself to invite Kyle to Simon's 30th. Since they had arrived at the pub, and Simon had had the crap scared out of him, Daisy had attached herself to Kyle's side and had barely left it since. In Tess' mind this was why Daisy had suggested the party in the first place. They had certainly eaten their dinner at an indigestion inducing pace as Daisy had seemed anxious to get to the pub. It wasn't because she wanted to do something nice for Simon; it was because she wanted to spend the night with Kyle and gradually infiltrate him in to the group. Will looked at Simon, he was heartbreakingly unaware, he followed Daisy around the room with his eyes. Still as in love with her as he had been on his wedding day. The fact she was cracking on to another man right in front of him passed him by completely. Sadly it hadn't gone unnoticed by Kyle's wife who looked in a similar state to Tess. Will didn't have it in him to deal with another drunk and ranting woman. She looked like she was about to tear Daisy limb from limb, only able to hold her self back through good manners alone. The only saving grace (and possibly why Kyle's wife had not completely lost it) is that Kyle is utterly oblivious. Daisy could be dancing the dance of the seven veils in front of him and he wouldn't care. It's not that he's stupid, it's that he's not interested. Will logs all this to tell Tess. Not that it will help the situation. Daisy is besotted but at least Tess can be sure that it's not reciprocated.

"Shall we go and rescue that poor bastard?" Stuart's voice breaks through and Will is suddenly aware that Daisy has crossed the line of acceptable behaviour and other people have noticed. He and Stuart get up and walk across to the awkward threesome.

"Daisy, would you mind going and checking on Tilly and Tess? They went to the loos a while back and obviously we can't go in." Will smiles as he says it but it's a definite order.

"I'm just in the middle of ..."

"Now please. Thanks a million Daisy" Will smiles at her but the smile doesn't reach his eyes.

She goes. She can't really not. Thank goodness for manners; although they're all behaving like animals, middle class breeding means none of them have the audacity to be rude to each other's faces. As Daisy heads off to the toilets, Kyle, Kyle's wife, Stuart and Will make awkward conversation and refuse to let Daisy join in when she returns far too quickly. Daisy eventually gives up and spends the rest of the evening with Simon although she ensures the party wraps up slightly earlier than planned now she can't spend it with her beau. A green-faced Tilly and a swaying Tess do not complain at the early ending.

Chapter 23

Tess puts her phone down. She was desperate for this 'star' to get back to her and had willingly spewed out her email, work number and mobile number to anyone vaguely connected to her. She was repeatedly checking her phone. The minute this woman called her back she could go home, she didn't want to leave it hanging over her head till tomorrow and have weird dreams about work. She's had too many of those lately. 8-01 pm. Come on you bugger. RING.

She sees she has a text from Daisy. Daisy likes to text. Lately though the texting has gone in overdrive. Daisy is aware that she behaved badly at Simon's birthday party. But rather than apologise and explain her behaviour she is pretending it never happened but sending a lot of random texts. The texts are to see if Tess replies and if she is in a mood with her.

Tess makes a mental note to reply to Daisy later (she is in a mood with her) and makes one last appeal to the universe for this celebrity to call. She is rewarded by an email arriving, from the lady herself, saying she hopes to be in touch 'soon'. It suddenly dawns on Tess that even if she got all the information now there's no one still working to pass it on to. She shuts down her computer and goes home, where she finds Will waiting for her. She turns down his offers of food and after the briefest of debriefs about her day she collapses in to bed, barely noticing when Will gets in beside her a few hours later.

The next morning Tess surveys the rapidly growing pile of clothes and gives it a half hearted kick. It's so well stacked that it barely moves. She'd waved goodbye to Will half an hour ago reassuring him that she would just jump in the shower and join him in the office in under an hour. Despite their relationship being an open secret around the workplace she still couldn't bring herself to walk in to the office with Will. So she staggered her arrival so she always arrived about fifteen minutes after him, clearly today the arrival would be not so much staggered as gaping. Every outfit Tess tries on looks ridiculous at best, care in the community at worst. There is barely anything left in the wardrobe as she tries clothes on then rips them over her head and throws them on to the clothing mound in the corner of the room. All the dressing and undressing means that soon Tess is boiling. She walks over to the window and heaves it open, treating her neighbour opposite to the sight of her in a pair of jeans and a bra, her hair held back from her head with a pair of (clean) knickers.

Tess had never quite mastered the art of a capsule wardrobe. She merely bought what she liked without really thinking how it would fit in to her wardrobe as a whole. Tilly was able to create 15 outfits out of three articles of clothing. Tess found a jumper she liked and wore it with everything until it went in the wash and then she forgot she owned it and moved on to another piece of clothing.

Slightly cooled, Tess sits on the floor and starts to work on her face. In all the years she's lived in the flat she's never quite got round to hanging the mirror and so simply sits on the floor to do her make up. Will keeps saying that he can put it up for her. But she keeps batting him off. She's not sure she's ready to become a couple that do DIY at weekends. The face that stares back at her in the glass is sweaty and blotchy. Thanks to tears of frustration that hit during the clothing crisis, her eyes are glassy and red and the trails of the make up that she failed to take off last night are working their way down her cheeks. She has a brief pang of nostalgia for the days where no one at work noticed what she wore. Now she was the MD's girlfriend she had to be more groomed than ever before. Not for Will's sake. He couldn't give a monkey's what she wears (which in itself is annoying as sometimes she needs to be told that an outfit is shit. A point driven home by the incident Daisy still refers to as 'Beyonce-gate'). But she has to look her best for the hordes of women who have come out of the woodwork to stare at her and answer the perennial question 'What does he see in her?'. Therefore Tess has learned to rise a half an hour early, to kick Will out and then prance around in front of the mirror holding things against herself, then apply airhostess levels of make-up.

"And here's Nick with the 8-30 news". Tess looks at the radio in horror and as if on cue the tears which haven't quite been beaten, bubble over and make their way down her face. The clothing pile gets kicked again and then a wave of determination sweeps over her. She wipes her face down with an old t-shirt then slaps on foundation and taking a thick black eyeliner she covers every inch of her eye with it. No mean feat given the weeping has reduced them to piss holes in the snow. Why this couldn't have been done an hour ago is beyond her but undaunted she adds mascara and just enough bronzer to look alive but not so much that she looks like a cast member of TOWIE. She flings on a decent top (which inevitably was the first thing she'd tried on that morning) and rams her feet in a pair of heels. As she makes her way out of the bedroom a last look in the mirror confirms that her face is beginning to deflate. By the time she gets to work she should look slightly more human.

She goes to the kitchen and takes out the lunch that Will made the night before and left for her in the fridge. Irritation at this is only superseded by actually wanting the lunch. She gathers together her oyster card, keys and phone. She sets up *EastEnders* to be recorded that evening. She turns on the hall light so she doesn't have to come back to a dark flat. She places an eyeliner in her bag so she can make regular touch ups throughout the day. She picks up her bag, she throws it on the floor, she walks across the landing and goes in to the bedroom. She gets in to bed and pulls the covers over her head and sobs in to the pillow.

"You poor thing", Will says, rubbing her shoulder as he walks past. "Have you had one before?"
"Not for years. I used to get migraines when I was a teenager, thought I'd grown out of them."
"You should see a doctor."
"About a one off migraine? I don't think I need to rush for medical attention." Tess wishes he'd let the subject drop. She'd chosen a migraine as her excuse as it needed little explanation and she could be better in twenty four hours. She dreaded to think how much interrogation would have taken place if she'd told Will the real reason she hadn't gone to work. She tried to imagine his face as she told him she had called in sick because she was too sad and couldn't stop crying.
"Well just take care, you look awful." Will says.
Tess is about to object but lets the subject drop. She does look like shit. She spent the day alternatively revelling in having the flat to herself and enjoying wandering around knowing that she wasn't going to be forced in to conversation or asked what she was thinking and feeling guilty that she wasn't at work (she had never called in sick before and she felt what Tilly called 'S-skivers guilt') both of these emotions were punctuated with bouts of ferocious weeping which took her by surprise. One moment she absolutely fine and thinking about lunch the next she was staring at a loaf of bread and weeping so copiously she could barely see.

Will had rushed over after work and had not batted an eyelid at her ravaged face and mismatched leisure wear. Instead he had made her a meal and insisted she sit and rest while he tidied around.

He sits on the sofa and pulls Tess to him. She rests her head against his chest and his hand plays with the nape of her neck. She sighs with lazy satisfaction and gently stokes his chest with her hand.

"So how was your day?" she asks.

As he tells her stories of the office and recounts the details of his day, Tess closes her eyes.

A few hours later Tess kisses him goodbye on the doorstep and waves him off in to the night. Both having agreed that she needs her rest. She shuts the door and smiles to herself. Perhaps she's cracked it. That was a really lovely evening. She looks at her phone. Inevitably she already has a good night text from Will. She replies with a simple 'xxxx' and flicks off the lights and heads to bed where she sinks in to a sleep that is happy and contented.

At 3am, her eyes fly open and her sleep is over for the night. All rest is replaced by unnamed panic. Her chest contracts and there is an unassailable fear which means that all attempts at sleep are gone. She briefly considers calling Will but as she is unable to articulate what is wrong is unsure of what she will say to him. Instead she drags her duvet to the sofa and begins to channel surf. Challenge TV comes to her rescue with an old episode of *Funhouse* and Pat Sharp driving a tiny car fills the rest of her night.

Chapter 24

"So don't tell Tilly," Daisy concludes.

"OK." Tess agrees although she doubts she could cobble together anything to tell out of the breathless tales Daisy has just divulged "Why not?"

Daisy had begged Tess to have lunch with her and not invite Tilly. Tess had assumed it was to discuss a wedding present or hen do or something. It's actually to discuss Kyle. This annoys Tess beyond words and as a result is not the audience that Daisy so obviously wants.

"Well I know that Tilly thinks I am being funny with her and I suppose I am a little bit." Daisy says "It's just I know that she's always looked to me and Simon as a happy marriage and with her wedding coming up I don't want to shatter her illusions in love what with, well, my situation."

"The interesting thing is that she actually thinks there is a situation." Tess says. Safe in the knowledge that Daisy had only decreed Tilly shouldn't know Tess was keeping Will fully informed. "I had to point out to her that she still does have a happy marriage and if she doesn't the person she should be talking to about it is probably Simon. But to be fair I don't think there is anything she can tell him, I think she needs to get this out of her system. It's like she's creating drama for the sake of drama. It seems to be all stolen glances across the photocopier and 'bantering' emails. She printed some of them out to show me, I'm now certain that Kyle isn't in on it. Especially after what you said about him at the party. They read like something I'd send to you."

Will gestures to himself sat on the end of the bed in just his pants. "Not the greatest analogy" he observes.

Tess grins "OK, like something I'd send Geoff." Geoff is the cuttings manager at work. He is notoriously smelly. He works in the basement and has used that as an excuse not to wash. Tess comes over and straddles Will. Pushing her hands in to his hair. "Oh actually that's not a great example either. Geoff and I are absolutely filthy."

Not that Will isn't desperately interested in Daisy's fictional love life but Tess is rarely spontaneously affectionate these days and he isn't one to muck about. Turns out they don't go out for dinner that night and Tess sleeps soundly for the first time in weeks.

This working for a living is hard going and seems to be getting harder. Whereas weekends for Tess used to be fairly active and involved epic plans now they seem to be based around getting as much sleep as humanly possibly as she seems unable to get more than four hours a night during the week. She is aware that this is not fair on Will and so attempts to be awake for at least 10 hours a day. When she wakes up on Saturday it's clear that Will's been awake for hours and is not happy about her late awakening. It does beg the question why he decided to sit around and get in a mood about it rather than getting on and doing something without her but she decides not to start a row and instead puts the kettle on.

She rallies briefly in the afternoon and she and Will go to the cinema. Curled in Will's arms she feels secure. The film washes over her and she laughs at the latest rom-com. Will is thrilled to see her so carefree and they spend a happy few hours. Until they walk out of the cinema and Tess immediately checks her phone. She has a missed call from Arrabella.
"Oh God, what do you think she wants?" Tess panics.
"I don't know. Could be anything, you know what she's like. Ignore it. She can't expect you to answer on a Saturday." Will is

practical.

"I must have forgotten something. Think, have I said anything to you about what I was meant to do this weekend?" She rattles off a list of D grade celebrities, desperately trying to trip her brain in to remembering what she should have done.

Will simply takes his phone out of his pocket and dials Arrabella's number.

"Hi Arrabella, it's Will how are you? Yep, yep good. Listen I'm with Tess and it looks like she's missed a call from you. Her phone's playing up. Is there anything I can help you with? Yep, OK, I'll let her know. OK, yep, you too. See you Monday."

He hangs up, Tess looks at him.

"Can you remember to bring 'One Day' in on Monday. You said you'd lend it to her." He says.

Tess sags with relief.

"Why can't she text?" she asks.

"Tess, she can barely read. Can we get on with our day now?" Will is beginning to get frustrated.

"Do you think she knows about us?"

"So what?"

With that Will reaches the end of his tether. It's hard to get annoyed with Tess. Mainly because he fancies her and to be frank she could vomit all down herself and he wouldn't be put off, he's pretty enamoured, but also because she's clearly on edge about something. She's lost her 'Tessness'. Her (and he hates that this word comes in to his head, he blames the X Factor for even knowing it at all) swagger. All he can do is love her more and hope that sorts it. But as a short term measure he takes her phone out of her bag, inputs her password (she's never told him it but he knows her birthday) and turns her phone off.

"What?"

"Please Tess. You need to switch off."

He's right. She's twitchy and on edge. Tess is nervous, she seems to be unable to keep a hold of anything in her life at the moment, and she's not going to lose Will through being crap. She puts the powered down phone in her bag and slips her hands in to Wills.

"Sorry. Now, could I tempt you to a drink?" she asks.

She can and they do. And gradually real Tess returns and they have an excellent evening, which turns in to an excellent night. Tess is amusing, witty and scathing. Will is charming, kind and funny. As they tease the best out of each other they are unaware that another cloud is brewing.

After spending the night at Will's and having a lie in, Tess heads for home around midday and for once Will doesn't try to walk her. She potters along and enjoys the weak sun on her face as she looks in shop windows and buys a coffee to keep her company. Then she turns the corner to her street and sees Hannah sat on the doorstep of her flats. All relaxed feelings are immediately gone.

Chapter 25

Tess goes for the obvious; she's not good under pressure.
"What are you doing here?"She asks.
"Well you'd know if you answered your bloody phone, I've been calling you since yesterday Tess, I had to call Mum and Dad to get your landline number, which meant I had to face the Spanish inquisition." Hannah is properly pissed off. Tess is impressed that even though this has almost nothing to do with her Hannah has managed to make this Tess' fault and put her on the back foot.
"Sorry I was at Will's", Tess apologises. "My phone was off. It's a long story but I was...it doesn't matter. It's in my bag somewhere. Look here it is. I'll turn it on now." Tess turns her phone on and holds it out, almost like it is evidence to support her story. Hannah looks at her with absolute disgust. Tess tries to salvage the conversation. "How are Mum and Dad?"
This was almost definitely not the right thing to say. Hannah fixes her with a dead eyed stare. Tess finds it hard to believe that a few short months ago she had had a laugh with Hannah about people trying to get her to date. This Hannah is terrifying. She doesn't know if it's pregnancy hormones or she is revisiting her teenage years but she is unsure as to why it has landed on her doorstep.
"They're fine Tess. As am I. Thanks for asking." Hannah snaps.
If it hadn't been for the fact that Hannah looked like she was about to cry Tess would have turned on her heel and gone back to Wills. Instead she reverts to the role she has always had and tries to placate Hannah.
"Oh good, well that's nice. Anway good to see you." Tess goes to hug her but Hannah steps back.
"I'm not in the mood." She says.
Brilliant. Tess finds it hard to believe that they have said less than ten words to each other and they are already having a row.

Honestly she likes nothing better than when people turn up, out of the blue and totally uninvited to her house and pick a fight with her. Nothing gets her day off to a better start. However she wants to nip it in the bud so doesn't rise to the bait. Instead she gets her keys out of her bag and reaches past Hannah to unlock the door.

"Are you coming in?" she asks.

Hannah doesn't reply. Merely picks up her bag (bag????) and waits for Tess to hold the door open for her. Tess is confused for a second, wondering what she is waiting for, then twigs and opens the door and leans past Hannah to hold it open for her. She barges past Tess and makes her way in the to communal hallway. Tess has a slight twinge of satisfaction when she has to walk past Hannah to show her the way as Hannah has never been to here before and doesn't have a clue which is Tess' flat. When she opens the door to her flat Hannah attempts to keep the strop momentum going by pushing past her so she is the first one in. It's a slight over reaction but Tess lets it go; she is quite intrigued as to what is going on with her sister to make her behave like such a twat. In one way it's quite enjoyable, Hannah has been firmly ensconced in yummy mummydom for quite some time so it's entertaining to see her regress so much. Hannah flounces in to the living room and flings herself in to an armchair. Tess wanders through to the kitchen and opens the fridge and sniffs the milk.

"Tea?" She calls through to the living room. "Or are you not doing caffeine?"

"I'm doing it," Hannah replies. "Tea would be great."

As she waits for the kettle to boil she has a quick tidy around. Not that there is much laying about in her usually pristine house it's just she doesn't want to leave anything around that Hannah might read. She found Tess' diary when she was fifteen and can still recite whole passages of it. As can her friends. Hannah issued them with copies.

Tess takes the tea through to the living room where Hannah is still sprawled in the chair. She's opened all the windows and there is a near gale blowing through the room. A photo from the mantelpiece has blown off and is face down on the carpet, Tess resists the urge to go over and return it to its rightful place. Hannah twists herself round to accept the mug of tea that Tess proffers. Looking at her as she squirms in to place Tess forgets that she is a married mother of two with another child on the way and is instead reminded of student Hannah. She holds up a couple of Tess' books, clearly she's been through the book shelves and helped herself to whatever she likes the look of. "Are these any good?" she asks.
"Yeah not bad." Tess replies. "I preferred his earlier stuff but it's well written, very readable. You can borrow them if you like."
"Thanks", Hannah says. Tucking them in her bag. "Do you mind? I liked his first book and I'd like to see what…"
Tess loses her patience and cuts her off. "Hannah what are you doing here?"

There is a pause then finally Hannah speaks in a voice so quiet that Tess has to strain to hear her.
"I've left Garry."
Of all the things Tess should say at that moment she knows that 'Do Mum and Dad know?' isn't the best question to ask but that is what comes hurtling out of her mouth. She gets the look of disgust that that comment deserves.
"No of course they don't know." The contempt in Hannah's voice is clear. "I don't know what I am doing. Why would I tell them? And you're not going say anything either."
"What do I say if Garry calls?" Tess asks.
Hannah looks as though she is going to hit her. "He's not going to call you Tess, he'll call me. I've got my phone, I've not done a midnight flit, he knows where I am. Jesus Tess, I was hoping for

slightly more support from you than some weird preoccupation with Mum and Dad and how you should answer the phone."

"You're right. I'm sorry. It's just come at me a bit out of the blue. Do you want to talk about it?" Tess offers.

"No."

"Right," Tess stands up. "Great, well nice of you to show up. How long are you staying?" Hannah might be sticking to her teenage role but Tess sees no reason why she should have to stick to hers.

"A week?" Hannah suggests.

A week! Tess isn't sure she can stick a week of this. Especially if she keeps this mood up. Tess is fairly up and down on the moodometer herself at the moment, she doesn't need Lucifer coming to stay. But it doesn't look like she has a huge amount of choice in the matter. She certainly not going to argue, Hannah has a look on her face like she is going to stab someone soon.

"Great", Tess says. Plastering a shit eating grin all over her face. "Right, well do you fancy going out for lunch of something?"

"Why not."

"Brilliant, well I'll sort myself out. Make yourself at home."

She already has. She's got her feet all over the chairs and is leafing through Tess' books and magazines whilst she drinks her tea.

A week, she can't stay a week. There's no way Tess can put up with her for that long. Especially if Hannah stays in this mood. A fundamental difference between Tess and Hannah is that Tess assumes that no one wants her around whereas Hannah assumes that it is an honour and a privilege to house her and can't see how anyone could object.

Tess goes through to her bedroom and plugs her phone in to charge. As it starts gaining in battery she sees the missed calls and texts start to build up. Most are from Hannah, a few are from Daisy and Tilly and there are some from an 'unknown' number. That will be her parents. They are paranoid about identity fraud for some reason. Anything that has their name on is immediately shredded on its arrival in the house. Phone numbers are guarded like a state secret (although they do answer the phone by quoting their phone number). In contrast they haven't checked the batteries in their smoke alarm for the last five years. Presumably they'd see a massive house fire as a way to destroy all the details that shredding can't reach. After a quick change of clothes and dashing off a few texts to Tilly, Daisy and Nina, Tess slaps a bit of make up on and decides she can't put off talking to Hannah any longer so walks back through to the living room where Hannah is halfway through an episode of *The House of Elliot*. Given that Tess hides this particular DVD box set Hannah must have had a really good rummage. Hannah looks at her as she walks in "Should I ask why you have this?"

"No. Are you ready?"

She is and they leave to head to a pub about five minutes away. Tess attempts conversation but Hannah responds with a few half hearted grunts. It is difficult to believe that this is the same sister who was cheerfully taking the piss out of her and regaling her with stories about the boys not so long ago. She's wearing low cut jeans and a fitted tee- shirt and doesn't look pregnant at all. Not that Tess is sure how pregnant she is or how she should look. In her mind maternity wear is all about smocks and those funny trousers with expandable pockets. They arrive at the pub and look around for somewhere to sit. Despite the warm day Hannah refuses to sit outside as 'there might be people smoking out there' so they head to a dingy corner of the pub. As she follows her sister Tess wonders if they give out new personalities with pregnancy hormones. Hannah used to smoke around the back of the shed when they were teenagers, their mother had found all her fag butts once and Hannah had blamed it on a tramp. Their Dad had kept quiet; Tess reckoned he'd added quite a few of his own over the years. They sit down and an awkward silence descends. Tess picks a topic that has never been known to fail in the past.

"So how are the boys?" She asks.
Hannah's face lights up and she is quite transformed. "Oh they're lovely. Finn was so cute yesterday; he wants to do everything Jake does. So they were out in the garden and …." The anecdote is actually quite sweet and Tess loves hearing stories about her little nephews. But what is interesting is the change that comes over Hannah. She is animated for the first time since she got here. The attitude and rudeness that were already tiresome were gone and in their place was a contented and happy woman. She's totally enamoured. She gets photos up on her phone and flicks through them, showing selected ones to Tess, who smiles and nods in approval. As Tess offers comment and admires the boys she can't help but think that something must have gone seriously wrong with Garry to make Hannah leave them. Even if it is only for a week.

The food they ordered arrives and Hannah is forced to stop talking as they accept cutlery and food and turn down offers of condiments and other drinks. Tess immediately wishes she hadn't tried to win the sibling higher ground by ordering salad. Hannah has a Panini and chips and it looks amazing. Tess' in comparison looks utterly unappetising, she smothers it in salad cream, immediately defeating the point of having a salad and starts picking the bacon out.
"So how are you feeling, what with the pregnancy and everything?" Tess asks her sister.
"Fine. Why are you eating your salad in such a weird way?"
"There's a shit load of lettuce so I'm trying to eat around it. It was a bad choice. How's yours?"
"Why did you order it then?"

The most animated conversation they've had all day and it's about Tess' menu choices. Tess decides to change the subject. "So. What's going on, what's Garry done? Why are you here?" As questions go it's pretty direct but she is still surprised when Hannah answers her.

"I'm just so fucking angry with him, " Hannah spits out. She lays down her knife and fork and picks her napkin up and presses it to her eyes. Tess wonders if she can make a grab for a chip but decides to concentrate on the issue at hand.

"Why? What's he done?" Tess was about to say they seemed fine last time she had seen them but then remembers that that is a lie. However Hannah is on a roll and Tess can just sit back and let her go.

"He's so fucking smug and he thinks that he can talk me in to doing whatever he wants just because he earns all the money. He doesn't get that he wouldn't be able to do half the things he wants to do if it wasn't for me but he doesn't see what I do as work. I slave for that family and he thinks I just sit around all day. But when I try and do something for me he doesn't like it. Every time I try and do something that doesn't directly benefit him, or isn't quite what he wants, he shuts it down. He's always finding ways to keep me in that bloody house. Don't get me wrong I love the boys, love the boys, of course I do but day in day out talking about PowerRangers or fighting or who'd beat who in a battle of superheros, or toilets or pants...it's too much. Then I feel guilty that I'm not enjoying it so I throw myself in to it more but I need some time for me. Just me. Garry doesn't get it. HE thinks my whole life is one big doss just because I'm not in an office. He doesn't get it at all. So he can have the boys, have the house, he can have it all. See how he likes it."

Hannah finishes her outburst and picks up her drink and knocks it back. Tess can tell she wishes it was something stronger than sparkling water. She's taken aback. All this time she thought Hannah had it made and it turns out she's been living with the

UK's answer to Joseph Fritzel. And what's with all the swearing? Tess had said 'crap' in front of the boys once (Jake had ridden his bike full speed in to her arse down a hill when he couldn't find the brakes and was in a bit of a panic) and Hannah had reacted as though Tess had had a full blown Tourette's attack. As Tess had pulled the bike out of bottom and checked for internal bleeding she was astonished she wasn't being congratulated on her restraint.   Now Hannah was effing and jeffing like Roy Chubby Brown. This outburst by Hannah makes Tess choose her next words carefully, for all she knows they could be her last.
"Oh, OK. I thought all was rosy with you two. What with the new baby and all."
All she gets in return is a gigantic 'Huh'.
Faced with the return of Kevin the teenager Tess decides to go for the plunge.
"Hannah." She doesn't quite know how to say this. "Errmm. Are you entirely happy about this baby?"
Hannah wells up. Oh shit. Why had Tess attempted this on her own? Would it be rude to call for back up? She's about to get her phone out to call Will when Hannah speaks.
" Yes. No. Oh I don't know." She stops suddenly but Tess doesn't leap in to fill an awkward silence. She lets it grow between them and eventually Hannah continues. "It wasn't planned. I was on anti-biotics and they must have interfered with the pill or something and the next thing you know I'm pregnant. I feel quite guilty actually, Helen next door is trying and having no luck then I muck up once and I'm knocked up again. But yeah, Garry's over the moon, he thinks it's a chance to have a girl. But it's not what we planned. It's not what we agreed. We agreed two. I don't care if we have a girl. I'm happy with the boys."

She stops. Tess considers it all and garners the relative information from it. Ignoring poor Helen from next door.
"OK well firstly, far too much information about your contraceptive habits." Hannah smiles, the first genuine smile

since she's got here, encouraged Tess continues. "It must be hard if it's not what you planned but surely it's not going to change things too much?" Tess knows nothing about their domestic arrangements but is trying to placate her.

Hannah looks up at Tess, her eyes bright with tears. When she speaks she speaks slowly, as if speaking to the village idiot. "But it was going to change. I was going to get to be me again. The end was in sight. Finn would go to school and I'd go to work. Oh only part time, I wouldn't rival your illustrious career that is all Mum and Dad can talk about." She looks bitter, "But for around five hours a day I could be Hannah again rather than Mummy. Garry and I agreed. We agreed I'd be at home with the boys until they went to school then I would go to work. Something in a shop maybe. I don't want to set the world on fire I just want to do something. And then this happens. Garry's trapped me again. Another five years of 'yes darling', 'oh lovely darling' admiring paintings and bored out of my brain. I've spent the last five years doing everything for that family. Cleaning up poo, and if it's not poo it's sick, and it's always me that has to do it. It's all my responsibility. Never Garry's, long as the money goes in to the account every month then his job is done. I love the kids but I hate my life. If I have another child I'll go spare. I can't do it again."

She's getting fairly over excited and although Tess wants to calm her down and stop her causing a scene she can't let a few of the very obvious holes in her argument go. As much as she would like to the pedant in Tess won't let them lie. She looks at Hannah and says in what she hopes is her conflict resolution voice (she was sent on a training course once; she'd tried the techniques she'd learnt on Arrabella who had looked at her then said 'why are you talking like a fucking half-wit?')

"Hannah. You're blaming a lot of this on Garry", she says. "If it was an accident then you both need to deal with it. Surely you could go back to work anyway. Lots of people do. When the baby's a bit older. In a year or so?"

Hannah slumps in her chair. She looks defeated. "Apparently", she does strange air quotes thing. Tess can only imagine she's taking the piss out of Garry. She does it again. "'Apparently', it's not fair to treat the kids differently. How would this one feel if its Mummy didn't love it as much as she loved their brothers? Besides whatever I earn wouldn't cover the cost of childcare and Garry says that he won't pay, so I have to stay at home. Heaven forbid that things change and Garry has to step up. Far, far better that I stay at home and am as miserable as sin." She's working her way up in to quite a state. Her Garry impression is pretty poor. When ever she pretends to be him she speaks in a whiny, high voice when everyone knows that Garry's voice is a manifestation of his personality: boring and monotone.
Tess is aware that people in the pub are beginning to look at them "Calm down Han. It'll be OK. Have you explained to Garry how you feel?"
Hannah gives her another look "Yes of course 'I've explained to Garry how I feel'". This is said in a child like mocking tone which Tess takes to be an impression of her. Hannah is turning in to quite the Mike Yarwood. Although Tess does sound quite like Garry according to Hannah's repertoire. Or perhaps she has been spending too much time around the boys and can only do whiny five year olds. She carries on, this time in her own voice. "The moment I knew I was pregnant I sat him down and told him how I felt. I thought I was being mature and responsible and it was something we could sort out together. I told him I felt trapped and things had to change. I told him I wasn't sure if I could do it again."
She stops, lost in her own thoughts. Tess prompts her "and what did he say?"
Hannah doesn't hear her and carries on. "I told him I couldn't do it and that I wanted a termination."

Tess looks at her agog, despite all that had gone before she hadn't seen this coming. Yes, she'd kept saying that she couldn't do it and yes she had walked out but Tess had been fairly certain it had been a way of holding Garry to ransom to get a Nanny or something, not this.

"Close your mouth Tess you look mental." Hannah comments. Tess complies, Hannah is ranting and raving in a pub but she is the one who looks odd.

"Garry said we'd take some time to think about it." Hannah continues "It was still really early days so we had a bit of time to think about what we were going to do. I thought we were being really sensible and grown up about the whole thing. Then a couple of days later we went to Mum and Dads and he told you all and the boys that we were having a baby." Her voice cracks and creeps up a couple of octaves. "He told the boys Tess, he trapped me. He completely trapped me and now I don't have a choice. I'm stuck."

She winds to a halt. Tess can see her phone vibrating on the table. It's Will. She sends it to voicemail then looks at Hannah. "You would have had an abortion?" Tess asks.

Hannah looks at her, wounded. Then she pushes her chair back and begins to head for the door. "I knew this was a mistake, I'd hoped you'd understand."

Chapter 26

"Hannah". Tess puts down her drink and rushes after her. She is aware of the looks of the other customers and feels like she is some particularly bad episode of *Home and Away* but resists the temptation to tell them all to "rack off" and follows Hannah out on to the street. She easily catches up with her; she hasn't got very far, although she keeps trying to walk away from Tess like she hasn't seen her.

"Stop, oh Hannah don't be a dick, I know you can see me. Hannah! Come on. Where are you going to go? You're staying at my house and I've got the keys." Tess shouts but Hannah keeps walking.
"Seriously?" Tess shouts. "Oh sod you then." She turns on her heel and walks back to the pub. She's not too sure of her plan but she's buggered if she's going to have Hannah stropping around her flat while she sits and watches. She plonks herself on a bench in the beer garden and texts Will.
"Hello lovely. What a day. Are you still coming round tonight? Do you fancy a takeaway? Hannah is here. Long story. Call you later? Xx"

"You alright love?" A voice shouts and she looks over and sees a man who had witnessed their altercation inside and is now having a fag outside, right by the children's playground.
"Yes thank you." She shouts back.
"Where's your girlfriend?" he asks.
Oh brilliant. She decides to use it to her advantage and wanders over to him.
"I don't know. Women hey? Can I have one of those?" She gestures to his fag packet and he offers her one. She takes one and then bends her head to light it from his proffered match. She hasn't smoked since she left university but some how she

needs one now. As the first drag hits her lungs she feels simultaneously sick and like she's come home. Before she starts coughing (which in turn would lead to, she fears, vomiting) she thanks the man and heads back over to her bench and the picnic table.

She fires off texts asking Daisy and Tilly how their days have been and is about to text Nina when Hannah slopes in to the garden and sits next to Tess.

"Smoking?" Hannah asks

"Yep" says Tess and stands up and rearranges herself to sit on the table, her feet on the bench next to Hannah. She blows the smoke over Hannah's head. It's not quite the answer to passive smoking but it's the best she can come up with at the moment. Hannah still isn't talking. Tess' phone beeps and she reads the text from Will. "You Ok? I'll be over about 7, will bring Turkish, with enough for Hannah. Think I just saw Bob Holness in Comet!"

Tess replies "Great see you then. Bob Holness is dead. Things must be crap in heaven if he's haunting Comet."

A few more minutes of uncomfortable silence pass, even the man watching them gives up and goes back inside. Tess grinds her fag out, flicks the butt away and positions herself back on the bench next to Hannah. Hannah reaches in to her bag and passes Tess anti-bacterial hand gel (of course). Tess uses it, her hands reek, and then passes it back to Hannah. Finally Hannah ends their silent dance.

"I thought you'd understand." she repeats.

"No." says Tess. "You thought I'd agree with you."

"But you don't want kids."

"For me. So I don't have them. I'm not Herod. I'm not starting a holocaust of newborns."

"But you can understand why I feel like I do." Hannah asks.

"Honestly? No." Tess replies. "But equally I couldn't understand why you wanted the boys"
Hannah looks at her in horror.
"Oh don't look at me like that", Tess continues. "I love the boys you know I do. I just find it hard to believe that anyone actively wants kids and is pleased to be pregnant. It's my issue, not yours. And now you come here and tell me all this and expect me to be on board. You can't expect me to be thrilled at one pregnancy and not at another. And expect to know which is which without you saying a word. For the last six years, no before that, you've been all about the kids. How many you were going to have, what they're names were going to be, you wanted a family and now you've got it. All I see is you and Garry playing happy families, you got what you wanted and now you're telling me the opposite. What am I meant to think? The boys were a mistake?"
Hannah shakes her head and goes to speak but Tess speaks over her.
"You need to decide what's important. Unless you and Garry have just been pretending with all the happy family stuff."
"We are happy. Well we were till this came along." Hannah tries to explain.
"You make it sound like this has nothing to do with you."
"It doesn't."
"Hannah." Tess is incredulous.
"This is not my baby Tess. It's not. I have no connection. The boys are my children and I have to put them first."
"So it's only a baby if you want it? It's a collection of cells if you don't." Tess queries.
"I didn't know you were so pro-life." Hannah says.
"I don't know what I am." Tess says "I don't know what I'd do. This isn't a political discussion. It's not about the rights and wrongs. It's about you. I want what's best for you. But you're not being you. You've turned up and hit me with this and expect me to be on your side. I don't even know what the sides are. "

Hannah is unmoved, as far as she is concerned if Tess isn't with her then she's against her. "People think with kids that it's come one, come all. I can't have another child. It's not fair on me; it's not fair on the boys. I am not doing it again."

Tess already hates herself for what she's about to say but she can't stop the words from leaving her lips. "It's Garry's baby too."

Oh fuck, she's unleashed hell. Tess longs to return to the awkward silence.

"Is it?" Hannah shrieks. "Well someone should tell him that because he pays fuck all attention to the two kids he's got. I do the washing, the cleaning, the worrying, and the never ending drudgery of it. He gets to have his life. He can go to stag weekends, he can play golf, he can play football, he can go for drinks after work, all it takes is one phone call to me to tell me, TELL me, that he'll be late because he's going for a drink. I go out once in a blue moon and it's all planned a month in advance and Garry 'babysits'. Babysits. His own kids. And I'm home by ten. And then at weekends he has a lie in because he's been working all week. If I could be a father then I'd have another child, I'd have another ten because it makes no difference how many there are. But I'm a mother and these are my kids. Mine. I get to decide what happens to them and any others that come along."

It's a good speech. Tess is impressed. But Tess is still thrown. She doesn't want to talk about this. She doesn't want to know this. "Or don't come along." She says and this time it's Tess that gets up and walks off and Hannah follows.

Hannah catches up with her along the high street. Tess is going at quite a pace.

"Have you spoken to anyone else about this?" Tess asks.

"Like who?"

Good point. It's not really the kind of thing she's going to mention in the playground or bring up at a PTA meeting which are really Hannah's only forms of social interaction. Tess is impressed though that Hannah is having a conversation with her. A mere ten years ago this would have descended in to a slanging match. She can't decide if they've matured or if Hannah has run out of options and had to throw her lot in with Tess.

"Can I still stay?" Hannah asks. Tess nods and they continue meandering home.

"I thought you were odd that weekend at Mum and Dad's. Plus you've barely spoken to me since," Tess says

"I hit Garry that night."

Tess grins, she can't help it. Anti-abortion but pro domestic violence. She's learning a lot about herself today. She turns her head to try and hide it but Hannah catches her and to Tess' surprise Hannah laughs.

"Thank you. I need to be with someone who gets me. Who doesn't think the sun shines out of Garry's arse."

Tess wants to nip this in the bud "There's still a lot to think about Han."

They walk the rest of the way in silence.

Chapter 27

Tess strokes Will's hair. His head is in her lap. After a meal eaten almost entirely in silence (Tess and Hannah didn't know what to say to each other and Will had more sense than to try and get between them), Hannah had announced she was tired so Tess and Will had offered to go and sit in the kitchen so she could get an early night. Tess found linen and pillows for her and placed them on the sofa. They heard her plodding around, using the en-suite off Tess' bedroom and then eventually it went quiet. Although they had started off on the uncomfortable kitchen chairs they soon sat on the floor and cuddled up. They were whispering. Partly so as not to disturb Hannah and partly so she doesn't over hear. Tess is thankful for Will's support. He's achieved a fine line in being both non-judgemental and being on Tess' side. Supporting her indecision. As loathe as she is to use the phrase 'just being there for her' he is and it feels amazing. And unusual. She's spent the day feeling like she's been battered from all sides and finally she can stop and just be.

Will talks about his brother, his family back in Ireland. How he feels about not living in the same country, about being in the family but slightly removed from it. They forge a closer bond that night and rarely Tess doesn't want 'me time' at the end of it. They talk until they grow chilly sat on the floor. Having to whisper is making them laugh and they are getting a bit giddy, they know this is heading one way and they make their way, smothering their laughter, to the bedroom. They are kissing and Will bumps the door open with his bum, not breaking his lip lock on Tess. She's impressed and sliding her hands under his shirt she pushes him in to the bedroom. Only to be confronted by Hannah fast asleep in her bed. Her and Will spring apart. Tess goes to shake Hannah awake but Will stops her and begins to pull her out of the room. She breaks away and on a hunch opens the wardrobe. As she suspected all Hannah's clothes are hung up, she goes through to the bathroom and finds her toothbrush relegated to the side of the bath as the sink, shelf and surrounding areas are filled with a plethora of beauty products without which Hannah is unable to get through life.

She walks back to the kitchen and Will follows hopeful that they will resume their activities in there. When Tess shuts the door he turns to take her in his arms and begins to kiss her neck, a known weakness. Tess however is not easily placated. She moves away from him and starts a whispered rant.
"I should have known she'd do that. She's so bloody entitled."

Will goes to hold her again. Soothing her and kissing her forehead. "It's fine, come and stay at mine. Grab what you need and we'll leave her a note."
"I don't know where everything is. Especially now she's moved everything. Sorry, sorry, I know it's not your fault. Ugh. You go. I'll stay here; I'll sleep on the sofa or something. I'll see you at work tomorrow. "
"You can always stay at mine whilst she's here."
"Thank you. "she kisses him. "Thank you darling. I do appreciate that. But I feel I should be here to mark my territory. I wouldn't put it past her to change the locks"
"Just don't piss around the sofa." Will warns her.
"Oh she's used to random puddles of piss."
Will laughs and goes for one last seduction attempt. He is surprisingly successful and he leaves half an hour later with a spring in his step. Tess meanwhile goes to the bedroom, strips the duvet off Hannah and makes her way to the sofa with it.

Tess' sofa is extraordinarily uncomfortable. She should have known. She can barely sit on it for an hour without getting pins and needles in her bum so she was pushing her luck thinking she could sleep on it. As she flings herself around in the night, trying to get comfortable she is driven to the point of tears knowing that she has an incredible comfortable bed the other side of the wall. Eventually she realises that the crying is pointless and instead channels her energy in to planning Hannah's death. Far healthier and far more effective. Finally morning arrives and she barges in to the bedroom to get herself ready for work, determined to be as loud and inconvenient as possible. She's incredibly unsuccessful. Hannah merely ignores her aside from the odd muttered complaint about 'some tart nicking her duvet'.

Chapter 28

"So do people not wear clothes in New York?"
Tess is sat on Nina's bed half-heartedly sorting through her
jewellery and putting it in to piles. She has spent the last twenty
minutes trying to untangle a necklace and despite being
repeatedly told by Nina to leave it, she's become slightly
obsessed and is now viewing it as a personal challenge. Nina is
emptying her wardrobe in to three heaps: pack, ship and bin.
Tess has secretly created a fourth pile: give to Tess. The pack pile
has three items in it, the ship has a few horrendous sentimental
items and the bin pile is threatening to topple over.

"I just don't think the clothes I have here are going to cut it in
New York," Nina justifies, flinging yet another top on to the bin
heap. Tess nudges it into the 'Tess' pile with her foot.
"That's as maybe but you may want to take some clothes with
you, just so you don't have to impulse buy an entire wardrobe
the second you land or go to work in your pants," Tess reasons.
"True, fling that blue top in to the shipping pile." Nina concedes.
Tess reluctantly takes it out of the Tess pile and throws it on to
the small heap by her feet; she returns her attention to
separating the necklace out of its tight knots. She rams the post
of an earring in to the mess and wiggles it about a bit.
"So have you given any more thought to your leaving do?" she
asks.
"Oh no, I just want to go I don't want a fuss. Perhaps just a few
of us can go for drinks or something?" Nina says.
"Nice idea but I don't think you'll get away with that. You know
they're going to force you to do something formal."
"Ugh, can't we just slip away?" Nina sinks to the floor and sits
on the bin pile. She reaches over and grabs her diary out of her
handbag. "So I leave work on the 20th. Say they do force me to

do something we could endure that and then we could go for dinner on the 21st. You and Will would be up for that?"

"Count me in."

"And Will?" she asks.

"Ask Will." Tess replies.

Nina knows Will and Tess are dating. Of course she does and if Tess is unwilling to confirm it then she'll just assume that is what is happening and treat Tess accordingly. She's a bit insulted that Tess is keeping her in the dark actually. It's not like she's going to blab to anyone at work (although everybody knows anyway).

Tess knows that Nina knows. She doesn't care that she knows but she also knows that Nina is thinking that this is a together-forever-till-death-do-us-part relationship. Which it may or may not be. But she has no desire to be joined at the hip to Will, she doesn't want to control his diary, to answer invitations for him; in her mind it's a slippery slope to buying his family birthday presents and cards on his behalf, why would she do it when he is perfectly capable of performing all these duties himself? Equally she is capable of replying to a social invitation without consulting Will, if he can come too then lovely, if not then they'll catch up another time. She's spent the best part of 30 years turning up to places on her own, she's not going to lose the ability now.

"It's like that is it?" Nina sounds offended.

"I don't know what it's like Neen." Tess throws Nina's necklace down next to her and flops back on the pillows. "This is fucked by the way; try putting some olive oil on it. I know you think there's some great passionate love affair going on but there's not, there's really not. I don't know what the hell it is and I know that you're Will's friend as well so it's not fair for me to start banging on about him behind his back. It's just something I've got to work through."

"Work through?" Nina questions. "That doesn't sound good."

"That's the thing though. It is good. I really like him. I just don't like the indelible bonding of our very souls. People seem to think we are one."

"I think you're reading too much in to it love. Now sit back up, you're crushing my jacket."

Tess lifts her hips off the bed (who said that one Pilates class hadn't come in handy) and pulls the jacket out from underneath her.

"I don't want you to go." Tess pulls an exaggerated sad face and speaks in a Deputy Dawg voice 'It makes me very, very unheppy."

Nina looks at her. She's not fooled by the stupid look or voice, Tess is unable to express an honest feeling without hiding behind something. "Well snap out of it dear. You'll be fine. I'm the one heading to the other side of the world, where I don't know anyone and I have to work in the most blood thirsty city in the world." Her tough love stance is slightly compromised when she wells up and sobs, "I don't even own any Manolos!"

Tess puts her arms out and Nina crawls in to them joining her on the bed. They lay there for a while until Nina's sobs subside. Tess eventually breaks the silence "I always thought they were pronounced MAN a lows. Like they were named after Barry."

"You'd be beaten to death in New York."

"As long as you aren't."

"Now, now, now." Tess lifts her foot out of the box and Nina immediately slams the flaps down. Tess turns and sits on the box whilst Nina begins to plaster it shut with duct tape.

"Is it safe to get up?" asks Tess.

"I think so. What I'm going to do is completely cover it in tape, all the way around."

"What if customs need to open it?" Tess asks.

"Then they can repack the bloody thing." Nina pauses. "It's strange you know. Seeing all your life come down to boxes." "Boxes and one hell of a mess, " Tess says, surveying the wasteland of Nina's flat. "Do you want to stay at mine? You could borrow my clothes as well, you're going to struggle to piece together outfits out of what you've got left." Tess isn't sure where Nina could stay in her already crowded flat but the offer is there.

"Nah, I'll be OK. I might nick a few bits and pieces to see me through but I want to stay in my flat as long as possible. What am I doing Tess?"

Tess looks at her and pulls a sincere face. One she has copied directly from 'ER'. "The right thing", she says.

It takes a second for Tess to crack before she starts laughing.

Chapter 29

"Do you want these?" Daisy asks.

"Ermmm, what are they?" Tilly asks.

"Individual Omelette pans in a variety of sizes." Daisy reads from the label.

Tilly and Daisy are wandering through a department store looking for presents to put on the wedding list.

Tilly pulls a face, "No I think we'll pass. Remind me again why I didn't just cut out of all of this and ask for cash?"

"Because you don't get to sit and unwrap cash and it's nice to get presents, isn't it?"

"Well this is slightly taking the element of surprise out of things." Tilly grumbles.

"Oh they'll always be people who will go off list. We've spent years trying to drop that vase Simon's Aunt Ruth got us. Flipping thing's unbreakable." Daisy says.

"Don't you feel obliged to get me, I mean us, anything. What with the hen night and everything you and Tess are already having to fork out a load. Plus staying in the hotel two nights."

"Oh don't be so silly," Daisy says "You'd be horribly annoyed if someone turned up without a gift, I would have been livid."

"Oh I know but it sounds so awful to say that doesn't it. It sounds so grabby. And obviously I don't want anyone to bankrupt themselves or anything but I want a card at least, some kind of acknowledgement that my life is changing and I want them to be a part of it."

"Do you think your life will change?" Daisy was genuinely curious.

"I think so. How could it not? Yours did, didn't it?" Tilly asks.

Daisy puts down the icing set she is holding and wanders over to a dining room table, pulls out one of the chairs and sits down.

Tilly joins her, holding two forks that she is trying to choose between.

"We were so young, none of it really felt like change." Daisy remembers "I was off to do my PGCE and Simon had just started his first job. It was almost like we were playing at it. We set up house and we scrimped and saved and it was fun but I'm not sure it was marriage. I feel more married now, like more is changing now than I ever did when we got married."

Tilly looks at her. She even puts the forks down.

"Is this the seven year itch?" She's trying to sound light hearted but she's genuinely concerned. As selfish as it is, she cannot cope with Daisy losing the plot now. She needs cheerleaders around her, to be surrounded by people who love marriage and weddings and think that every decision Tilly makes is the right one. She also doesn't want Daisy to be unhappy. And on a very practical level, a thought that she keeps trying to push to one side, she doesn't want to redo the flipping table plan again and separate Daisy and Simon. It's taken her hours to do that thing. She was unaware so many people in her family had issues with one another until they all decided they couldn't sit next to each other for a mere three hours.

Daisy seems to pick up on the fact that she's not selling the perfect marriage. "Oh no, no, nothing like that. I'm just saying that I kind of sleepwalked in to it. I was so young, someone proposed and I said yes. I was lucky it was Simon really, I could have ended up with someone awful." She laughs, a laugh that does nothing to reassure Tilly. "You know you just think of all the things you'd do differently if we'd been a bit older or had a bit of money. Like changing my name. I did it then, I didn't really think about it. Whereas if I was older, had done something under my own name then I might have wanted to hang on to it. But it's a bit late now. I don't think Simon would be too understanding if I changed it back."

Tilly is now convinced there is something wrong. Daisy has always been Mrs traditional. She would have bet money on Daisy convincing Tilly to change her name not to be sat in a pretend kitchen doing a fair impression of Germaine Greer.
"Daisy", she starts "I err, I mean would you..."
She trails off and Daisy leaps in.
"So what's Tess up to today? Has she got new-couple-itis?"
"Will's working; she just wanted a bit of time on her own." Tilly says.
"What do you think she does with all that time? Why do you think she has to be constantly alone?" Daisy is I the mood for a gossip. Sadly Tilly isn't.
"Daisy. I don't know – ask her. Now why can't I change my name?"
"Do what you want. I'm just saying don't underestimate what it means. I mean it's all romantic now and you get a shiny new bank card with a brand new name on it but ten years down the track you wonder why you did it."
"But we're building something new together. I want to have the same name as him." Tilly is certain.
"Then get him to change his." Daisy says.
"He'd never do that."
"So why should you?"
"Why did you?" Tilly asks.
"I don't know. I don't know why I do a lot of things. Why does anyone do what they do?"

Tilly has found that once you announce you're getting married, everyone has an opinion and apparently the answer isn't 'do whatever is right for you' but 'you have to do what I did otherwise you're weird'. Most of the time she let it go but after a haranguing from Barbara in accounts about how her wedding would fail because she wasn't having 'little' bridesmaids she was in no mood to deal with Daisy rewriting history.
"Would you change being given away by your Dad?" she asks.

Daisy looks up "No, of course not, that was a wonderful moment, he was so proud."

"And would you give away your engagement ring?"

"No, I love my ring." Daisy turns it carefully around her finger.

"Well both of those are symbols of a patriarchy and you don't see people turning those down. Not all tradition is wrong. You do what you want; call yourself Umbongo Jones for all I care but I am taking Stuart's name. If I regret it, it's my problem." Tilly is in the mood for an argument. She's had too many opinions thrown at her lately.

Frustratingly, Daisy doesn't bite. She picks up her phone instead.

Tilly is beginning to really regret her bridesmaid choices. One has no concept of organisation or urgency and has to be spoon fed jobs as she has no idea of what a wedding involves. The other seems to (despite being married for seven years and having had her day) hate marriage and all it stands for and wants Tilly to join her on some kind of campaign against monogamy. If she could combine the Hitler aspect of Daisy with the 'hello trees, hello flowers' attitude of Tess then she would really have something useful. As it is it's like a wedding special of the Chuckle Brothers.

She knows she should take time out. Calm Tess down. Convince her that it's OK to be in a relationship and she should stop fighting it. Talk to Daisy, find out what's going on. She's not stupid, if she hears the name 'Kyle' once more she's going to scream but she should work out if it's a harmless crush or something more serious. She knows that Tess knows but she also knows that one of Tess' most annoying characteristics is loyalty, however horrifically misplaced. But she also knows that she gets one shot at marrying Stuart, the time is fast approaching and although she shouldn't begrudge Tess her happiness and new couple status and she should support Daisy she wishes they could have done this some other time. As much as it pains her to say it, this is her day and she's going to enjoy it. People will have to save their dramas until there's a ring on her finger.

She makes a token attempt at cracking Daisy.

"How's Simon? Haven't seen him in a while." She says.

"He's fine. Have you made any menu choices yet?"

Ah her kryptonite. The next hour is filled with the benefits of chicken over lamb.

Chapter 30

If Will had had any thoughts of progressing his relationship with Tess to the co-habitee level then Hannah has pretty much ruined it. Wet towels decorate Tess' flat. She is forced in to a 10pm bedtime or she loses her bed. Hannah intermittently wants to talk non-stop about her situation and then doesn't want to talk about it at all but wants to sulk around the house. Will feels as though they have skipped a couple of years worth of their relationship and they now have a stroppy teenager. They get a couple of nights alone and their days are free at weekends when Hannah visits the boys. The upside of her visiting them means a fairly relaxed Tess (once she's tidied away all the mess, ready for Hannah to start untidying afresh on her return), a semblance of a normal couple in the early days of going out and sex without having to keep an ear out for a terribly confused and incredibly angry pregnant woman. The downside was the fall out. Hannah would weep for hours when she returned, Tess has to stay up till all hours counselling and consoling her. Will knew his role in all this. Make tea, make food and keep out of the way. Then step in and tell Tess that she's doing the right thing.

Both he and Tess were certain of one thing though. Despite the tears, the heartache and the self-denigration Hannah was still pregnant. And getting more pregnant by the day.

"Yes of course darling. Come the bank holiday weekend. Would be lovely to have you."

Tess was confused. One of the flies in the ointment of her happily single life was the feeling that she was somehow failing her parents. Now she was fairly certain that Will wasn't going anywhere she had broken the news to her parents that she was seeing someone. And that yes it was the nice young man who had so entranced her Mother when they had been in London. Her parents had taken the news calmly. So calmly in fact that Tess wasn't sure they had understood. She appreciated it was a hard concept for them to grasp – her having a boyfriend. They had kept this attitude up, asking after Will in passing but concentrating on Tess and more so on Hannah. Tess had decided to grasp the nettle and invite herself and Will down to her parents for the weekend. She had expected bunting, 21 gun salute, an announcement in The Times. Instead she got benign acceptance.

"Oh. OK. Well don't sound too excited." Tess humphed.
"Sorry darling, we're watching Mastermind. No, of course it will be nice to have you. I'll make up the beds." Replied her Mother. Plural. She'd break that to Will on the way down there.
"It'll be nice for you to meet Will properly. Perhaps Auntie Susan could come over." Tess asks.
"Mmmm. Yes, well let's not get ahead of ourselves."
"What does that mean?" Tess queries "Auntie Susan came over when you buried the cat, she bought a wreath! How is this less important than a cat funeral?"
"It wasn't a funeral Tess. Don't be silly. It was a memorial. No of course Sue can come over I just didn't think you wanted us to make a fuss. But yes, we'll do something." Her Mother is non committal.
"Good."
"I'm quite pleased actually darling, I never thought it would last this long."
"Thank you mother. People ask me where I get my innate self confidence from; I can only put it down to a supportive family."
"Oh you know what I mean."
"Enlighten me." Tess asks.

"Well you spent your childhood desperately trying to get away from people. You spent your life up a tree or behind the shed reading. We had to take the key out of the garage as you'd lock yourself in there and sit on top of the washing machine. I could never get a load on. The minute we'd invite people round you'd say hello then disappear. You were forever putting yourself to bed when people came to dinner." Tess sighs, her mother picks up on this and continues, "it's not a criticism dear; it's just the way you are. I just find it funny that you of all people have ended up with a house full of people."

It's hilarious. Tess wakes up every day roaring with laughter.

"I know. What can you do? And this time I don't have a garage or a tree." Tess says.
"Oh it'll be fine darling. Go to the library. No one's allowed to talk in there." Her Mother is sanguine about the situation.
Tess laughs and begins to sort out the cutlery from the draining board in to the drawer.
"Are you playing the tambourine?" her mother asks.
"Yes, I've taken up Morris dancing."
"That's nice dear. It's the Sahara, Harry, not the Gobi. I want a point for that."
Tess hears her father protest in the background and feels it time to draw this conversation to a close.
"Right, well I'll let you know when I'm coming, when we're coming," she corrects. "I don't know about Hannah, she seems to be seeing the boys every weekend. Oh I don't know what you're meant to know by the way, so don't drop me in it."
"Oh Garry's filling me in. Don't you worry. Shep!"
Assuming this is the answer to a Mastermind question rather than her Mother finally losing her mind she hangs up.

The more and more that changes the more and more Tess clings to Will. Everyone she normally would turn to seems to be either under going huge life changes (Tilly and Nina) or having a personality transplant (Daisy) or swinging between mother earth and Satan (Hannah). Matt used to be good in situations like this but he is still ignoring her. In fact he seems to have dropped off the face of the earth, no one has heard from him. Will is her constant. Not that Will's getting an enormous amount out of this. Gone is the independent, witty and intelligent girl that Will lusted after for years. Instead he has a weepy, irrational mollusc. His reaction to Tess' personality change is to cosset her. To love her problems away and so he responds in kind. Which makes Tess feel more at sea and so Will tries harder. It is to their eternal relief when Hannah announces that she is going to visit the boys for the day.

"I haven't left them," she announces piously at the breakfast table, "I'm simply estranged from their father."

Will busies himself with the scraping the last of the jam from the pot whilst Tess raises her eyes to the ceiling.

"Hardly estranged, he's still funding you and you talk to him every day." Tess says.

"We have a family, I can't just walk away from my responsibilities." Hannah says in a manner that Tess is sure she has copied from Princess Diana in the Panorama interview.

With that she leaves her cereal bowl, dirty mug and the tissue she had fixed up her make up with on the table and walks out taking Tess' keys with her as she can't find her own.

The door slams

"Freedom," whispers Will. "What shall we do?"

"Well whatever we do either has to be housebound or one of us has to stay here as she's naffed off with my keys."

"I can think of something fun to do that involves staying in the house," says Will and winks.

"Oh god I'm going to get cystitis," thinks Tess.

Obviously Tess had experienced stress before. Exams, driving test, all the other various rites of passage that make up modern life. But it was always for something. This just seemed to be constant, on going heightened fear. She is constantly anxious. Constantly waiting for something awful to happen. It doesn't seem to stop so she's not sure she could be described as stressed. It would be more likely to be described as 'life' or as 'just the way things are now'. She can't put her finger on what it is. Everything should be good. But she's unbearably sad. But she can't explain what she's sad about.

So she does what she always does. She controls what she can. Her home life is out of her hands. So she concentrates on work. She works harder. She proves her worth. Sadly the only person who really notices is Will and he only notices that she has less free time to spend with him. On the plus side she gets to spend more time with Nina who is sorting out her hand over and wrapping things up in the office. Then one day someone asks a question and Tess knows the answer. Someone needs a suggestion. Tess has the answer. She begins to become an integral part of the team. Obviously this means her Arrabella responsibilities increase as Arrabella gets jealous. With achievements, however, come side effects. Paranoia (is that person who's on the phone to Geoff ringing to complain about her?), long hours (just to finish up one last thing) and an inability to switch off. She no longer reads the papers in her free time. They have been tainted by work. If she hears a song on the radio by one of their clients she becomes convinced it's a subliminal message and there'll be a problem with them when she arrives at work. So she stops listening to the radio.

It's irrational. It's annoying. It's bizarre and most of all, it's tiring.

It also doesn't seem to be making anything any better. She's still steeped in sadness.

Chapter 31

It's been a long day. A friend of Will's (or Wilbert as she has taken to calling him, just to annoy him) had thrown a 'Best of British' party and they have spent the day getting very drunk on Pimms. The reasoning had been that after the Royal Wedding, The Olympics and the Jubilee there was a lot of bunting and alcohol left over and it needed to be used up. It was now, they are sure, all gone. Tess and Will are now back at Will's flat recovering from the day.

As they had walked home, slightly merry from drinking nothing but alcohol since ten o'clock this morning, it had turned chilly so Will had offered her his hooded top which she had gratefully accepted. She was still wearing it now and had teamed it with the bright blue dress she had been wearing all day (the dress code being 'red, white and blue') and a pair of thick socks she had flinched from the host when the weather turned cold. She still had her heels on and had become inexplicably attached to a plastic union jack bowler hat and so was still wearing it. She looked ridiculous. Will had never loved her more.

Tess was sprawled on the floor, another Pimm's in hand, putting stickers in to her Royal Family sticker album that she had found in a newsagent. She claimed it was ironic but given the number of hours she had put in to it and how carefully she placed the stickers in their allotted places Will suspected otherwise.
"I had no idea you were so patriotic," he said. He was fairly merry himself and also had a glass of Pimm's in his hand, they had decided it made more sense to make a jug.
"I love the Royals," she said. "I had a sticker book of them when I was younger, I loved it. No one to swap stickers with in the playground though."

"You surprise me." Will sympathises.

Tess carries on, not acknowledging his sarcasm although well aware of it.

"I used to go to the library and read all the Royal biographies, all of them. My favourite was Princess Marina's. Did you know aqua-marine is named after her?"

"I don't think that's true. Isn't it a mineral?"

"Not according to the woman who wrote that book. If we were at my flat we could play my Royal Family board game." Tess says.

"Damn it, why did we come to mine? Another regret in my shoddy little life."

Tess grins. Will laughs and stretches his leg out from the armchair to rub her back with his foot.

"I reckon I could list all the Royals back to 1066," she boasted. "Oh and the line of succession, that's how I used to calm myself down, reciting the line of succession as far as I could go. Got me through my A levels that did."

Will decides to call her bluff. "Ok, who's nineteenth in line to the throne."

"Oh a challenge. OK. Well let's see, I have to take in to consideration that Margaret has died since I last did this and there's been more children born"

"Of course."

Tess rolls on to her back, providing Will with a tantalising glimpse of her pants through her tights. She begins to count on her fingers and murmur under her breath.

"Margarita Armstrong Jones." She finally announces.

Will merely raises his eyebrows and looks questioningly at her.

"Fine." Tess takes a deep breath. "After the Queen comes Charles, obviously, then William, little baby George, Harry, Andrew, Beatrice, Eugenie, Edward, James, Louise, Anne, Peter, Savannah, whatever their youngest is called – Barry?, Zara, Mia, David Armstrong Jones and Charles Armstrong Jones, then providing they all get wiped out King Ralph style then Margarita takes over."

Will had actually only raised his eyebrows at the name of Margarita as he was only really familiar with it as a type of pizza. The fact that she has expanded and was able to expand pleases him no end. He looks at her, her face flushed with the success of her royal knowledge, in her silly hat and cobbled together outfit and his heart contracts.

"I love you," he says.

It's only later in bed, when they are both drifting off to sleep, that she suddenly answers him. Almost as though she's needed time to properly assess her feelings.

"I love you too," she says.

And she does. She finds it odd and unsettling but she knows that deep down and in her own way she really does.

Chapter 32

"Have you got a spare? This one looks like I've had a stroke."
Tess says.
Daisy and Tilly are sat at on Tilly's sofa, glasses of red wine in
hand, putting invites, reply cards, maps and information in to
pre-labelled envelopes. Tess is sat at the table, painstakingly
writing out all of Tilly's 120 invitations. She is not allowed a
drink of any colour; although she has nice handwriting she is
notoriously clumsy. A glass of Rioja is on the side, her reward for
when she has finished.

Tilly talks of plans, of all the issues the wedding has thrown up.
Family members who have suddenly come out of the woodwork
and now cannot survive without an invite to the wedding of a
great-niece they haven't seen in twenty years. Of people who
haven't got a plus one and by being single are screwing up the
table plan, creating odd numbers everywhere. Apparently giving
them a plus one is not an option. Throughout this Tess feels
'other'. This is not a brilliant description but she doesn't seem to
have the combination of words to describe what 'it' is. At first
she thinks it is annoyance at Daisy. Despite what she tells Tess
about the state of her marriage, of her love (don't get her
started) for Kyle, for her future plans, she sits along side Tilly
talking about her wedding day. What she did, what she'd do
differently, what Tilly should do. Tess' input is limited; she can't
really talk from experience. What annoys her, no not annoys,
confuses her (and it is that confusion which annoys her) is why
Daisy is talking about her wedding day like it was the best day of
her life.

"Perhaps it was," reasons Will. "Just because she's not happy
now, doesn't mean that she wasn't then."
"Oh don't be so reasonable." Tess snaps.

Will doesn't get it.

Tess understands that people change. That people grow apart. What annoys Tess is that Daisy is living in a work of fiction. She's pinned her hopes on a man who doesn't reciprocate. Who isn't even aware of these feelings. She's blaming a lot on Simon yet won't talk to Simon. Tess doesn't want to know about this yet she is the only one who Daisy will confide in. This puts her in a mood with Daisy, sadly it doesn't stop Daisy sharing but it stops Tess confiding (or really in any real way talking) to Daisy. A relationship she has relied upon over the years has crumbled and she doesn't know why.

It has also, inevitably, affected her relationship with Simon. Something that is baffling to both of them. Baffling to Tess as it has been affected by something that doesn't really exist and yet she is forced to lie to Simon, lie by omission (never mentioning Kyle, not acknowledging that Daisy is behaving like a lunatic) and so their easy going relaxed friendship has gone and that really bothers Tess. This is because, whisper it, she met Simon first. Yet somehow over the years, by virtue of female friendship or voodoo she has become Daisy's friend and Simon is her husband. When in actual fact Simon was her friend, she introduced him to Daisy and she became the third wheel. This also effects how she feels towards Daisy. Each action leads to a reaction and puts Tess further and further away.

She finishes the invites and is rewarded with a glass of wine. She settles on the floor and reads through the instructions Tilly has printed out for her guests. These include details on where they're registered for gifts (Tess and Will have got them a spa mini break, Tess enjoys having her budget increased by virtue of being in a relationship and this is possibly the first wedding present she has bought that she is happy with. Normally she buys something from the wedding list that is fairly low down.

She finds it hard to believe that anyone really wants a gravy boat yet she's bought a hundred of them), where to park, details of hotels in the area and the like. Tess spots a spelling mistake but viewing the growing pile of envelopes she decides to keep it to herself.

Tilly looks beautiful. This is love. Think Tess. It's messy and it's not what you expect but looking at Tilly she knows it's worth it. Daisy and Tilly are discussing flowers. Tess has nothing to add. It seems to her that she is always playing catch up. Always two steps behind. She finally gets a boyfriend and everyone gets married. She rolls on to her back. She wants to sleep. To wake up in a month or so. Or to pause. What was that sitcom? A girl put her fingers together and the world stopped. Her Dad was a crystal. She starts to sing snatches of the theme tune.
"Would you like bah bah bah bah. Something moon beams something la la."
"What are you singing?" Tilly prods Tess with her foot.
"I can't remember the name of it. I think it was on when we were kids." She hums the tune again "Would you like to bah bah bah."

And this time Daisy, almost as though compelled to, sings "Woah woah woah."
Tess laughs. And sings the second line. Again Daisy replies with her refrain.
"What was that?" Daisy asks. "Was she an alien?"
"I don't know." Tess replies. "I think her family might have been. Her Dad was in a crystal or something."
"Did she live with her Mum?"
Tilly suddenly interjects, "Out of this world!"
"Out of this World!" Daisy and Tess shout in joy.
"That was it, thanks Tills," Tess happily sings the song again.

Tilly and Daisy look at each other confused. Then they look at Tess who is laying on the floor singing to herself whilst repeatedly pressing her fingers together.

Chapter 33

Tess never thought that she would be able to summarise her life using Take That lyrics. Now that she can she doesn't know whether to feel a sense of resentment that her life can be summed up so simply or relief that Gary Barlow has encapsulated so neatly what she is feeling. In short – 'Everything changes but you'. As the world around her goes mental she is delighted that Will is a constant. She feels she is on a bed of constantly shifting sands. All the certainty she once had has been replaced with doubt and unpredictability. She doesn't know why. Yes Daisy has gone mad, work is horrendous, Nina is going, Matt has gone, Hannah – well that's just, who knows – and Tilly is lost in a world of satin. Whereas once Tess would have taken all of this in her stride, now she is out of her depth and is relying on Will more and more. Could she cope on her own?

More than anything the feeling is that she wants to escape. She has stopped listening to Desert Island Discs as it fills her with resentment that she can't escape to an island and spend her days catching fish, listening to music and lolling about in the sea. Totally alone. She craves solitude more than anything. She wants to shut the door on the world. Then she remembers that she has to be nice to Will, she can't push him away. If the last few months have shown anything it's that she can't rely on friends to fill the gap where a boyfriend goes. If she does that she'll end up totally alone. And while that might be what she longs for, practically she knows this won't work. No one actively plans to be found five years after their death in front of the still-on television.

Throughout the first heady days of going out with Will Tess was aware of neglecting her bridesmaid duties. Luckily Daisy seemed to be taking most of these on. At first this pleased Tess as it meant there was less for her to do but when Daisy told her it was so she could spend time away from Simon and had a handy excuse to go and meet Kyle then Tess felt a lot less pleased and a lot more worried.

"You're meeting him now? I mean outside of school?" Tess asks.

"Well no. Not yet. But when we do then the wedding is a perfect excuse."

The ennui continues. There's nothing wrong, yet there is a relentless panic to all situations. She wakes up feeling anxious yet when she considers it there is nothing that needs to be worried about. She wakes up every morning feeling awful. Most mornings as she lies there dreading the day ahead and feeling unsettled she runs through a checklist to work out what it is that is ailing her. She works from top to bottom:

Headache – no
Sore throat – no
Swollen glands – no
Chest pain – no
Stomach pain – no
Lady pains – no
Any miscellaneous bumps or bruises – no
Unstoppable crying – Yes. Constantly.

And so the mystery continues, it's like knowing you have a cold coming but not actually getting a full blown dose. Something is wrong but it doesn't have a name. She tries to articulate this to Will one night on the phone.

"I know what it is," he says.

Finally an answer. "Go on"

"You're doing too much, you need a break. You need to do absolutely nothing." He says.

Bliss. Yes that was what it is. The wedding, Hannah, work, she needs a weekend of nothing. When Will presents her with a voucher for a spa weekend she snogs his face off with gratitude. Swimming, massages, crap TV in a hotel room. If she plays her cards right she could go forty-eight hours without talking to anyone. It is only when she looks again at the voucher that she realises Will is coming too. Disappointment, quickly followed by guilt, fills her. She looks forward less and less to the weekend and then spends the weekend itself having painful massages where she is constantly told to relax and enjoy it. She constantly has to reassure Will that she is having a lovely time and is a lot less stressed. This is punctuated by trips to the toilet and on one occasion a sauna where she cries her eyes out because she feels so awful and doesn't know why and then cries with guilt that she has so much, including a lovely boyfriend who buys her spa weekends and yet she feels so unhappy and doesn't appreciate it. She also discovers that it is very dehydrating to cry in a sauna and that many beauty treatments give the same effect as weeping in a toilet. Although that activity possibly can't be sold as a luxury mini break.

It is the fear of being a crap girlfriend and friend that ensures that the mystery illness (Tess needs to stay off Google, this week she is convinced it's dropsy, so far she has had cholera, TB, chicken pox, shingles and a nasty bout of Ebola) doesn't grind her life to a halt. Tess is not good at letting people down. So after a weekend spent helping Nina do her handover notes, having lunch with Tilly and Daisy and asking supportive questions about the wedding and trying not to antagonise Hannah it gets to Sunday afternoon and Tess feels she has neglected Will. Hannah is with the boys and so they finally have some time to themselves. The minute Will expresses pangs of hunger Tess leaps in to action and volunteers to cook. Inspection of the cupboards means that a trip to the shops is in order and Tess immediately says she will go on her own.

As she walks to the shops she looks at her watch and decides that at 3-30 it is unlikely that she is going to get to Sainsbury's before it shuts so it's a choice between the petrol station and the Happy Shopper corner shop. Sadly, planning ahead not being her strong point, Tess knows the layout of both of these shops rather too well and decides that on this occasion that the corner shop is her best bet as it has a rather extensive freezer section. The last time Tess prepared a meal for Will he had been less than impressed with her menu of hummus, pitta bread, chipsticks and celery, with an offer of a bowl of cereal if he was still hungry after that feast. She arrives at the shop and is greeted by name by the guy behind the till. She says hello and asks after the family and then begins her search. She has no idea what she is looking for but can disregard most of the stuff on offer. She doesn't want a breakfast in a tin, she doesn't want hot dogs that come in a jar. She spies a slightly suspect aubergine in a vegetable basket and picks it up. If she got some bacon, onions, a tin of tomatoes and some pasta she could cobble together something resembling a meal, if she covered it with cheese she could almost pretend she had followed a recipe.

She wanders through the shop picking up ingredients and deciding what goes with what. She is in no hurry and quite likes that for the first time in a while she is simply 'out' and no one knows exactly where she is. She heads to the back of the shop to have a look in the freezer section. For some reason boys demand pudding. She is a bit over the look of disappointment on Will's face when she is content for a meal to end without an overload of sugar. A while back they had had a conversation about the meals of their childhood. Both being children of the 80's they had happily reminisced about the various monstrosities that had been considered acceptable to give to children.

Tess had a particular fondness for horrible squash that came in a plastic cup and had a small layer of film stretched across it, she'd only ever had them on school trips but had always been excited to repeatedly stab at the drink with a flimsy straw until she gained entry. Top that off with a packet of iced gems and Tess was in seventh heaven. Will meanwhile had had grandparents who had embraced every convenience and modern thing that came their way. According to Will a trip to his grandparents' house was akin to going to Willy Wonka's Chocolate Factory. Forced to eat vegetables and fruit in his own home thanks to his grandparents he now had enormous fondness for vile, pre-packaged 80s food. Arctic rolls, Vienetta, Pop Tarts and Lucky Charms all delighted him. It was on this basis that Tess found his criticism of her "cooking" so annoying. But she found his childlike enthusiasm quite endearing and she thought if ever she was going to find some of these treats it would be in a shop such as this. There was a strong chance that there would be an original from the 80s in this shop. So she headed to the chest freezers to have a look for something that would make Will happy. As she peers in to the waist height freezers and slides back the top to have a rummage, Tess' vision starts to swim. She pulls her head out, convinced that it was a sudden rush of blood to the head that caused it but it doesn't ease when she is upright. She rests herself against the edge of the freezer and is alarmed when the floor starts to roll and buck under her feet. She hangs on and tries to catch her breath, she can't breathe. Well more accurately she can't breathe out. She gasps and gasps and is vaguely aware of the shopkeeper coming out from behind the counter and heading towards her. She has dropped her basket and the contents are rolling all over the floor, she is beginning to make a bit of a spectacle of herself. Normally this would be Tess' worst nightmare but she is so alarmed she doesn't care. She needs help. She grasps at her throat, at her chest, tears streaming down her cheeks as she gasps and gulps for air. As she doubles over, her vision begins to tunnel and she considers the very real possibility that she is going to die in a corner shop. Her happiness at no one knowing where she is fades rapidly as she faces the possibility that no one is going to know she's dead for quite a while. This is going to wipe the smile off the Happy Shopper's face. And that is her last thought as she eventually blacks out and bounces her head off the freezer on the way down.

Chapter 34

Not that Tess had been planning on keeping it a secret or anything. But she would have liked to have controlled how the news emerged. As it was Asif the shop keeper had sprung in to action. After calling an ambulance he had gotten Tess' bag and found her diary whilst some fellow customers tended to her in the shop. There at the front of the small book was a list of contacts, and he had called 'home'. Despite being nearly thirty and having never actually lived in her parents' current house she still had her parents down as 'home'. When her mother had answered the phone he blithely told her that her youngest daughter was currently passed out on his shop floor. As panicked as her mother was she had enough presence of mind to realise it would take them at least three hours to reach London and so she had called Hannah, who hadn't answered as she was with the boys and considered that sacrosanct. So the next call was to Daisy's mother to get Daisy's number and ask Daisy to call Will. Daisy had also called Tilly. No one thought of calling Tess' landline – which would have tracked Will down in half the time. Her mother, rather sweetly, thought that Will didn't stay over. The result was that there were a lot of people all clamouring to be kept up to date with the unfolding drama and all looking faintly disappointed when they found Tess sat up in bed playing with the adjustable settings.

There is a relief that comes with letting go. Admittedly Tess probably would have chosen not to let go in such a public manner but now she was sat in bed and being offered tea and valium (she said yes to both, she'd never tried valium and felt it was important that she tried new things) it all seemed to be out of her hands and became clear that things would be decided for her. She was also fairly confident that she wouldn't have to go to work tomorrow. She was slightly less thrilled that the news had got out quite so quickly. If pressed she would confess that she would rather deal with this on her own. There would be an argument to suggest that that is how she got in this mess in the first place, so she would be willing to concede and admit Will in to the circle of trust. He was here now actually, he'd gone to get magazines and stuff for her. It was a good job he was here. She wasn't quite with it and was having very strange conversations with people. Tess had come round quite quickly in the ambulance. Smacking her head in to the freezer had led to a cut (or laceration as everyone kept calling it) on her forehead and a hell of a headache. It would seem that heads like to bleed as when she came round in the ambulance and she was asked for information, she had seen her clothes covered in blood and being a squeamish sort had passed out again. Tess wondered if this was a new personality for her, she'd never fainted before in her life and now she'd racked up two incidents in less than twenty minutes.

With the patient unable to give any sensible answers, concussion was suspected and Will was forced to answer questions and fill out forms on her behalf whilst she was preoccupied with inhaling the best part of a cylinder of oxygen and trying not to be sick from the headache that was rattling around her head. Therefore it was Will who kept people in the waiting room, who found out when she was going to be discharged and what the next steps were. It takes some time as the A&E department is heaving. Three children had been bought in with food poisoning and were not very good at aiming their vomit into the cardboard trays and there's a man without trousers threatening to blow up the whole department. They dread to think where he is hiding the dynamite but are happy for him to take priority. Tess chatted away merrily about three subjects repeatedly and Will answers as best he can. No he didn't mind that she wasn't going to be cooking him dinner (especially as Asif had recounted what had been in her basket as he thought it might be medically significant – it would have been more medically significant if Will had actually eaten the hideous feast Tess was going to prepare), no he didn't think the nurses had stolen her clothes and no he was sure that wasn't Jimmy Tarbuck (it was a lady). After a long time of these circular conversations he let Tilly and Daisy in; both of whom promptly burst in to tears. Tess tried to cheer them up by showing them how her bed worked and pointing out Lady Tarbuck but it soon became clear that she was fairly out of it and it would be best if she was left to sleep.

Will sent everybody home and Daisy saved the day by offering to put up Tess' parents and intercept them before they got to the hospital and settle them in. As they file out waving their goodbyes Tess is in tears; she tells herself it is the headache but she is, in truth, completely overwhelmed and feels like a kid on the first day of school watching her parents say goodbye. She is sure at some point this story will be turned in to an amusing anecdote but right now it just feels horrendous. She's been told it was a panic attack but she's not too sure it is – what does she have to panic about? Her over-active imagination is building it up in to something and nothing and by the time Will comes back in the cubicle she is jaggedly crying and convinced she's had a stroke. Will handles it beautifully. He pops the oxygen mask back over her face and performs a rudimentary stroke check based on the television advert. By the time he has her lifting her arms and smiling with both sides of her mouth she is in a much better place and able to drink the tea that Will has bought her. She tries to convince Will that they should leave and that she is fine but he is adamant that she waits to be seen by a doctor. The combination of drugs and concussion has made her difficult to reason with so in the end he tells her that her he can't find her shoes, which seems to appease her and get her to stay put.

Tess has been told not to go to sleep until her head injury has been assessed and so Will reads the papers and out of date magazines to Tess and enjoys her slightly bizarre answers to the crosswords. Unfortunately the on call psychologist comes in just as Tess is amusing herself by rocking backwards and forwards. He gives her a bit of a startled look but ever the professional he goes straight in to the spiel.

"Hello Tess. Do you mind if I call you Tess? My name is Dr. Himesh."
Tess shakes his hand and then Will introduces himself. Dr. Himesh checks that Tess is OK for Will to stay during the examination. The fact that it would probably take surgery to remove Tess' hand from Wills convinces him that she's fine with it.
"Could you tell me a bit about what happened today?" he continues.

"This is my moment," thinks Tess. "I can do this and then we can finally leave this place. We could be in Starbucks in five minutes".
"Well I'm not sure," she says. "I think it was all a bit something and nothing. It was very warm in that shop and I think I must have overheated or something and I hit my head on the way down."
"I see. Have you ever fainted before?" Dr. Himesh asks.
"No. Never. But I suppose there's a first time for everything."
"Well yes. But there's a normally a reason for these things. Now tell me Tess. Are you happy?"

This floors her. She wasn't expecting that at all. And suddenly she can't pretend anymore. A sob starts in the bottom of her chest and before she can stop it, it bursts out and she is crying like a baby for the umpteenth time today. Except this time she is doing it in front of medical professionals which holds more weight than crying in front of Will.

"No. No I'm not. And I don't know why." She ignores Will's stricken look and weeps silently whilst Dr. Himesh runs through her treatment plans. He hands her anti-depressants and painkillers, explains that he will call her GP and get her an appointment for the following week where they will set up a long term treatment plan, he also hands her leaflets about therapists and support groups and finally gives her a small leaflet about concussion, which is beginning to seem like the least important part of this whole escapade.

Once the diagnosis is complete things move quickly. Her head is checked and it's considered that the stitches will hold. Then it's back home for a bath and a change of clothes. All supervised in case the concussion takes over and she sinks beneath the bath water or accidentally smothers herself with a jumper. Then it's round to Daisy's where she is greeted by her parents, fed and falls asleep in a chair. Every time she stirs and opens her eyes she is greeted by everyone staring at her, making sure she's not dead. She gives a little wave and falls back to sleep.

"This feels like a celebration." Tess looks around her as the waiter pushes her chair in for her. She's arranged her hair over her forehead and smoothes it down as the waiter busies himself handing out menus. They smile their thanks and he discretely slips away. It is Monday evening. Will had taken the day off work and they had spent it with her parents. Well Will had. Tess had spent most of it asleep. She awoke to find her mother had tidied the house and was berating Hannah for making so much mess. Tess had had to check that the bang on the head hadn't done a 'Freaky Friday' and taken her back to 1994. After waving them off in their Volvo Will had instructed her to get her glad rags on and then she had been whisked away to this fancy pants restaurant.

"I suppose it is a kind of celebration in a way," Will says. "I know you don't want to go on about it but I just want to say I am really proud of you. This is crap for you but you'll get through it and I am really proud of the way you're tackling it head on. I also want you to know that I am here for you and although one of the things I love about you is that you always put people first but for now I really want you to put you first and be selfish for once."

Tess smiles at him but Will's not done.

"And... I spoke to my friend Gav the dodgy pharmacology student from my year at university and he reckons the anti-depressants won't have hit your system yet so we are quite safe to get absolutely ratted tonight."

"Oh fantastic. I like your style." Tess says.

"Why thank you Miss Acraman. May I also say that tonight is coming courtesy of Mr Visa so price is not to be considered. Tonight we drink from the end of the wine menu."

"Ooh la la."

"And I think a wine per course, don't you." Will says, looking at the menu.

"Why the hell not." Tess agrees.

There is a reason why Tess has never matched her wine to the courses of her dinner before. Tess gets drunk pretty fast. After a couple of glasses she may as well be knocking back diesel. She's more interested in the effect than the taste. She plays along though and obligingly sniffs and swills each wine that is offered. Her and Will chat easily but it is clear that there is something on his mind. It takes until the cheese course for him to come up with it.

"It's not me is it?" He asks.

"Oh I thought it was the camembert, good grief what have you done?"

"Not the smell. The ... you.. the ennui?"

"The black dogs? The terrible sadness? No Will it's not you."
Tess smiles kindly at him. "It's unfortunate timing. But you are
not the cause. I am the cause. I'm just a bit...shit."

She laughs, expecting Will to join in. "You're not shit. Don't you
ever think that. I think you're amazing and don't you forget it."
Tess softens. "I know." She pauses. "Thank you."

"I don't think you do know. You're uncomfortable with any kind
of affection coming your way. You deserve to be cherished and
I'm going to do it. You need someone who loves someone to
distraction." Will says.

Tess is slightly alarmed by this promise/threat "That's very
sweet of you but I don't think depression can be 'loved' away."

"Can't do any harm though can it? Shall we give it a go?" Will
asks.

"It's not a reflection on you if this doesn't go away
immediately." Tess wants to stress this. She doesn't really want
to be responsible for Will's feelings as well as her own.

"I know."

Tess lets it drop.

"Coffee?" she says.

"I reckon I could go one more drink how about you?" Will
replies.

"No, I'm good. I think I need to claw it back a bit." She pauses.
She doesn't want to ask but she can't not. "Will?"

Will is perusing the wine list, possibly trying to find one they
haven't drunk yet. "Mmmm?"

"Are you OK with this? I mean you don't normally drink with
such...ferocity. I know this isn't what you signed up for. I'd be OK
if you ...."

"God, no. No, I wouldn't leave you like this."

"That's reassuring." Tess deadpans.

"No. Came out wrong. I don't want to leave. I love you Tess and that's that. Now come on. I'll join you in a coffee. Then you're staying at mine. No excuses. You're going to have a hangover to remember."
"There's a promise."

Although this conversation should have been reassuring it actually unsettles both of them. Tess is now terrified Will will leave and that she needs to behave slightly better in order to keep him. She needs to stop being so independent and pushing him away. She needs to include him more and put a braver face on things. Will is equally as scared that Tess will decide that maintaining a relationship is too much hard work when she is feeling like this (in some ways he is spot on with his diagnosis except she finds relationships too much hard work regardless of her mental status). In order to both reassure themselves and each other they finish their meal and go back to Will's where they have terribly meaningful sex in order to reassure one another. Needless to say it is horrendous and they both lay awake minds and stomachs churning. Both trying to convince themselves it's the cheese rather than the situation.

One of the bonuses of dating your boss is that when they insist you take time off work it is difficult to refuse. Tess isn't entirely sure that a whole week off is the best thing to do. Stopping and thinking is the last thing she wants to do but Will is insistent. Doctor appointments aside (she is definitely mental and is given a longer prescription) she has very little to do so amuses herself with a great deal of sleeping, watching terrible television and catching up with friends. She would like to read, do the crossword, do all sorts of things but it would appear she is able to focus on very little and can not absorb information. She reads the same pages of books several times and is still unable to follow the plot. She tried to comfort herself by reading 'Ballet Shoes' a book she reads about three times a year but even that doesn't work. So she gives up and instead reads nothing more taxing than the Metro that Will brings home.

"You sure you don't want to come to Mum and Dad's with me?" Tess asked.

Hannah and Tess had both regressed and were lying on the floor with a tube of Pringles between them. As a courtesy Tess had put some celery and carrot on a plate but she was dipping them in peanut butter and then using them to pick up Pringles, so there were no illusion of healthy eating.

"Can't. Boys." Hannah sprayed her answer as her mouth was jammed full of crisps.

"They could come too...."

"Now that actually is a good idea." Hannah says.

"I am full of them." Tess boasts.

"Full of something," Hannah replies.

This week off has been spectacularly helpful for her relationship with Hannah. Now that Tess isn't trying to rush around and get to work, make time for everyone and perhaps occasionally eat she is less resentful of Hannah laying on her sofa all day, doing nothing more taxing than watching Homes Under the Hammer. Tess was going to head to her parents house at the end of the week for more supervised rest and relaxation. Will was going to come down on the Saturday, spend sometime with her and her parents under less bizarre circumstances than an A&E department and then drive her back. She was being trusted to get the train down on her own but she knew the presence of Hannah and the boys would reassure everyone that she wouldn't suddenly get on a train to the White Cliffs and say goodbye forever.

It is surprisingly difficult to leave Will. She's never had issues with saying goodbye before and she's always loved train journeys. Seeing them as an opportunity to eat as much as possible and get drunk, as everyone knows that calories eaten in transit don't count. It's a shame that airports and train stations are so expensive as Tess really likes to test this theory. But since this has all kicked off she is finding that she relies more and more on Will. Then she worries that she's too needy and withdraws and then wonders if she's being cold.

It's a lot of fun for Will.

Not that it's a barrel of laughs for Tess. She is desperately hoping that the tablets kick in soon. Everyone seems to have an opinion on her taking the tablets and all are very happy to share their opinions with her. Tess is regretting being quite so jolly about sharing the information. Top of people's concerns are that she will become 'numb'. Quite frankly Tess is up for a bit of numbness considering the rollercoaster ride of emotions she's been on of late. As she sobbed to Will the other day 'if I lose the highs at least I lose the lows'. Then he pointed out that was a Will Young lyric then she sobbed some more. Partly because she was losing the ability to think for herself but partly because her boyfriend was so readily able to recognise Will Young lyrics.

Tilly, in particular, is adamantly against Tess taking tablets and has recommended her taking up exercise (which would surely only lead to misery) and perhaps taking St John's Wort. In return Tess suggested that Tilly stop taking the pill and try the rhythm method or perhaps hollow out a lemon to use as contraception. Oddly it is her father who provides the sanest reaction.

They are walking across the fields in Bath. Hannah is having a nap and so they are walking the boys, in her Mother's mind small boys are quite similar to Labradors. Her mum keeps sending the boys ahead to find random objects; pine cones, a dock leaf and the like so they can talk without little ears listening.

"So how are you Darling?" her Mother asks. "Are you ready to go back to work? You mustn't if you feel you can't cope."
"Oh I'll be fine," Tess lies. "It's just one of those things. I know Arrabella gets me down but it'll be OK."
"So what is it you're taking?" Her father asks
"Seroxat."
"And what, you just take one when you feel it coming on?" He queries.
"No, you take it every day. It's preventative rather than Nurofen."
"Oh like me with my prostate," he says and that seems to be all there is to say on the matter.

Inevitably Hannah is discussed. Both her parents are of the opinion that Tess should kick her out, that she is enabling her by giving her somewhere to stay. Tess argues that she is not enabling, merely unable to get Hannah to leave. She is not completely surprised that Hannah's behaviour is her fault. She sees her mother having stern words with Hannah in the garden one day. Tess is washing up and can see her Mum gesturing angrily at Hannah's stomach and a hand movement which is either 'boys' or 'dwarf'. Hannah gestures that the dwarves are important to her and then walks off. Unusually her mother follows Hannah, Tess cranes her neck round but they walk down the side of the house and she can't see anymore. She is also slightly distracted by Jake trying to pull her dress down. When the children are in bed her mother restarts her campaign and insists they all sit in the living room and talk. No telly and most unusually for them no wine. Tess is allowed tea, Hannah isn't even allowed that. Tess keeps quiet about the far from nutritious diet she's been feeding Hannah.

She's got to hand it to her Mother. She has style. She starts an innocent conversation about their great aunts. By some amazing coincidence it turns out that they had two Great Aunts (who strangely have never been mentioned before, even by their own siblings) and one had suffered from 'the blues' and one had got pregnant unexpectedly and wasn't pleased about it. Tess looked around and was stunned to see that Hannah was lapping it all up; she really wanted to know that it was all going to be OK. She had failed to work out that this child that no one was keen on would have been their Aunt or Uncle and yet they had never heard of their mother. Hannah was asking questions, how long had it taken to come around to the idea, had it affected the marriage? It occurred to Tess that Hannah had never been on the receiving end of one of these chats before whereas Tess could name several off the top of her head: the Aunt who had had platinum hair (when Tess wondered why she was albino when the rest of her family could pass for Italian), the Aunt who had been a nightmare as a child but was wonderful now (when Tess was locked in the shed by Hannah and it had taken four hours to realise she was missing - Tess wondered if there had been an Aunt with Altzhiemer's to explain the fact her parents hadn't noticed she was gone).

After her Dad went to bed the conversation became a little more serious. Hannah mentioned that she knew she had to make decisions. Her mother pressed home to her the fact that it wasn't about her anymore. Tess drifted off in her chair (perhaps there was an Aunt with narcolepsy) and when she sporadically surfaced from her napping she was convinced they were talking about baby names.

The arrival of Will breathed fresh air in to the house. Even a phone call from Garry announcing that he was coming on Sunday to pick up the boys (and Hannah if she wanted) couldn't bring the mood down. Will was a delight. He charmed her mother, gently teased Hannah and was prepared to be used as a human climbing frame by the boys. Tess was happy to watch him interact with her family. His behaviour reflected well on her, it made her look good. As they packed themselves in to the car ready to leave, complete with a pack of sandwiches and a blanket - presumably her mother thought this drive was taking place in the 1950s - they said their goodbyes and Tess felt genuinely better for the short break. She hugged her parents goodbye and when she hugged her Dad he whispered, "Just make sure you're happy."

It was unsettling and she didn't really want to unpack what he meant so instead she told Hannah that if, IF, she was coming back then she should let her know.

Hannah came back.

Chapter 35

Monday came round far too soon. It was like her first day at school, only she was sure she wouldn't get away with a bit of light colouring and wetting herself. She was so pale and nervous on Sunday night that Will questioned whether she was actually up for going in. She reassured him she was and then lay awake all night. At 6am she decided that she would just get up and get on with it and so was at her desk by 7-30.

As always it takes forever for her computer to boot up so she flicks through the post and the press cuttings and sees that everything seems to have gone to plan while she was away. It would also seem that Arrabella is too grand to open her post and it has simply piled up on Tess' desk. As a result Arrabella has missed the RSVP dates for some parties Tess knows she would give her right arm to go to. This amuses Tess as Arrabella has really shot herself in the foot with her own laziness but then she realises that this will somehow come around to being her fault and so she makes a note to ring the organisers and try and get her in. .She scrawls a brief explanation on to a couple of post-it's attached them to the invites and then slings the lot on to Arrabella's desk. With the basics taken care of she is then clear to do her actual job.

By now the computer has come on, its tardiness down to the fact that it has lain dormant for a week. A quick flick through her emails confirms that nothing of any drama has come to pass whilst she was eating Pringles and having heated discussions with Hannah about what they would do with Nick Knowles. By the time the others begin to arrive she is ready to face them. Will thoughtfully brings her in a coffee when he arrives and this helps bolster her to answer everyone's questions on how she is feeling and if she is better. The only person missing now is Arrabella. And then there she is. Shiny red shoes and a shoulder padded power suit. (She once went to a conference on how powerful women dress. When she has important meetings she can barely get her quarterback shoulders through the door. Will and Tess once worked out the equation of width of shoulder equal to lack of knowledge.) The outfit signals it's going to be hard day. She looks at Tess, looks at the pile of post on her desk and then back to Tess.

"Did you not have time to look through this Tess?"

Tess hates herself for the quiver in her voice. "Morning Arrabella, I've been through all that but it looks like it's all for you."

"Yet you've had time to get yourself a coffee." Arrabella says.

"I got that for her actually Arrabella," Will interrupts. "If I had known what time you were coming in I could have picked one up for you too."

The fact that Will is a man turns Arrabella in to a simpering simpleton.

"Oh I'm trying not to drink so much coffee now as I've heard it gives you cellulite and I also want to sleep better." She giggles and tosses her hair back. Will backs off in alarm.

"Right, well I'm going to that...meeting," he stutters and then heads off to hide in the loos for a bit.

"Coffee please Tess," snaps Arrabella the moment Will has left the room.

Chapter 36

Normally Tess would take any opportunity to get out of work. She's been known to skip her way to the dentist. But today she would do anything to stay and listen to Arrabella bollocks her way through a simple press release. As the clock clicks down to 3pm Tess begins to procrastinate. She tidies her desk, putting everything away neatly and making an all-encompassing to-do list ready for the next day. She is just filing her emails when suddenly her phone bings and at the same time an email falls in to her inbox. The email is from Tilly, the texts are from Daisy and Nina. All say the same thing – Good luck.

She looks up and sees that Will is looking at her. He smiles and she almost cries; she really doesn't want to do this. She collects her stuff quickly and walks out the office. Will is hot on her heels.

"Are you sure you're going to be OK?" he asks.

"I'll be fine."

"Let me know when you're out." He requests.

"I will." She promises.

"And are you still meeting Daisy? Because I can leave early if you need me."

"You've got that meeting." Tess protests.

"I can cancel it if you need me to." He offers.

"I'll be fine. It's the first one. I doubt we'll talk about anything."

"Well take care. Let me know how you get on."

Will pulls her close and kisses her on the forehead. She clings to him and he eventually had to prize her fingers off his arm. He walks her out of the building and hails a cab, handing the driver a bundle of notes and telling him the address. Tess smiles her thanks and waves as the cab pulls away.

For some reason Tess had expected a hippy. Paisley skirt (possibly decorated with mirrors and beads), long hair and a stench of patchouli. What she wasn't expecting was a woman about 45 who looked like Yasmin le Bon. Yasmin le Bon on a really good day. Her councillor was absolutely stunning. Tess immediately felt intimidated. Tess was led through to the kitchen and Yasmin, or Georgia as she kept insisting on being called, made her a cup of tea. The kitchen was perfect. Shaker style units, granite worktops and all utensils shiny stainless steel. Held up on the fridge by magnets were photos of Georgia and her family – two stunning little girls and a husband who looked like he modelled for catalogues. "I have nothing in common with this woman," thought Tess. "I can't share anything with her she's got no idea, her life is so different to mine, she wouldn't understand." Then they go through to Georgia's study and Tess is offered a comfy chair. One carefully asked question later and Tess is in tears and doesn't give a shit.

Neither does Georgia. She hands Tess a box of tissues and lets her carry on. Words pour out of Tess, she doesn't think she is making sense then Georgia will ask "and how did that make you feel?" and Tess realises she's right there with her. And she cares. Not in a friendship way but in a wanting to sort someone out way. An hour goes in a flash and Tess knows instantly she cannot not come back next week. Her sanity is hanging by a thread and she thinks Georgia might be the key.

"It's a depression. You're probably pre-disposed towards it but it's been triggered by real life events. I'd hazard a guess that it's not the first episode you've had but it's probably the first one you've not been able to get over. " Georgia comments.

Tess simply nods. She doesn't particularly want to be here but she has to admit that this therapist has a point. She could probably list five or six occurrences where she has not wanted to exist. Has felt like an outsider, has felt unable to cope, felt incompatible with life. Felt...pointless. Felt on standby and unable to reboot. She thought that was normal. It's quite something to be told that it isn't normal, that everyone else doesn't feel like this. She thought therapy was meant to make you feel better not confirm you're a freak.

"Sorry" Tess weeps. Daisy looks a bit stricken.
"Just carry on, " Tess advises. "Pretend it's not happening."
"You've never really cried have you Tess? I suppose there's no point crying if there's no one to comfort you. Perhaps now you've got Will you're able to let go." Daisy makes up her own theories.
This actually helps and the tears begin to grind to a halt. "Good Lord Daisy you're mental. Firstly I'd slightly challenge the idea that an emotion isn't worth expressing unless there's an audience. Secondly it's not like I've lived in emotional torment and Will has spoken to me miracle worker style. It's just happened. It's no more puzzling or wondering than that. I wish it hadn't but it has and now I just have to get on with it. As do you."
"But don't you feel safer with Will." Daisy presses.
"I veer. Sometimes I don't know what I'd do without him other times I just see him as one more thing to deal with. He's been so good with everything... but is life better? It's different."
"But different good. I mean no one wants to be on their own." Daisy says.
"That is the received wisdom." Tess agrees.
"Oh don't pretend you didn't want it. I know you put a brave face on it but you wanted someone. Any one who says otherwise is lying"
"This isn't really an argument I can win is it? The more I deny it the more you'll think I'm in denial so I am just going to change

the subject. Oooh do you fancy seeing that new Nicole Kidman film."

"I don't like her." Daisy says.

"She's acting it won't be her." Tess reasons.

"No, I know but I'll spend ages trying to decide whether she's doing a British accent or whether that's her acting style and then I start thinking about Tom Cruise and what she was thinking and then I lose the plot of the film."

"Odd." Tess feels she has the power to make these judgements.

"It's not. I'd never make you sit through a Keira Knightly film. " Daisy says.

"I've sat through a Keira Knightly film."

"*Love Actually* doesn't count. Colin Firth, Liam Neeson and Alan Rickman cancel out Keira Knightly." Daisy argues.

"Is it like how you can watch *Four Weddings and a Funeral* despite Andy McDowell because you want to turn John Hannah."

"Exactly. Or *Peter's Friends* because of Hugh Laurie."

"Oh let's watch *Peter's Friends*. We could buy Malteasers? Please........." Tess begs.

Chapter 37

Tess isn't very good with people being sympathetic. She just wasn't very sure what to do with it. She was far more comfortable with her mother's methods. A method based on "Oh dear you're not well, you'd better stay away from everybody else, we don't want it." It was an approach Tess found both practical and comforting. If she's coughing her guts up she doesn't really want cheerleaders or observers. Sometimes she has had her mind taken off feeling sick by attempting to keep Tilly out of the bathroom, so desperate is she to help. Tess once made Daisy cry when Daisy mentioned for the 300th time in an hour that she didn't feel very well (and somehow expected Tess to be able to cure her). Tess offered to take Daisy outside and beat her to death to put her out of her misery.

What she really, really wants right now is to be left alone. She knows this will pass. That it will all be fine. Yes. This is singularly the most terrifying thing she has ever gone through. She feels out of control, scared, sad and desolate. But there's a rational part of her brain (that she is clinging on to for dear life, for once that goes she knows there is no way back) that tells her that one day this will be over. Either she will get better or she will end it all because she can't live like this. And as extreme as it sounds, it's very comforting. It will go away. And the one thing she really doesn't want to do is talk about it. She has no idea what 'this' is.

Which goes some way to explain why she, Hannah and Will are all laying underneath the window sill. Tess was absent-mindedly standing by the window, tuning Hannah's latest whine out when she saw Daisy turn the corner of the street. Without really think it through too much she instinctively dropped to her knees and lay out of sight on the floor.

"What are you doing?" Hannah asks, momentarily distracted. "Get down." and for once Hannah did as she was told. As did Will. In his defence when you walk in to a room and there are two women laying on the floor hissing at you to get down then you do as they say as you assume there is logic behind it. They had to stay down for quite a while. Not only did they have to wait for Daisy to clear the road but they had to lay silently whilst Daisy stood and banged on the front door (she had the security code to the main door).
"Why are we doing this?" Will whispers.
"I can't be bothered to emote." Tess explains.
Hannah gets the giggles. Tess puts her hand over her mouth. Which then makes Tess laugh. So Will puts his hand over her mouth. They lay there snorting in to each other's hands until Daisy retreats. Then they get up and dust themselves off. None of them, including Tess are quite sure why what has happened has happened.
"I'll put the kettle on," says Tess. And walks out of the living room. Hannah and Will simply look at one another.

Chapter 38

The plan for Nina to stay with Tess for a few days before she went to New York was shot to ribbons by Hannah and to some extent Will. But Nina had given up her flat and had to go somewhere so Tess housed her luggage (and tripped over it) whilst Nina resided in a Travelodge around the corner. Tess found a huge amount of solace in Nina's spartan, boxy room. It made a nice change from the Big Yellow Storage Unit/ Youth Hostel that she was currently living in.

"What time is your flight?" Tess asked. She was making a cup of tea for them both, trying to split a minute carton of milk fairly between the two of them.

"11 in the morning, so need to be there about 9, so leave here...what, 8 do you reckon? Heathrow on a Tuesday morning – shouldn't take that long but there's no telling what the traffic will do. You still OK to check Mum and Anna get home alright?"

Nina's mother and sister were coming down the night before, squeezing in to the hotel room with Nina and then going to the airport with her. From there they were going to navigate the Piccadilly Line to Kings Cross where they would get the lunch time train back to Durham. It was their first trip to London and, although they would more than likely be fine, it was Tess' job to ring them and make sure they had made it safely on board and weren't weeping and shaking whilst shuttling repeatedly between Cockfosters and Rayners Lane.

"Yep, fine." Tess confirms.

"I feel bad leaving with all this, all you've got on." Nina gestures to Tess, Tess' stitches are out now but her head still sports a fairly livid streak of red across the top. Tess had discovered fairly early on that trying to put make up on the cut was not only astonishingly painful but also turned the skin over the scab an oompa loompa orange. It was like travelling back in time to her 14 year old self and trying to cover up spots with a Clearasil stick which seeming only suited those with the skin tone 'tangerine'. Not that it had stopped her slapping it on, leading to some rather alarming school photos. Tess wondered if leaving the cut alone to heal on its own was a sign of finally being a grown up.

"Don't worry about it. I'll be fine. If I hadn't smacked in to the freezer then nothing would have been diagnosed and we'd all be none the wiser," Tess rationalises.
"Well it's good that you did then as something is clearly wrong.." Nina isn't going to be fobbed off.
"I know but it's not bad enough that you need to stay."
"I must say I feel better knowing you've got Will. Although you need to kick that sister of yours out."
"Tell me about it." Tess agrees.
"You need to concentrate on you."
"I'm not pregnant though, am I? She is. We all know that's the trump card. I can't kick a pregnant woman out"
"True. You will call me though. And email and Skype and whatsapp." Nina says.
"Yes, yes, buy me a webcam and yes . And you too. What you're doing is far more important than whatever the hell this is."
"It's not a competition." Nina says
"Not one I'm winning." Tess agrees.
It was a strange evening. As the time clicked down on the rather unpleasant clock radio on the MDF bedside table both Nina and Tess were aware that they were basically filling time until they had to say goodbye. They both dreaded its arrival and

desperately wanted it to be over. All conversation seemed redundant. They were reduced to random and wild exclamations of "I can't believe you'll be gone in 36 hours!" and "Wow this is really happening!". Eventually there was a knock on the door, Nina opened it and Will was there with a bottle of champagne.

They sat on the double bed; Will and Nina drinking from the hastily swilled out mugs and Tess swigging from the bottle and ignoring Will's glances at her. She wasn't meant to be drinking on the anti-depressants. But Tess had taken that advice with a pinch of salt. She'd drunk through umpteen courses of anti-biotics over the last ten years and she'd yet to lose a leg to gangrene or have her liver dissolve. She saw it more as a helpful hint, like hand washing your bras, than as an actual directive.

"Well Nina." Will was good in these situations. Tess smiled at him, grateful he was there and could take control and sum things up. "We've had the work goodbye, we all know you're irreplaceable and this 'Barry ' or whatever he's called is a mere pretender to your throne. I'm sure within two years you'll be ruling the earth and will have bought us out and a dozen companies beside. But speaking as your friend and on behalf of Tess, who...Oh Tess." Tess has dissolved in to tears and when Will reaches out an arm she tucks herself under it, and Will kisses the top of her head in comfort and carries on "I was going to say I know you hate me talking on your behalf but I guess you're beyond it?" Tess hiccups her agreement and disentangles herself from Will and crawls in to Nina's arms where they stay clamped in a weepy embrace. Will can sense he's fighting a losing battle.

"You'll be missed," he concludes. "Enormously. Don't forget us, stay in touch and most importantly don't forget it's aluminium not alooominum."

They toast Nina well and leave. At 11am on Tuesday they sneak away from their desks and go outside the building and wave at planes that fly overhead. They then go back to their office and try and acclimatise to a Nina-less world.

Chapter 39

Tess can hear Hannah and Will talking in the kitchen. How can they have anything to say to one another? They were up until 2 yammering away and now a mere, she rolls over (carefully so she doesn't fall off the sofa) and looks at the clock, bloody hell, a mere six hours later they have found some more shit it's absolutely vital that they talk about.

She hears one of them move around, scraping their chair back, of course, and put the kettle on. She plays dead. As much as she would love a cup of coffee she would rather die of thirst than go out there and join them. She has nothing to contribute to the conversation and is a bit over being called 'miserable' or 'grumpy' when she doesn't contribute to a conversation about absolutely bollocks. Not that she wants to sit around discussing Proust. She doesn't want a conversation about anything. She would like some peace and quiet. She's not sure when her flat became party central; possibly around the time Will stopped going home. She never realised how difficult it was to get people to leave your house. As a result she has two squatters.

Hannah wouldn't leave, even if she was asked directly. Will has never been asked to leave and so has never gone. To ask him to go doesn't really seem like the actions of a loving girlfriend so Tess has said nothing and is now feigning up to fourteen hours sleep a day.

Which she can get away with because of the "depression". She remembers this and reaches in to her handbag left lying by the sofa and takes out her packet of tablets. She pops a Seroxat out of the blister pack and swallows it down dry. She wonders why it has hit now. Oh she knows the spiel. Depression is an illness; it has to be treated as such. But why now? Things are looking better than they have for years. Boyfriend, friends, job – she's firing on all cylinders. Hannah's laugh echoes through the walls. It's like a dog with asthma. 'The timing,' she thinks, 'could be down to the fact that everyone in my life has gone fucking mental and it's some how my responsibility to sort them out." It's coming to something when the sanest person in your life rang you in tears at half past one this morning because a hundred and fifty napkins have arrived and they are cerulean not azure.

"And then Stuart," Tilly had hiccupped out, "Stuart said 'I thought we were going with blue.? Blue! And he found some in a drawer left over from Amanda's baby shower and said 'Why are we spending two hundred quid on serviettes? Why can't we just use these?' I mean why don't we take a dump on the table?"

Tess had laughed which had made Will pop his head round the door and see if she wanted to join Hannah and him. She had smiled, gestured to the phone apologetically and walked in to the bathroom. She could still hear Hannah's rasping, breathy laugh in there so she retraced her steps and stood in the hallway. She could still hear her. Finally at a loss she took her keys, grabbed her coat and went and sat in the tiny communal courtyard that was shared by the eight flats in her block.

"So why are you up?" Tilly asked. "I was going to leave a ranty message on your voicemail. I didn't expect you to pick up."
"Couldn't sleep. I don't know whether it's the world's most irritating house guest or whether it's the latest symptom of this flipping depression. It could be that I spend so much time pretending to sleep that I have exhausted my reserves."

There is silence. Tilly doesn't really 'believe' in depression. Tess doesn't really think that it's something you have to 'believe' in. It's a fact. It would be like deciding you don't really 'believe' in cancer and all these melodramatic people cluttering up NHS beds claiming to be ill could cure themselves with fresh air and positive thinking. But this is not a row for today. Particularly at this time in the morning in a communal courtyard. So Tess breaks the silence.

"Still I get a lot done. Never been so ahead at work. Besides I'll go back to bed soon and hopefully get a few hours then. Are we still lunching tomorrow?"

"Yeah, although can you check with Daisy? She's being really bloody weird with me." Tilly says.

"Ummmmm," is Tess' non-committal reply. "I'll check with her. I wouldn't take it personally. She's got a lot on at the moment."

"Really Tess? Compared to you and me? Perhaps she could deal with it in her thirteen weeks holiday a year." Tilly gets four weeks a year. She is bitter.

"She has to use that for planning and marking." Shit, when did Tess get indoctrinated by the teacher manifesto? "Anyway, it's not a competition, I'll see you tomorrow and I'll call Daisy. I'm going to go in now. I'm bloody freezing. You normal now? No more weeping at table wear?"
"Wait till it's you and Will, then you'll understand. There are websites and bridal forums I could show you that would make you realise that I am being remarkably sane."
A shiver goes up Tess' spine the second Tilly mentions her and Will and marriage in the same sentence. As is traditional she goes on the attack and is unable to resist a dig.

"You know for someone who doesn't believe in mental illness you're doing a fair impression of a grade A nutter." Tess says. "Your only problem is that you don't know how lucky you are. You've got everything a girl could want. You need to start appreciating it and realise that life isn't a fairy-tale." Tilly counters.

Tess accepts defeat. She's not going to argue about life being a fairy-tale with a woman who is going to wrap herself in a white lace dress and throw a party in a castle.

"Don't ever volunteer for the Samaritans will you Tills? I'm going to bed now. If they find me swinging from the shower rail remember you made me do it."
"If you can wait until lunch I'll suffocate you with two hundred cerulean napkins." Tilly promises.
They say their goodbyes and Tess makes her way back to bed. Will and Hannah have finally stopped talking and said their goodnights. He's also taken pity on Hannah and so Tess is greeted by Hannah's sleeping form in her bed. She considers getting in next to her sister but goes through to the living room and when she sees Will on the sofa, vulnerable and open, deep in sleep, she smiles and curls up next to him. She is lucky she thinks. Most people would kill to be in her position. She snuggles in closer, half to get closer to him, half to avoid falling off the sofa. Will throws a heavy arm over her and she is saved from an arse first fall on to the floor. A mere two hours later and she is finally back to sleep.

"Only to be woken by the loud bastard brigade five minutes later," Tess grumbles as she reaches about for her phone; she tries to work out in her head exactly how little sleep she has had so she can gauge her resentment properly. She sees she has had a text from Daisy. If Tilly refuses to acknowledge depression then Daisy cannot stop acknowledging it. She is alarmingly supportive. Perhaps Tilly's right she thinks. Perhaps she is living in a fairy-tale. Goldilocks – trying to find exactly the right level of friendship support. She wonders if Daisy is trying to prove that she is a 'good' person. As if to offset the Kyle situation and then she realises that Daisy is just being Daisy.

It hits Tess suddenly that she really misses Matt.

Chapter 40

"So don't tell Tilly," Daisy concludes.

"OK," Tess agrees, although she doubts she could cobble together anything to tell out of Daisy's breathless tales. "Why not?"

Daisy sighs. She had agreed to lunch on the proviso that she and Tess met first to discuss the Kyle situation and now Tess was just being plain obtuse.

"Well, I know she thinks I'm being funny with her and I suppose I am a little bit. It's just I know that she's always looked to me and Simon as a happy marriage and with her wedding coming up I don't want to shatter her illusions in love what with, well, my situation."

Tess continues to look at her blankly. Her brain desperately screams 'say something supportive' but it doesn't actually help her by conjuring anything up.

"So how are you?" Daisy asks. "How's the errr stuff?"

It's like Daisy has been reading an etiquette book. She is aware that it is rude to monopolise the conversation and only talk about yourself and it's polite to ask the other person in the conversation what is going on with them but as Tess is not getting married, not having children and her relationship with Will is stable she is unaware of anything else in her life apart from the mentalness.

"Well the counselling has hit a dry spot.. I've started to feel a bit of a fraud for going. At first I couldn't stop talking to her and thought she had all the answers but now the more I think about it the more I am convinced it's chemical and it's not really a reaction to anything. Do you remember second year at uni?"

"The uncontrollably weeping over a pair of trousers and only eating Frosties?" Daisy recalls.

"Yep. Looking back I think that might have been something. And it certainly wasn't lifestyle related. Who could really have anything to complain about when they only have three hours lectures a week and have a part time job in a bar?" Tess says.

"True. I suppose we were all slightly highly-strung twenty year olds. You staying in bed for a week may not have been normal but we were all revelling in the fact that we could. Should we have done something?" Daisy asks.

"No. If I didn't twig why would any one else? And it passed. As did the one at 25."

"My life is meaningless I must work for a big corporation...." Daisy recounts.

"And look how well that worked out! Anyway. Yeah, having a bit of a life reassessment. But I suppose at least it's got a name. And I might not be able to drag myself out of this one but maybe a bit of help won't go amiss."

"And you're in such a better place this time. Will is amazing." Daisy says.

"Mmmmm."

"He'll be there for you."

"Seems unfair to dump it all on him." Tess confesses.

"Give and take, isn't it?"

"Yeah, so anyway... What you up to this week?" She asks.

"School stuff mainly. Reports to write. I need to redo the displays on my wall before parents' evenings. Some of that stuff has been up there since the last one."

"Double mounting on sugar paper?" Tess asks.

"Yep, going to stay late and do it."

"Can I help, I used to bloody love that. Lining it all up on the guillotine. I could come by after work and help if you're going to be there late."

"Great, I'll probably be there till about 6."

"Oh. Well I don't finish till 6."

"That's a shame. You could have spent some time with Kyle."

"Awww Shucks." Tess pulls an exaggerated disappointed face."

"Tess." Daisy is put out.

"I can't have this conversation again. Simon is my mate. Sort it out Daisy."

Daisy goes to protest. But Tess stops her

"Or I'll cry. I'll get a bowl of Frosties and I'll cry. If you argue with me I'll be irrevocably mentally damaged. And I'll cry. In public."

Tess is open about the mentalness. Even if Will winces every time she uses the term 'mentalness'. He seems to think it is something that should be suffered through stoically and silently. Something that should be referred to in public in an obscure and oblique terms. Like a yeast infection, which come to think of it Tess had also shared with anyone who asked how she was.

Tess is not a subscriber to suffering in silence. She shares pretty much everything with those around her. The office has seen her through deaths (grandparents), a migraine when she had been spectacularly unwell and just the day-to-day grind of looking after Arrabella. She doesn't see why this should be any different.

"But it is different." Will argues.

It's early morning and they have the office to themselves. They've given up the pretence and now freely walk in together. They assume Arrabella knows, there have been a few comments but she won't say anything to them. This, Will maintains, is because Arrabella 'has her head rammed up her own bum'.

"How?" Tess asks.

"There is a fundamental difference between calling in sick with a headache and calling in sick because you're too sad to get out of bed."

"But why?"

"There just is." Will says.

"Do you think less of me? Think I should be stronger?"

"Sweetheart, no of course I don't. You're ill. I'd do anything to take this from you. I'm your boyfriend, I will be there for you every step of the way." Will replies. His answer a little too practised.

"You're also my boss and you don't think it's a valid reason not to come to work?" Tess argues.

"You're wasted here. You should be a lawyer."

The door opens and the first of their workmates arrives. Will is distracted but Tess hasn't forgotten that he actually dodged the question.

Arrabella was one of the few people who didn't know about Tess' issues. Not because Tess didn't want her to know but because she had no idea how to have that conversation. With others in the office she had simply dropped it in to conversation. 'This bruise on my head? Oh I smacked it against a freezer in a shop. They reckon it was some kind of panic attack." This statement was accompanied by a 'what can you do?' kind of shrug and she'd find people would either say 'Oh that's awful' and then concentrate on the physical injury or recount some tale of mental disorder of their own (which mysteriously always happened to a friend of theirs). There was, of course, always the risk that she would become the sounding board for every kind of upset in the office. She had no desire to be in a misery club. She wasn't running an outreach programme. She was also fairly certain that sad Linda in accounts hadn't been diagnosed with anything and was just living a sad little life. Arrabella meanwhile was bananas. There was no way to tell how she would take it. Ironically if ever anyone were a prime candidate to be diagnosed with some sort of personality disorder it would be Arrabella. But she remained highly suspicious of anyone who admitted a flaw. She was the type of person who believed in mind over matter. She hadn't quite told Uta to think her way out of her wheelchair but Tess expected it any day. This view was of course suspended when Arrabella was ill. Sympathy was ordered and the merest hint of a headache was diagnosed as a brain tumour. Surprisingly, positive thinking was eschewed in favour of, not painkillers, but whinging. Tess found that a hit of anti-histamine made things a lot better even if she was the one to take it, not Arrabella.

The weird thing was that anti-anxiety, anti-depressant tablets had caused Tess unimaginable levels of stress.
She had always been a 'get up and go' kind of girl. Clothes were fished out the laundry basket, hair was brushed on the bus (or sometimes not brushed at all) and breakfast either got skipped or was eaten around 11am in the office. Now, however she had to remember to take a tablet every single morning. This happened most days, but there were occasions when Tess was travelling to work, head bouncing off the bus window as she slumped against it in her seat when she was suddenly racked with the notion that she hadn't done something, she retraced her steps and soon came to the conclusion that she had forgotten to take her daily dose of happiness. And with that she was racked with uncertainty and panic. Ironically really given that not so long ago she hadn't been on them and knew no better and would easily get through the day. Where as now she was convinced serotonin couldn't survive more than a day in her body and would abandon her mid morning, leaving her an emotional wreck. The anxiety and panic this would cause made her wonder if taking the tablets was in fact worth it. But there was a huge fear of being without them. "Is this addiction?" she wondered. "What a shit addiction to have." She would of course lie to Will when he asked her (as he did every day) if she had taken her prescription today and if she was OK. She could barely manage her own worrying; she couldn't deal with carrying Will's as well.

She could only assume that at some point she would have a huge amount of serotonin swimming around in her and soon missing a day or two wouldn't bother her. Still, she thought it was worrying how quickly she had come to rely on something she hadn't even thought of before. Which did pose the question why she was taking them but then she remembered that she had been up for a whole hour and hadn't thought about tipping herself under the bus so she assumed there was some positive effect.

She got her phone out to text Tilly. Although Tilly seemed to think she was the cause of Tess' breakdown, Tilly seemed to be of the opinion that there was a limited amount of happiness in the world and she had some how stolen Tess' share hence the desolation. Tess found it hard to believe that Tilly could subscribe to this theory whilst also believing that the brain was the one part of the body that didn't get ill. She actually loved being around Tilly. Uncomplicated joy was something she was more than happy to get on board with. A world where the most stressful thing involved was finding the time to break in your wedding shoes was the kind of world Tess wanted to live in. Sadly she lived in a world with Arrabella in it.

Chapter 41

Whenever Daisy thought about it she wanted to die. And she couldn't stop thinking about it. She saw reminders of it everywhere. She read Burger King as Burger Kyle. She watched EastEnders and was reminded of the time that Kyle had said he had watched it. She then remembered how at the time she had taken the fact that he watched EastEnders as a sign that they had an enormous amount in common and that they connected on a deep and meaningful level. Now she could see that about nine million people watch EastEnders four times a week and she's about as connected to the other 8,999,999 as she is to Kyle. And then she's back to wanting to die again.

Sadly dying is not really an option. So she has opted for the less messy option of laying on the bed, reliving the terrible moment and dreading the arrival of Monday. If there was any kind of redeeming aspect to this sorry situation is that Daisy had chosen to completely humiliate herself on a Friday. This meant she didn't have to see Kyle again for two days. On the other hand she had two days to build and twist things and torture herself with what is going to happen. She seems to have a talent for building things up in her mind. She groans and rolls over and buries herself in to the pillow. Below the front door opens and slams shut and she can hear Simon go about his rituals. The chink of the keys as they hit the stairs, the two dull thuds as he kicks his shoes off. He shouts for her and she doesn't reply. She hears him walking in to the kitchen and then the living room. She knows he's on his way upstairs but she can not be bothered to reply to him. As she hears his feet pad up the stairs she lays perfectly still. Like a child playing hide and seek, if she can't see him then he can't see her. She tenses as the door opens.

Simon is completely baffled. Is this the next stage of his marriage? For six years he was met by a smiling happy Daisy. When he used to get in from work she would greet him with a smile and a query about his day. Often there would be a meal on the go. Not because they had a super traditional marriage or because he expected it but because Daisy tended to get in at five and he got in at 7. Plus Daisy loved to cook . For the last six months or so he has been greeted by an irrational, moody Daisy. Instead of a meal he was often told that she had already eaten and he could sort himself out. She would sit in her pyjamas on the sofa and grunt in reply to his questions about her day. He was given the distinct impression that his very presence annoyed Daisy no end but he had no idea what or how to change. For years she had loved what he did and who he was. Now she couldn't tolerate him. Was a weepy wife the next step?

"Daisy? Daisy sweetheart. What's wrong?" Simon sat on the bed and tried not to wince when Daisy rolled away from him and instead stroked her back which was now turned towards him. "Daisy are you ill?" he asks.
A shake of the head.
"Is everyone alright? Your parents?" Simon persists.
"They're fine." Daisy replies.
Well, he supposed words were progress.
"Can I get you anything?"
Nothing.
"OK. Right, well I'm going to get us a drink each because I don't know about you but I sure as hell need one and when I come back you can tell me all about it and we'll sort it out together. If can't be that bad can it?"
Daisy snorts.
"OK. Well back in a bit." He yanks his tie off and throws it down as he walks out. Not the start to the weekend he had been hoping for. Then he feels bad. Daisy's not been easy of late but he wants to get to the bottom of this. He walks back down the

stairs and hunts around for a bottle of wine. He was convinced they had the remains of a bottle of white somewhere. He remembered opening it the other day and he was sure he had put it in the fridge. He shuts the door after a fruitless search and then spies the now empty bottle on the table next to a glass with a tell tale lip stick mark on it. Explains where the wine went and also accounts for the state of Daisy. He sighs and flicks the kettle on and starts spooning the coffee in to the mugs, he slops a bit of milk in to one and adds sugar to the other. Almost on auto pilot. He leafs through the post as he waits for the kettle to boil. When he's made the coffee he carries it carefully upstairs. He tries to open the door with his hip but can't manage it, so he gently kicks the door.

"Dais? Daisy? Can you open the door? I've got my hands full." He calls.
There's no response so he carefully puts the cups and the plate of biscuits down and blows on his knuckles where they have slightly burnt on the hot cups. He pushes on the handle of the bedroom door and it doesn't move. They don't have a lock on the bedroom door. This means that Daisy has pushed something against the door or wedged a chair under the handle.
"Daisy!" Simon shouts. He is worried but also irritated. He could do without all the drama. If there's a problem can't they just talk about it rather than go through all this 90210 rigmarole? It's been a long day and he was hoping for a pleasant evening with his wife. He knocks loudly on the door. "Let me in Daisy. I don't know what I've done but can we just talk about it? "
A voice floats through the door. "You haven't done anything."
Progress. It's not exactly what he's looking for but at least she's responding.
Simon tries again. "So why have you wedged the door shut?" He uses his most reasonable voice, he's impressed that even in this ridiculous situation he is managing to be civil.

"Because I want to be on my own!" Daisy screams – she's clearly not on the same page.

Simon snaps. "Fine," he yells back. "You could have just asked rather than scream at me and behave like a child. I would have gone to the pub and had a nice time with people who actually want to spend time with me and had a good time rather than coming home and seeing my fucking miserable wife."
He stomps back down the stairs in a foul mood. All the positivity that he had walked through the door with has evaporated; he can't see the rest of the weekend going well now. Bloody Daisy. Her moods inevitably became his moods and he was sucked in to a place he didn't want to me. If there was a genuine problem then he wanted her to share it with him. If not, then he just wanted her to get over it without all these hysterics.

He gets a beer, not from the fridge – there used to be a time when Daisy would put a few in the fridge for him when the shopping was delivered. Now she put the wine they ordered in the fridge and shoved Simon's beer bottles to the back of the larder, leaving Simon to sort himself out. Which is fair enough he supposes, he is thirty, but it was nice to feel that Daisy cared enough about him to accommodate him and think about him. Now he is left to his own devices he finds that he constantly forgets to plan ahead so when he desperate for a drink, much like now, he is forced to drink warm beer.

It doesn't put him off though – he drinks three. He tries to read the free paper, he attempts a crossword but he mainly sits there and seethes. He knows he should be worried about Daisy but quite frankly he's too pissed off. He sits and stews on the situation; occasionally his thoughts are interrupted by a buzzing. He assumes it's a fly or the washing machine or something. It's not until the fourteenth or fifteenth time that he hears it that he stirs himself from his stupor and works out what it is – a mobile phone ringing on vibrate. It's not his, his is in his jacket pocket and he always keeps his on loud. It must be Daisy's. He looks around for it but he can't see it. He's not too bothered, he assumes it's either Tess or Tilly; the three of them can barely let a second of their lives go by without informing the other two. When it rings again he thinks he'd better tell which ever of the two it is on the other end to stop ringing and (he can't deny it) get a clue as to what is wrong with Daisy.

He tracks down the still vibrating phone to Daisy's jacket pocket. Inevitably it stops ringing just as he finds it. Without really thinking he unlocks the phone, her password is their wedding anniversary, and sees that she has twenty-one missed calls.

He assumes something is up with one of the girls. Between Tilly's wedding and Tess'... whatever it is, he must ring her actually and let her know he's here for her to help her with ...whatever it is, there's always something going on. So he goes to the list of missed calls to discover which one has needed to speak to Daisy twenty one times. But it isn't Tilly or Tess' name that he sees when he goes to the call log. Instead there is just one name listed again and again. Kyle.
Who the fuck is Kyle? Almost on autopilot he dials the voicemail and listens to the messages that have been left.
"Daisy, I think we need to talk about this. Can you call me back?"
Delete
"Daisy, can you give me a ring please?"
Delete
"Daisy, this is Rachel, Kyle's wife. Can you give me a call please?"
Save.
Who the fuck is Kyle? Why is his wife ringing Daisy? He goes to the phone book and scrawls through the numbers. He presses one and waits for it to connect.

"Hi Dais." Tess is breezy, unconcerned. Simon can hear her crashing around, putting the kettle on.

"Who's Kyle?" he demands.

The clanking stops.

"Simon." She instantly sounds more alert.

"Well who is?" He asks.

"Erm isn't that the guy she works with? I think he was at your thirtieth? Blond guy. Really pretty wife?" Tess says breezily.

Simon's known Tess for ten years. He knows how she lies, the slightly too studied nonchalance, too many details, a fake air of 'everybody knows this'. He'd just never been on the receiving end of it though. And never thought he would be.

"Tess. Daisy is locked in our bedroom, I've got twenty one missed calls from Kyle on her phone and a few messages from his wife. What the hell is going on?" Simon asks.

Tess drops the act. "I don't know Simon. I honestly don't. I know... ugh, look she's not been. I don't know."

"Who is he?"

"She works with him, I don't think there's anything going on? Simon, shouldn't you be talking to her?" says Tess.

"I've tried. She's ignoring me."

"Well she'll have to come out at some point – you never did get around to fitting that en suite."

"Tess please."

"Look. I'm 100% sure there's nothing going on. I don't know why he's ringing her. You know what Daisy's like, she likes a drama. She probably wants choirs of small children singing a lament so she can announce the new date of the school play."

"Tess..." Simon's not happy, he can slag Daisy off but he'd rather her friends didn't join in.

"Sorry, look. It'll be fine." Tess is desperate to get off the phone before she says something she shouldn't.

"Great, thanks." He hangs up.

Daisy is lying on the bed. Staring in to space. If truth be told she hadn't really thought this far ahead. She knows she'll have to come out eventually but she's too embarrassed. She wishes with all her heart that she could turn back time. Every time she thought about it her stomach muscles contracted with embarrassment and she felt the bile rises up in her mouth. She just couldn't get the look of panic and sympathy in Kyle's eyes out of her head.

They had been giggling over the list of children for next year's intake. Amongst the swathe of Chloes, Olivias and Georges there was a smattering of the inevitable Baileys, Madisons and McCauleys. But what had pushed them over the edge were the new methods parents had used to torture their young. Joining them next September would be three Nevaeh's. Daisy had assumed it was an Irish name until Kyle had pointed out that it was Heaven spelt backwards. In Nevaeh Heaven Riley's case this was particularly unfortunate. But it had been Tibernius Alfredo Hutchins that had pushed them over the edge.

"Star Wars or Roman Empire?" Kyle had asked.
"Star Trek you idiot," Daisy had gently corrected.
"I may be an idiot but at least I'm not a geek," he had laughed. She jokingly shoved him and he banged his elbow in to the side of the low wooden and cloth sofa, the type of furniture that was unique to school staff rooms and public libraries.
"Ow," he had winced, and without thinking she put her hand on his elbow where he had bashed it. This had meant they were knee to knee and facing each other. She had reached her other hand towards him and touched his cheek.
"Daisy?" Kyle is confused. Sadly Daisy is unable to pick up on the nuance between confusion and uncontrollable lust.
"Oh Kyle," she breathes and launches herself at him. Their lips connect but just as Daisy puts out a tentative tongue Kyle

ricochets backwards leaving Daisy with her tongue poking out whilst she leans rather threateningly over him.

"Daisy, what the fuck are you doing?" he says, panicked.

"Oh Kyle, don't be silly there's no one around."

"I don't give a shit who's around, what the hell are you doing? Why are you trying to kiss me?"

"I thought, thought, well, isn't this what you wanted?" Daisy is confused, this is not going the way of her day dreams.

"Why would I want this? I'm married, you're married. I don't..." Kyle suddenly recovers himself, he doesn't want this but he realises he doesn't need to destroy Daisy in the process. "I don't like you that way Daisy. I'm sorry. But no."

Daisy isn't stupid. She knows he was about to blurt that he didn't fancy her. Luckily at that moment Helen, the headmistress, walks in and Daisy takes the opportunity to leave. She goes back to her classroom, doesn't bother to pick up any marking or work for the weekend, gets her bag and walks out to the tube.

As she lies on the bed she is consumed by a wave of nausea. It is part embarrassment and part most-of-a-bottle-of-wine-on-an-empty-stomach-at-4-30-in-the-afternoon. There is a hammering on the door. Simon again. He's yelling all sorts about what will happen if she doesn't open the door. Daisy's not too concerned. He hasn't got an aggressive bone in his body. He'll hammer and shout and then he'll go downstairs and make dinner, probably making sure it's something she likes, she thinks. She despises him in that moment, his weakness, his lack of masculinity, how easily she can control him.

Suddenly the door comes off its hinges and Simon is lying on the carpet whilst the door hangs broken and drunkenly behind him. The chair she propped under the handle now has two broken legs and lays on it's side.

"Well that worked better than expected," Simon says.

Chapter 42

"In Sex and the City 2, when Carrie kissed Aiden, Big bought her a piece of jewellery so she'd remember their marriage vows."
"Are you fucking kidding me?" Simon is incredulous.
"That didn't come out right," Daisy apologises.
"No it didn't."
"What I meant was..." Daisy starts to clarify but Simon talks over her and she trails to a halt. They had put time aside to talk about their marriage. Daisy had all but killed the conversation dead with her opening gambit. She tries to claw it back but Simon is well away.
"You try and wreck our marriage and then you try and justify your actions and you're using films as a point of reference and I'm meant to sit here and listen like you're making sense? It's bad enough you made me watch that film let alone use it as an argument"
"What I meant was," Daisy uses her classroom voice, "he accepted that she acted in a certain way because of the way things were in the marriage. I'm not saying you have to buy me jewellery but I'm saying you need to look at why I did it."
"No." Simon replies.
"No?" Daisy asks.

Simon looks deadly serious and stares at Daisy. She can almost see him gathering his thoughts and assembling them in to an argument. She dreads what he is going to say; he's always been erudite and clear when arguing. She can't match him. She normally cries, but she doesn't think it's going to work this time. They've never argued about something that would have a cataclysmic effect on their marriage. No one's going to 'give in' as there is nothing to give in about. This is something that has to be talked about and then decided if what they have is worth continuing with.

Simon starts: "1. Things were fine in our marriage before you decided, let me finish, before you decided to blow apart all we had. Now you're trying to blame it all on me. " Daisy makes a snort of protest. "Fine," Simon concedes. "Share the blame with me so you can justify your behaviour. Although it's worth noting that if things were so bad that you felt the need to cheat and I was aware of this – that I didn't do it. Just you. 2. I sat through that film with you and we both agreed that the ending was fucking ridiculous. I don't need to remind you that you are married. You are married. See that ring on your finger? I put it there. Even before I put it there I was under the illusion that we were a unit. If you forget that you're married then maybe it's because you don't want to remember. 3. If our marriage was so awful, if you were having such an horrific time then why didn't you talk to me?"

"You wouldn't understand." In the face of rational argument Daisy falls apart.

"Cop out."

"Nothing happened." This comes out as a whine. She doesn't want to talk about this. She wants this to go away. If life had a rewind button then Daisy would be stabbing wildly at it.

"Stop saying that, stop reducing this to nothing. You've done this Daisy. You. Tess, Tilly I suppose they know all about it.

"Tess...."

"No." Oddly that hurts. Simon had thought he'd become immune but that's another blow.

"She didn't understand. She told me to talk to you."

"Why didn't she talk to me?" Simon decides to ignore the 'she didn't understand' part of the sentence.

"I asked her not to." Daisy says.

"You really are burning down the farm aren't you? Our marriage, our life, my friends, what have I done that you want to take everything from me?"

"NOTHING HAPPENED." Daisy shouts.

"So what did? Tell me. Tell me this beautiful tale of love gone wrong."

And it all comes tumbling out. To her credit Daisy doesn't stumble and she doesn't hold back. She speaks of the loneliness, of the lack of excitement, of being seen as a wife and not as a person, of being taken for granted, of finding lasting love, their marriage, dull. So dull that when a moderately handsome man was kind to her she misread it. How she took an innocent friendship and built it up in to something that only existed in her mind. Built it up to the detriment of everything else so it threatened her friendships, her job and her marriage. Yet it was all in her mind. She took an idea and ran with it; slowly isolating herself and hurting those she cared for in the process.
"I've been such an idiot," she concludes. "I'm just so humiliated." And then she cries. And she can't stop.
Simon doesn't blink; he doesn't make a move to comfort his crying wife. Instead he gets to his feet and walks to the door.
"Well that makes two of us," he says.
And with that he leaves.

Chapter 43

"How's your faith in marriage?" Tess asks.

"Oh my heart is shattered. I don't know what to think anymore. My whole wedding is a sham, how will I go on?" Tilly replies.

For all Daisy's protestations about wanting to shield Tilly from the breakdown of her marriage she has inevitably fled to Tilly and Stuart's house and forced Tess to get up from a nap to meet them.

Tilly hadn't, as Daisy had expected, gasped and sympathised but instead commented "You must take me for a right mug" and put the kettle on.

"Oh so now you're laughing at me too." This isn't really helping Daisy's feelings of victimhood.

"No one is laughing at you Daisy. But I think the time has come to be a bit more open and honest than we've been lately, perhaps if we'd done this earlier then we, you, wouldn't be in this situation." Tilly says.

"She wouldn't have listened," Tess interjects.

"Tess!" Daisy is outraged, she's never felt worse in her life yet it seems to her that people are queuing up to take shots at her and make her feel worse and worse.

"Sorry, it's the tablets."

Tilly smiles, she knows Tess is joking but as always Daisy takes it at face value and is immediately contrite. Tilly and Tess exchange confused/amused looks and then get back to the matter in hand.

"Where is Simon?" Tilly asks.

Daisy looks at Tess.

"I don't know," Tess replies. "Honestly I don't. And based on what you've told me he's not likely to be telling me anything any time soon, is he?"

"I can't say 'sorry' anymore." Daisy says.

"Well that's not true… and you've not actually apologised to me at…"

Tilly cuts her off. "There's no point constantly going over who said what and when and to whom. Daisy, now I'm up to speed, answer me this: Do you want to be with Simon?"

"Yes, yes of course I do." Daisy is immediate with her answer.

"So Kyle was…?" Tilly questions.

"I don't know what it was. I just… I don't know."

"Can I ask a question?" Tess knows she shouldn't but she is curious.

"Yes." Daisy is equally as cautious.

"What if Kyle had said yes?" she asks.

"What?" Daisy questions.

"What if Kyle had turned to you and said 'Daisy thank God, I feel the same way too'?" Tess is suddenly aware her Mills and Boon romance voice sounds unpleasantly mocking so she changes tact. "What if he had felt the same? What you would have done?"

Daisy thinks.

"I don't know. I know that's all I keep saying but I really didn't think. I was caught up in what it was then. I know I thought it was vital that I told him, I thought he'd feel the same way and then we'd tackle the next step together."

"So you were going to leave Simon." Tess wants to get all the facts before she makes her prognosis.

"I guess so." Daisy is hazy on the details but she's fairly certain that's true.

"So are you going to leave him now?" Tess asks.

"No. I love him." Daisy is certain.

"I know you do and I know this is some, I don't know, bizarre brain storm. But Simon is at home, or somewhere, thinking that you are with him because it's better than being on your own.

You were going to leave him, then your plans didn't work out so you'll stick with him. He feels like shit Daisy and you did that. And I have to say as Simon's friend if you are only sticking with him so you're not on your own then don't do it. He deserves better than that. He's worth more than being your back up. If he still is my friend. By the way thanks for getting me involved in all this. I really appreciate that..." Tess trails off. Her thoughtful question designed to get Daisy to open up and see the error of her ways but in a, you know, caring, sharing kind of way in which Daisy would see Tess as a wise guru has backfired and Tess is now laying in to her. But Tess isn't sure that she cares. Why is it important that she cossets Daisy and be desperately protective of her feelings? Daisy has been a twat. Tess has told her that she is being a twat for months now and has been ignored. Now it's all gone tits up and Tess is expected to provide non-judgemental sympathy. If she's honest as to what she wants, she wants an apology.

Tess is tired.

She would like to drop out for a bit. Although Hannah, Daisy and Simon don't really have anything to do with her, she feels involved in it and as though they are all leaning on her. Her head is all over the place. She logically knows that she is not well but there doesn't seem an opportunity to just stop for a while and get herself better. Everyone seems to be of the opinion that this is sorted by carrying on and Tess doesn't know if she can carry on. She's weepy, she's tired and she has very strange thoughts. The pills are working; she no longer has elaborate thoughts about how she would end it all. Well, not often, and at the moment she has decided that she would kill herself by laying out in the snow and drifting off in to hyperthermia. In her mind if you can only really kill yourself on perhaps two days of the year then you're practically normal. Certainly beats having to force yourself to stand further and further back on the tube platform in case you tip yourself in front of the train. In the end it had been easier to get the bus.

Finally the tears have stopped and Tess finally feels like she is getting her money's worth out of her therapy sessions and also doesn't feel so much that she is wasting Georgia's time. Despite Georgia's constant reassurances that she's not, she still feels like a bit of a fraud. Most of their sessions consist of Tess insisting about how bad she feels that she feels like this when she doesn't actually have any problems and she still feels awful and Georgia convincing her that that in itself is a problem and something she needs to investigate. This push me pull you continues session after session until Tess one day says 'I suppose that's just depression isn't it?"
Georgia could have kissed her. "YES. You're ill Tess. But you can get better."
Tess celebrates by going to the library and reading four chapters of a biography of Charles II. She tells Will the session over-ran. He is delighted she's so upbeat. He puts it down to the therapy. She puts it down to the library.

Chapter 44

Tess stands up, bolstered between Tilly and Daisy. The heat wave that the weather forecasters had been promising all week has finally arrived and has hit with a vengeance. There's no breeze to break the intense heat and Tess is sweltering in her thin black cotton dress. She makes her way to the front of the church and stammers her way through the short speech she has prepared. Half way through tears threaten to overwhelm her but she makes it through and stumbles her way back to her seat where arms reach out and comfort her. Weeks later she is back at work, people are walking on egg shells around her but she is polite and courteous and puts people at their ease. After a few months she realises you only get one life and goes travelling on her own. Half way up a mountain she savours the quietness and watches the sunset, truly happy for the first time in a long time.

Tess is no psychologist but she has a feeling that lying in bed dreaming an elaborate fantasy about your boyfriend dying and the life you'll have afterwards isn't the greatest of signs. She throws the covers off her and goes through to her very much alive boyfriend who's cooking breakfast in his kitchen.

She mentions it to Georgia when she sees her. Georgia doesn't press a secret alarm button or alert the terror services; instead she nods and labels it a coping mechanism.
'It puts you back in control,' she opines
"Oh grief I don't think I should be left in control," Tess laughs.
Georgia doesn't. "It was a joke," Tess clarifies.
"We often make jokes when we're uncomfortable," Georgia says.

"And when we're not," Tess complains to Will later. "I don't think cracking a joke is a sign of a mental disorder. It's not like I'm telling knock knock jokes whilst picking people off with a gun from a bell tower. I feel like I need to see another counsellor to deal with this one."

"You're going back."

"Yeah I know. Next week. Have to do Tuesday rather than Monday as Georgia's got an appointment at her daughter's school on Monday. She's got two daughters – both teenagers. The younger one is kind of having a tough time."

"Perhaps you'll go next week and talk about yourself rather than Georgia's daughters." Will suggests.

"I was being polite!" Tess protests.

"You're paying her – you don't need to be polite. That's not why you're going there."

"Hmmmm, so how was your day?" says Tess, changing the subject.

Chapter 45

Tess is sat at her desk. Her to-do list needs adjusting. Anything over two pages is bordering on ridiculous. Especially when one item seems to read 'Australia Doc Bumming'. As far as Tess knows she's not working on a documentary about Australian anal sex, although it won't be beyond the realms of possibility that Arrabella has taken on a project and just mentioned it in passing to Tess who now has to perform a million functions. She is sitting at her desk sorting through Arrabella's expenses whilst reading the latest news on-line. She has RRS feeds set up for their clients and is seeing if anyone did anything horrific over the weekend. She's also making another list of potential clients for them after the latest rounds of reality shows were screened on Saturday night. She notices that she's been jotting names down on a taxi receipt. She's about to do a search for tippex in the office when she notices that Arrabella got a taxi to Selfridges. She carries on making her list over the handwritten receipt.

As the office slowly fills up Tess breaks off from her task to say hello to people and catch up on their weekends. Her time on her own has come to an end and she needs to be sociable again. Home has always been her sanctuary. Her place to get away from the world. Now the world seems to be located squarely behind her front door so she has taken to getting in to work earlier and earlier to get some time on her own. She sometimes walks to work. Enjoying no one knowing where she is and what she is doing. She walked home from work the other day and lost track along the way. Hannah had tried to call her about starting dinner and Tess hadn't answered. So she had called Will who had informed her that Tess had left work nearly two hours ago. When she'd got in around 8pm completely oblivious to the state of panic she had created, Will had been frantic.. "I lost track of time" seemed a bit of a weak excuse to account for taking three hours for a thirty minute walk. Therefore slightly tighter tabs were being kept on her walks so the office had become more of a sanctuary. Not something she had ever thought would happen.

She has to leave on time tonight though as she is going out with Simon. Yes, Simon. Just the two of them. He had rung and suggested that they get together, like they did in the old days. So Tess assumes they are going to sit in her bedroom drinking tea and listening to Belle and Sebastian records. Still it would be nice to go out with just one of Simon and Daisy. Whenever she had been at their house lately, when both of them were there it had been awful. Daisy and Simon circled each other like tigers about to pounce and weirdly they both seemed to be flirting with Tess. Both competing for her attention and friendship.

She shoved her jeans on and threw her phone in her bag. Tomorrow launched the weekend of the hen and stag do's so tonight wasn't going to be a big one. She had called Will and left a message saying she'd probably be home about 10ish if he wanted a hand putting the finishing touches to Stuart's costume... Will still wouldn't tell her what it was. She put her head round the living room door. Hannah had come in from seeing the boys about an hour ago and was quite low. She refused to talk about it but Tess had tried to be helpful. It wasn't really appreciated so Tess had left her to it.
"I'm just going for something to eat with Simon. You sure you don't want to come? It won't be a late one if you're leaving early in the morning for the boys. Probably be home by 9-30/10?" Tess says.
She is rewarded by a grunt from Hannah.
"OK. Offer's there if you want to join us later. I've texted Will and told him I might be about later so if he calls tell him I'll call

him when I get in."

"You treat him like shit." Hannah replies.

"Thank you." Says Tess.

"I'm serious."

"I know. The lack of self-awareness is staggering. How is your husband?" Tess asks. It is amazing how quickly things with Hannah can deteriorate. Twenty minutes ago Tess had felt sorry for her. Now she thought she deserved everything she got. It was also worrying how quickly Tess could retreat back to being fifteen.

"You don't know anything about it." Hannah argues.

"I know enough. It's living on my sofa." Tess snipes back.

It was coming to something when getting involved in your friends' marital disputes was a welcome break from your own home life. She needed to talk to Hannah. This had to come to an end. Hannah had been here too long. It wasn't good for Hannah, it wasn't good for Tess and most importantly it wasn't good for the boys. They had moments where Tess thought they were making headway but then it would return to the default position of arguing. According to Tess' mother this is exactly the same way all Hannah's relationships were at the moment. Hannah would simply hang up or walk out on her parents if the conversation took a turn she didn't like and things with Garry were on incredibly shaky ground. Anytime it looked like things may have taken a turn for the better, Garry would say one of the mystery trigger words and Hannah would still refuse to come home. The only people Hannah was consistently normal with were Finn and Jake. Things had to change and soon.

Things also had to change in the flat. Tess was finding it harder and harder. The atmosphere was almost unbearable. Sadly only Tess seemed to be affected by it. Hannah almost seemed to thrive on the constant air of tension and unpleasantness. Tess meanwhile hated going home. She knew she could stay at Will's but she really just wanted to be in her own house. She also felt she should be slightly better company before she took up residence in someone else's home. She'd tried to explain this theory to Hannah but it was like trying to explain black holes. She also had the suspicion that the minute she left for any length of time Hannah would claim squatters' rights. She headed to Daisy's with a mixture of relief at being out of the house and fear of the night ahead.

She was amazed that Daisy had agreed to just Tess and Simon going out. Perhaps things were improving

Or perhaps Daisy knew nothing about it.

It became clear when Daisy answered the door that she has not been expecting to see Tess. It then also became clear that she was on her way out and so Simon's stand about reclaiming his friends lost a bit of its power. They weren't going to go out and have fun without Daisy., They were going out and about on a night Daisy had plans so Simon didn't have to make too much of a stand. Daisy does look slightly put out that Simon and Tess are going to go out but she seems more annoyed that they are going out for dinner which apparently she and Simon never do. She does give Tess a funny look but Tess finds a very interesting spot on the wall and stares at that.

"I thought you said you were out with a mate Si?" Daisy asks

"I am, here she is," Simon responds.

Tess stays mute but feels a bit like the kid from Kramer vs. Kramer. She attempts to lighten the atmosphere. "Simon gets me Wednesday and Thursday nights and alternate weekends," she smiles. They all watch as the joke curls up and dies in embarrassment.

"Right, well. I'll be back at 9," declares Daisy "See you then."

Simon doesn't answer, he's trying to work himself up to tell her he doesn't give a shit what she does but he can't bring himself to do it. Mainly because he does care desperately what she does but also because he's sick of the rows. They are going round and round in circles and only communicate in shouting or notes, usually left after one has sneaked out to work early. Simon sleeps in the spare room (following another row about why he should be the one to move when he hasn't done anything wrong). He just wants his old life back. He'd even take the irrationally angry Daisy of the last six months.

The silence is awful. Tess looks back on the terribly inappropriate child custody joke as a golden time of this conversation.

"Right, well OK," Tess says. "I won't imagine we'll be late so I'll see you then." She leans forward and spontaneously hugs Daisy which startles them both.

"We might be late," says Simon petulantly.

"Well don't wake me up when you come in," Daisy retaliates.

"Shall we go?" says Tess.

No one moves. Daisy and Simon are too busy staring at one another.

"Bye Dais," Tess says and walks out of the door. Simon doesn't emerge for a couple of minutes afterwards but finally they are on their way.

They used up all their conversation on the way to the restaurant and once seated they busy themselves studying the menu. Five minutes later and Tess has read it six times already. She could recite it.

"Why didn't we meet in a pub?" she thinks. "There's a quiz machine in the pub. Would it be weird to fire general knowledge questions at Simon in lieu of conversation?"

Just as she is about to ask Simon what the capital of Peru is, the waiter comes over.

"Have you decided?" he asks.

"Yes!" Tess is delighted to be able to use her words. "Simon, do you know what you're having?"

"Yes, after you." He insists.

Neither of them order starters but they do order a bottle of wine. This takes a very long time as the waiter suggests numerous wines to complement their meals and they let him go through the whole rigmarole before they order a bottle of house red.

"So how's work?" Simon asks.

"Yeah it's good. Arrabella's still mental but what can you do? Bit odd working with Will but we're just getting on with it really. It's just weird to be with someone all day and then go home with them. It's a bit...." Tess trails off. She's gabbling. "How are you?"

"Yeah good." He says.

Oh bloody hell this is hard work.

"How are your Mum and Dad?" she asks.

How are your Mum and Dad? Seriously? The last time she saw Simon's mum and dad was at Daisy and Simon's wedding, which was also the last time she thought about them. Simon just stares at her and then starts to laugh.

"Do you really care?" he asks.

"Not really." She replies.

"This is weird isn't it?"

"I know. Why can't I talk to you? We used to sit in the union for hours. What the fuck did we talk about?"

"Well we tended to be drunk. In fact hold that thought..." Simon waves at the waiter and orders two Sambucas.

"Will's going to kill me. I'm not meant to drink on these tablets."

"Well Daisy already hates me, let's go for the double."

Down in one.

They eat their meals in record time. They both want to go to the pub, re-find the them of ten years ago. The evening has shifted from a civilised meal to a desperate desire to recapture their youth and their friendship. This is no longer a meal out. This is now simply a fuel stop to line their stomachs before getting down to the serious business of drinking. The conversation is free flowing now; they talk of work, people they went to university with, including one especially odd person who they have both found out has an open profile on Facebook and now neither can start their day without checking in on what he's doing. They speak of news stories; they leap from topic to topic but don't talk of Daisy or of Tess' situation. They don't purposefully avoid it; they are just bogged down by living their own lives and tonight they want to get away from it.

Copious shots and two bottles of wine later and they bid farewell to their friend Dave the waiter. Tess has her photo taken with him and then they stagger out in to the night. They settle on going to the Queen Charlotte and find a seat in the corner. Tess gets a round in and gets pints and doubles to save them the walk back and forth to the bar. She weaves her way back to the table and dumps the drinks on the table. Wiping up the slight spillage with her sleeves.
"Mighty Mouse? Was that one?" Tess has spent a long time thinking about this whilst waiting to be served.
"It was indeed, congratulations to you Miss Acraman." Simon congratulates her.
"Why thank you Sir. Now your turn. N"
Simon pauses then slurs "Nother one?"
They both piss themselves laughing The barman, who hates them both with a passion he wouldn't have thought possible at the beginning of his shift, eyes them for behind the bar. They grin back, their teeth stained black by red wine.
"That's not a proper one." Tess complains. " Come on Nimon." She points to herself and laughs. "Nimon! There's one. No seriously. Simon. Simon." She rolls his name around her mouth.
"Cartoon character superhero beginning with N." Tess is a stickler for the rules, even when she's unable to articulate them.
"Mmmm I don't know. Seems a bit harsh you being so demanding when I let you get away with Cedric Sneer."

"He had a very big nose," Tess qualifies.

"He did," Simon agrees. "Like that fucker Kyle."

"Did he have a big nose? I thought it was fairly proportionate."

"In my mind he does. And a very small dick."

"Well of course he does. Minute." Tess hasn't actually given a huge amount of thought to Kyle's genitals but she's happy to agree with Simon.

"So how are you? Still got the errr thing?" Simon asks.

"Yes," Tess replies. "Not really the kind of thing which goes away over night."

"Sorry I've been a bit shit about it all. I kind of left Daisy to deal with it on my behalf. Sorry."

"Don't worry about it. I don't know what to say to me. Don't beat yourself up about it. Do you think Daisy would mind if I stayed at yours tonight?" Tess asks.

"I wouldn't have thought so, that said I've got no idea what goes through her head most of the time. You don't want to go home?" he questions.

"It's so far." Tess lets herself go limp and pathetically falls on to the table. "And I won't have a bed. And hey, it might help you and Daisy, you could have a row and I could stand between you and cry 'Mummy, Daddy please don't fight'. And you'd see me standing there and think 'what are we doing? We must think of the children', Then you'd make up and I'd simper delightfully in the background."

"That's a lovely plan," agrees Simon. "But where would we get you a Victorian nightdress at this time of night. It's also worth mentioning that you wouldn't get a bed at ours either. I'm in the spare room."

"Oh Simon." Tess is instantly contrite. She paws at his hand which is meant to give comfort but actually only succeeds in transferring a film of beer and peanut crumbs from her hand to his.

"I miss her you know," Simon says.

"I know you do."

"Why didn't you say anything to me?" Simon asks.

"I didn't know what to say. I still don't. It was all so strange. I don't think I took it as seriously as I should have. I don't know."

"This is weird." Simon is sad.

"I know," Tess agrees. "I don't know what Daisy..."

She is cut off. "This isn't about Daisy!" Simon explodes. Loudly. People at the quiz machine turn and look at them. Tess waves. "They probably think I'm his mistress," she thinks. "Brilliant. Still I could do a lot worse than Simon." She goes to shhh Simon but he's a on a bit of a roll and she can see he's working his way up to something. She knows him well enough to know that this explosion is a preamble to something and he's just trying to put his thoughts in order. Her patience is rewarded when he speaks. Thankfully at a lower volume.

"No. It is about Daisy but it's not all about her," he begins. "It's just I don't know. You were my friend first. And she took you and that was OK because I was with her and we could share but now she's gone and she's taken everything I was before her. I don't know who I am without her. I should be able to cope without her because I'm still me. But we've been us for so long I can't remember who me is. And my friends should be able to remind me but she's taken them with her. And she shouldn't get them because she's the one who did this. I haven't done anything wrong. I should get everything and I miss her. But I don't want to. But I do. And I miss who I am with her. I got married because I wanted to be married, to her. And I still want to. But if she doesn't then I don't really get a choice in it. I'm being forced out of a marriage I want to be in. But I love her and I miss her and it's all...just a bit shit." Simon grinds to a halt. He grins but his eyes are a bit too damp. None of that came out right. He sounds ridiculous. Tess is half smiling and he can't decide whether it's an understanding smile or simply relief that he's stopped talking. It's probably just that she's very pissed.

"I'm not a ball," Tess says. "You don't have to take it in turns to play with me and I'm not either one of yours to share. I don't live in a box when I'm not with you."

"That's not what I meant." He protests.

"I know it's not and that's not what I'm trying to say. Daisy's not gone. She's not," she reiterates when Simon shakes his head. "She's just, actually I have no idea what she is up to. I'm not sure she knows. She doesn't want out of the marriage, she's just lost her mind or something. It's not going to be easy, but it's fixable. I don't know what she's been thinking, it's completely beyond me but whatever it is you haven't lost her. And you certainly haven't lost me. But you need to decide whether you still want us?"

"How do you mean?" Simon drains the end of his gin and tonic and moves on to his pint.

Tess tries to explain, "Well me, it's not such a big deal. I'd imagine you've been trying to shake me for years." She pauses for a laugh but nothing happens so she carries on and tries to clarify what she means. "Our friendship has changed over the years. I was your mate, then I was the person who introduced you to your wife, then you were my mate's husband. Things change. Now we're at a crossroads. You're still my mate's husband and I know I've favoured Daisy over you but that can change. You're still my mate. You know that don't you?"

"I don't know. I don't know anything anymore." Simon is morose.

"Oh come on."

"No, I know, I know, I'm pissed, this will pass. I'll wake up in the morning and it will all be fine. But it's not fine. It's not. I want it to be. I want it to be OK. So much. But it's not and I don't know if it will be again." The words pour out of Simon and then to Tess' deep distress Simon starts to cry.

"Oh come on now." Never great in a crisis Tess becomes incredibly stiff upper lip and begins to channel an adult in an Enid Blyton novel. She tries to think of something to calm him. "Come on Simon, I'm meant to be the mental one."

It doesn't have the desired effect. "And I've been so shit over that," Simon wails.
Tess decides to nip this in the bud. "Come on Simon."

Simon attempts to calm down and starts to wipe his eyes on his shirt cuffs. Tess goes to the bar and grabs a wodge of napkins. When she comes back Simon is attempting to sort himself but has unfortunately reached the hiccuppy, self-perpetuating stage of crying and is unable to stop.
"Simon, you need to calm down. You're going to do yourself a mischief. Besides I want to show my face in here again. I've never had an emotional moment in the Queen Charlotte and I don't intend to start now."

This isn't the stern warning Tess thinks it is. Simon carries on trying to control himself and failing miserably. She supposes the warning loses something when Simon knows full well that although she may not have had an emotional moment in the Queen Charlotte she's done plenty of other things, many a lot worse. As the graffiti in the toilet would attest.

A couple of minutes and some ineffectual comforting later and Simon is calmer but words continue to pour out of him. "I had my life sorted at twenty two. I must have peaked too soon because now I'm thirty and it's all fallen apart."
"It's not all fallen apart," Tess protests.
"Really? If Daisy goes then I've lost everything."
"She doesn't want to go."
"But I don't know if I want her to stay." Simon replies.
"You want to break up?" Tess is concerned.
"I have absolutely no idea," and with that he starts to cry again.
Seeing her friend so low and so hurt sets Tess off. She feels herself well up and she helps herself to some of Simon's napkins.
"Why are you crying?" he slurs.

Tess attempts to explain, "You're so sad and this is all so silly and Daisy and I know and ... I'm such a bad friend. I'm sorry."
"Oh Tess don't be silly," Simon comforts. "You're a good friend and you had no real idea what she was thinking and," he stops as a realisation hits him, "and this really isn't about you."
"Oh God you're right, I'm hi-jacking. I'm evil," Tess wails.
To this day Simon can't really explain what he did next. But he picks up his drink which is half finished and throws it in Tess' face.

Tess sits there with beer dripping down her face and her mouth hanging open in shock. Simon's eyes are wide in horror at what he has just done but then he starts to laugh. And can't stop. Can't stop until Tess throws her drink in his face. "Bet you wish you hadn't persuaded me to get a pint now," she says.

Simon responds by chucking a handful of peanuts at her.
The barman responds by chucking them both out.
The walk home dries them both off but goes little way to sobering them up. Tess is desperate for the toilet and refuses to give in to Simon's frequent demands that she just goes behind a bush. He offers to keep a look out but she still refuses to acquiesce. Simon and Daisy's house is closest so they stumble back there and then Simon discovers that he has forgotten his keys. Daisy is less than impressed to have to let them in. She eyes them with disgust as she takes in their slightly damp clothes decorated with various stains.

"Hi Daisy, sorry about this," Tess gabbles. "I do want to catch up but I'm going to wet myself. Excuse me."

She darts past Daisy and up to the bathroom where she relieves herself and has a quick tactical vomit for good measure. She swills around some mouthwash then heads downstairs where she finds that a mini cab has already been called for her.

"Did you have a nice evening Daisy?" Tess asks.
Daisy doesn't reply.

"You know." Tess is aware that they probably do know but
makes the drunken decision to keep talking anyway. "You know.
You two are so silly. So silly. You're both unhappy, you both
make each other happy. Why not be happy together?" She
pauses. "Like the song."
"With respect Tess you don't know anything about it." Daisy
says.
"With respect Daisy I know a lot about it because it's all you
banged on about for months. If you want to cut me out the loop
now that's fine, it's your life but don't fuck this up." Both Daisy
and Simon stare at her. "I think I'll wait for my cab outside."
"I'll walk you to the door," Daisy says.
Simon doesn't say anything; he's fallen asleep on the sofa.
"Sorry Daisy," Tess tries to apologise, aware they are hosting a
hen night together later today.
"Did you talk about me over your cosy dinner?" Daisy asks.
"Yeah, he's really unhappy Daisy. Talk to him."
The light toot toot of the mini cab's horn gives Tess a decent
escape route.

Chapter 46

The room swims in to view. Tess squints at the light. She sees a coffee cup coming towards her face so she co-ordinates herself to sit up and puts her hands out.

"Thanks," she says taking it.

"Thank you," says Will.

"Oh god," thinks Tess, "why's he saying 'thank you' what did I do last night? Actually, why is he here? Why isn't he at his own house?" This slightly worrying thought is replaced when she sees Hannah walking out of the room. Why is Hannah bringing them coffee? This was both good and bad. Tess was relieved that her immediate living situation had eased with Hannah's attempt at an apology (being Hannah meant never having to say you're sorry) but this did come with certain caveats.

First rule of mental house: don't mention the elephant in the room. Quite literally in this case, Hannah was massive.

There was now a certain air of inevitability about the situation. She was too far gone. This was going to happen. Which led to the second rule of mental house.

Get Hannah out of mental house before they gain another resident.

She puts aside how Will ended up in her bed, given the thumping in her head and the slightly hazy grasp on last night there is every chance she rung him and invited him round. She decides to tackle the Hannah problem first.

"Morning." She says to Will.

"Morning. How you feeling?"

"Pretty rank. So what did you get up to last night?"

"Went out with Chris and some of the others. Thanks for letting me crash here, I really do need to move out of town." Will says.

So she did have a hand in this, she makes a mental note to check her phone. She grasps the bull by the horns.

"So what do you reckon to inviting Garry round one evening and letting him and Hannah talk it out?"

"Don't they see each other every weekend anyway and most days? And talk on the phone." Will doesn't immediately grasp the plan.

"Well yeah. But the kids are always there at weekends and if Garry mentions anything vaguely controversial on the phone then Hannah hangs up. Garry told Mum and Mum told me," she clarifies. "If he was here and we weren't then they'd have to talk about it."

"Don't you think you should be asking Hannah rather than me?" Will can be quite spectacularly irritating sometimes.

Tess explains it in basic terms. "Well. She'd say no. So I thought I'd talk to Garry. Tell him to come over. Before he gets here we cook a nice meal, then we say 'Oh dear there's no wine, we'll go and get some', then after we leave there's a knock at the door and she opens it. It's Garry with flowers."

"And then there's a terrible mix up and it ends with the vicar dropping his trousers and accidentally head-butting the Queen Mother?" Will suggests.

"What?" Tess doesn't understand what he's getting at.

"Sorry I thought this amazing plan of yours was taking place in a 1970s sitcom." Will can't really be bothered with this.

Tess however won't be put off. "If we can pull this off, then Hannah will go home. Evenings can be spent doing normal things, candle lit dinners will be for two not three. We could use the word 'pregnant', 'boys', 'expecting' and 'garage' again. We could eat soft cheese and pate again and not pretend we're boycotting them because of our political opinions about the French.

Will's still not getting it. Tess goes for a last ditch attempt.

"You wouldn't need to put trousers on before you make coffee in the morning."

"Fine."

Of all the days to get absolutely destroyed, the day before a hen night is not the best option. Tess has around 9 hours to turn it around and get back on it. She's struggling. Will is finding it hilarious. So Tess plays the bridesmaid card which helps him grasp the seriousness. He suggests a walk. Coffee, a walk, a power nap then straight out to do it again.
"You'll have to keep Simon going tonight." Tess says.
"He'll be fine. He'll bounce right back." Will is certain.
"As will I."
"That's it... positive mental attitude. Let's do this. Fresh air, caffeine and sleep. This is it Acraman you ready?" Will tries to psych her up.
"Yeah!"
"Louder!" Will shouts.
"Yeah!"
"I can't hear you!"
"I've got a headache." Tess complains
"OK let's get going, first stop Neros."
"Can I have crisps?"

It feels weird to Tess that she is in the park without Matt and is instead with Will. The park was always very much her and Matt's place. Which she is aware makes it sound like her and Matt were furious doggers or lived life on the edge by having sex on the climbing frame, possibly in full view of children. Whereas in reality all they ever really did was smoke on the bandstand or feed the ducks. Now she's here with Will she doesn't want the memories of times with Matt to overshadow now. She very much wants, in the words of Louis Walsh, to 'make it their own'.

Coffee and crisps have helped enormously. They have found a bench and they are sprawled on it. The changing seasons reflected in the trees around them. They chat easily and discuss all sorts of random topics. Tess tries to push back the nagging thought that she'd be having a slightly nicer time if she was on her own. Or had a book.

"Do you think the therapy is working?" he asks out of the blue.

"I think so. I think the main thing is just accepting that at our age we need to decide what are weird ideas we've picked up along the way and what is our basic personality." She says

"I suppose so. I've accepted that I am never going to understand rap music."

"So you've grasped the concept completely."

"Mmmm. I think you're fine the way you are. I just want you to be happy." Will says.

"Don't we all. I want you to be happy too. It's been a bit of a whirlwind since we got together. Hannah, Daisy and Simon, the mentalness." Will winces, Tess carries on regardless. "I haven't been a great girlfriend, sorry."

"Hey don't worry about it. If you're happy, I'm happy."

"Please stop saying that," thinks Tess.

Chapter 47

"It's the final countdown!" Daisy sings. Tess and Tilly knock back a shot and join in obligingly with the 'ba ba ba ba ba's.

Tilly had decided against a hen weekend in favour of a good old fashioned hen night (if truth be told she didn't want to spend a whole weekend away from Stuart). Nearer the wedding she, Tilly and Tess were going to go to a spa to be detoxed but right now they were toxing –up with a vengeance. For someone who prided herself on being cool, calm and sophisticated Tilly had embraced penis memorabilia and tack with untold glee. Tess and Daisy had planned the whole night. They had started fairly civilly with a private dining room in Tilly's favourite restaurant, they'd then gone to a wine bar and now they were, rather inevitably, in an awful nightclub in Leicester Square where the clientele was mainly other hen dos and you could get Sambuca shots for a pound a go.

Tilly's beautiful dress had a drink spill down the middle but it was partially obscured by a learner plate she had sellotaped to her front and a shot glass swinging on a beaded necklace. She sipped her espresso martini through a penis straw (complete with veins). She was messily beautiful.

"I wish it was just us three you know," Tilly bellowed under the illusion that she was whispering. "I mean don't get me wrong, it's lovely they all came but you guys – you're like my family."

"Awww," Tess and Daisy squealed whilst Pam from Tilly's work looked slightly put out and headed back to the main group. The three girls had snuck away from the rest and were doing some shots on their own.

"I'd better go and...." Tilly nodded towards the others.

"Be over in a sec," Tess shouted. Daisy was looking a bit peaky and Tess was feeling quite in love with the world tonight and thought she'd try and help. She stuck a hand out to stroke

Daisy's hair. Her appalling motor skills meant that it was more of an aggressive pat than the tender pat she had intended.

"You OK?" Tess asks her.

Daisy just looked at her with sad eyes. Tess reached for some words of comfort.

"Hey lady, turn that frown upside down. Let a smile be your umbrella."

"Oh stop. Please. I'm fine. It's just – look at her." Daisy gestures to Tilly who is doing a fairly literal dance routine to 'Reach' by Sclub7. "That used to be me. Now I've fucked it all up."

"You don't know that. I mean Simon is still here." Tess reasons.

"But for how long? Has he said anything to you?" Daisy asks.

"No." Tess replies.

Daisy looks at her.

"Honestly he hasn't. Oh you know I wouldn't say anything even if he had but he honestly hasn't. I think he thinks I'd tell you." To Tess' drunken brain this logic makes perfect sense. Daisy looks hurt .

"He hates me," Daisy says. It's what she has thought since this whole thing blew up but she's been too afraid to say it. The alcohol has made her bold.

"He doesn't hate you." Tess knows this is true. "He's embarrassed and hurt and sad and I think he's trying to punish you but he doesn't hate you. He loves you. That's the problem. There wouldn't be all this weird tension and problems if he hated you. He'd just wave goodbye. Write it off as a bad job, he wouldn't be sticking around."

"Why won't he talk to me?" Daisy asks.

Tess leans over the bar and orders another two shots.

"Right. I'm going to tell you something. Just hear me out, knock this back and then we'll go and dance with Tilly."

"I'm not going to like this am I?" Daisy has been party to Tess' 'advice' before.

"I doubt it." Tess is quite cheerful about this. "Right. Simon doesn't owe you anything. Yes he should talk to you, it would make this easier. But you should have spoken to him when this whole stupid Kyle thing came up. Oh I know it was all in your head." Daisy winces but lets Tess continue. "But it came about because you were looking for something else. Why didn't you talk to Simon rather than dream up all this stuff? Why not say to Simon you were unhappy rather than prepare to leave him? And he's probably pissed off because now there's no one to leave him for you decide to stay. He feels like second best. Like it's him or being on your own and that is your fault Daisy. You're making him feel like he's a fall back. Either way, you treated him like crap for months and let him feel like it was his fault. You can't expect him to suddenly be OK with everything and deeply committed to your marriage. You've got to let him be pissed off. Don't make him feel bad for not instantly leaping in to trust games and endless talking about his feelings. He's got to get through the strop first."

Tess downs her drink and waits for Daisy to do the same. "I'm trying to make my marriage work." Daisy says piously. There are many things Tess could say in reply to this. She thinks it's a slightly hypocritical statement if conveniently timed. It's not an argument she wants to have, least of all have it here and now. She chooses not to say anything.

"Must be nice to have it all figured out," Daisy continues bitterly. "I can only figure out other people's lives. Haven't got a clue when it comes to my own. Come on." Tess picks up Daisy's shot and drains that too.
They both head to the dance floor and help Tilly to interpret 'Wake me Up before you go go.' Tess is particularly fond of her 'yo-yo' move.

"I think I may have over subscribed to the theory of 'dance like no one is watching'." Tess says,

"And drink like you've never thrown up." Will replies.

Will is lying next to Tess on the bathroom floor. Tess is using the floor tiles to cool off her burning thighs. Will is dry retching in to the toilet – he had been on Stuart's stag do.

"I'm going to go Tesco's, I may be some time. What do you think will cure you?" She asks. Tess threw up last night, therefore this morning all her injuries are from exertions on the dance floor. She's not sure why people go jogging or roller blading or even yoga, just dance for 6 hours in 5-inch heels. Will however has not been so lucky.

"I don't know....I'd normally say fry up but oh God..." The mere thought of this sends Will back in to hopeless retching.

Tess rubs his back as he flobs hopelessly in to the toilet. When he lifts his head up she hands him a pint of water.

"You going to be OK if I go?" she asks.

"Yes", he smiles. "Besides we've got no food and I need....something."

"OK. Do you trust me to get something or shall I give you some options?"

"Options." Will flops back to join Tess on the tiles.

"OK.... McDonalds." She offers.

Controlled retch.

"Toast?" she tries.

Controlled retch

"Salt and Vinegar crisps and coke?"

Nothing.

"Say it again." Will orders.

"Salt and vinegar crisps and coke." Tess repeats.

"Yes that's it." Will could sob with happiness that soon this torment will be over. "Thank you." He smiles at Tess, the angel who is walking towards the door. An angel who is walking like John Wayne.

"No problem. Be back soon....and I'll bring you a nice egg custard tart."

She is treated to the sound of more retching as she heads out the door.

She laughs.

"You witch" Will's voice floats behind her as she giggles her way down the stairs.

She pushes the trolley round the supermarket slowly. She's got a coffee from the in store coffee shop and is using the trolley like a zimmer to ease the pain in her legs. As always she performs a brief mental health check. She seems to be doing ok. The insane crying has eased, the wanting to be dead comes and goes; she's favouring a light coma at the moment which is an improvement. The overwhelming feeling at the moment seems to be anger. She feels trapped, not physically, but she feels the weight of expectation upon her and she's not sure she likes it. Hemmed in. But if she was to say this to anyone they would rightfully point out that she can do what she wants. Which is true. She'd just need to justify and account for it. Still, she reasons, chucking radox bath salts in the trolley, short week this week as she has taken Thursday and Friday off for the build-up to the wedding before the big day on Saturday.

Chapter 48

"I thought you were out tonight." Hannah's bump enters the room before the rest of her. Tess is prone on the sofa. Which is now her bed. The more pregnant Hannah gets the more she needs an actual bed. So the sisters have performed a swap. It has been a hard day at work. Arrabella has gone in to overdrive. The less she understands, the more she takes it out on Tess and today has been a whirlwind of paranoia and coffee runs. She was also told that she was 'stupid' and 'couldn't be trusted'. The fact she'd emailed Nina and told her all of this made her think that Arrabella had a point and she hated it when Arrabella had a point. Nina hadn't replied. Too busy and important in New York, Tess reasoned, it was only now she remembered there was a time difference.

"No." Tess barely moves. Her eyes are shut and she's still in her work clothes. The only sign of the old Tess is that she has taken her shoes off and placed them neatly by the sofa.
"Is Will coming round?" Hannah can't take a hint and shut up.
"No."
"Are you going to Will's?" she presses.
"No."
"Do you mind if I put the TV on?" Hannah asks.
"Yes."
Too late. Unused to being denied Hannah had turned the television on before Tess had answered.
"Turn it off Hannah." Tess requests.
"Hmmm. I'm just watching this it, I'll turn it off in a sec."
"Turn it off Hannah." She repeats.
"Well are you going to talk to me? No offence but you're not the greatest company. I've been here on my own all day you know." Hannah huffs.
"Turn it off!" Tess roars.

Hannah turns, ready for the fight but is astonished to find Tess in tears.

"Tess, what's wrong?" Hannah is concerned.

Hannah doesn't know what to do. Tess is inconsolable, seemingly over Hannah watching TV.

"I want to help but I can't if you don't tell me what's wrong." She talks to Tess as she talks to the boys. Luckily Tess responds like a five year old.

"I've told you what's wrong. I want to be left alone. I want my flat back. I want my problems to be taken seriously. I want to matter. I want to sleep."

"You matter, what are you talking about? Is it the adoring boyfriend? The job everyone thinks is amazing? The friends who rally around you?" Hannah sneers.

"What is it Hannah? Is it the not working? The adoring husband? The two beautiful boys? The third healthy pregnancy?" Tess counters.

"You don't understand." Hannah says, turning back towards the TV.

"I understand perfectly." Tess says "Not only are we now talking about you again but once again my life is derided. I know why you're here: your life sounds shit. If I had your life I'd be swinging from the banisters. Yet everyone seems to want it. I'm weird for not wanting it. But you don't want it either yet your one aim in life seems to be to want to make everyone's life as bad as yours so you can convince yourself you're right. And yet you're here. You can't have it both ways. You're pregnant Hannah and everybody knows it. You haven't made one attempt to try and sort this out with Garry. This isn't you making a decision, this is you sulking. This is you attention seeking. You're not getting enough attention so you're throwing a tantrum."

"You're the one sitting there in tears! I can't believe you're throwing this at me. I was trying to be helpful. All I did was put the TV on." Hannah can't understand where this attack has come from.

"Go home Hannah. Get on with it. The applause has stopped. We're going to stop celebrating your every move. It's not about you anymore. Go home."

"You're a bitch." Hannah shouts "All this 'I've got mental health problems' boo hoo. You're just angry because you're alone and bitter. You tell me I need to get on with it? Look at your own life."

"Go home Hannah. Or go to Mum and Dad's. Go to a friend's if you've got any. Just go. You can't stay here." Tess isn't shouting. She is calm.

"You've always been jealous of me," Hannah states.

This is so staggeringly, shockingly untrue that Tess doesn't even reply. She just flops back on to the cushions exhausted. They've had this argument before. She won't win it. Hannah takes this as a sign that Tess wants to hear more so she continues. "You've seen me do everything that you should have done. I've got all the attention from Mum and Dad, they dote on the kids, Dad walked me down the aisle and you don't like that you're not the golden child anymore. I may have been a vile teenager but now I'm doing it all right and you're the failure and you don't like it. Oh they'll never say it but I bet if I had a problem and you had a problem then I'd come first because let's face it, I've got more at stake than you. If something happens to me the lives of quite a few people are at stake. Something happens to you – well."

Tess props herself up and looks Hannah in the eye. "You've been here for fucking months and the world's carried on. You're not that indispensable. She says.

"You're jealous." Hannah is convinced she's right.

"That's your go to argument – I'm jealous of the pregnant woman who's run away from her marriage."

"Least I had that; you're going to die alone." Hannah is sure she's right.

"You're going to die in about five minutes unless you shut up."

"Truth hurts."

"What hurts is that I put myself out for you. You know I can cope with other people thinking my life means less. Constantly accepting that I get second choice on holidays at work, accommodating other people's flexible working, looking on and beaming when parents rush off at 2 to go to a nativity play whilst I answer their phones. But to have it in my own home from someone who has really outstayed their welcome is another. I don't want your life." Tess desperately tries to make her point.

"You can't have my life!" Hannah shouts. "No one wants you! This isn't a choice. You've never found anyone who wants to marry you! If you had then you would have done it. No one chooses to be on their own, you just can't find anyone who wants to."

"What's Will?" Tess interrupts.

"He'll come to his senses."

"Garry never did. Then again he's so mind numbingly boring that he's probably inputting the activities of the last few months in to a spreadsheet."

"Don't slag of Garry." Hannah objects.

"Why not? I assume you married him because he asked, because it's what people do. Don't tell me it was a love match."

"Of course it was a love match!" Hannah protests.

"OK." Tess accepts.

Tess goes silent. This infuriates Hannah more than the row.

"I love him." Hannah insists.

"Yeah, course you do."

"I do!"

"Yeah, I believe you. All this arguing is probably my jealousy talking. I say Garry's dull but actually I want to rip off his pullover and rub lotion on his eczema."

"He's got a cream for that."

"Hubba hubba."

"You don't understand." Hannah says

"You're right I don't." Tess agrees.

"Well I can't stay here."

"No. That's what I was saying. You could have gone an hour ago and saved this row." Tess says.

"I can't stay with you anymore, not after what you've said."

"You can't stay here anymore because I won't let you."

"I can't believe my own sister...." Hannah is shocked that she's been treated so poorly.

"I can't believe my own sister is such a drama queen that she slags me off and somehow I'm in the wrong." Tess says.

"You called Garry boring." Hannah cries.

"Fuck off Hannah."

And to Tess' immense surprise she does.

Chapter 49

Tess is getting to work earlier and earlier. Partly to get some time to herself and partly because she gets so much more done when Arrabella isn't there. Despite a husband who works from home and a full time nanny, Arrabella has childcare issues so can not be in before 10 (despite the children starting school at 8-50) and has to leave by 4-30, therefore Tess can guarantee a few quiet hours to herself every day before she is forced to spend every day with a woman who sees Tess' bum being on a chair as a challenge. Being in so much earlier than Arrabella means that Tess has stopped providing her with a daily Starbucks. Whilst Arrabella could cope with a coffee that is a mere twenty minutes cold, she cannot put up with coffee (or what passes for it) that is nearly three hours cold. Arrabella is not happy about this new state of affairs.

"No coffee Tess?" Arrabella asks as she has done for the last few weeks.

This time Tess doesn't fold and nip out and buy her one (from her own pocket).

"No, no coffee," she pleasantly agrees.

"Oh lovely." Arrabella is playing to the crowd now, pretending to be put out to disguise the fact she really is put out. She's failed to notice that no one else is playing along as they are too consumed by embarrassment at this happening at all.

Tess can't be bothered to play along. "Well how thirsty are you? Were you really waiting till you got in at (checks watch) 10-45 before you had a drink?"

She sees Will and Uta smother laughs and become incredibly interested by their emails. Arrabella raises her eyebrows. She's not used to losing the upper hand. Tess presumes she is going to be killed. The reality is actually a lot more embarrassing.

Arrabella reaches under her desk and pulls out her handbag, she rummages in it and produces a ten pound note which she proffers to Tess.

"Frappuccino please Tess. Quick as you can."
Tess hand reaches out automatically and takes the payment. More out of shock that Arrabella is intending to pay for her own coffee. Then sheer impudence takes over and she puts the money down on her desk. Everyone is looking at Tess as though she's mad, Tess isn't mad but she doesn't really know where she's going with this. Will could stop this but he's watching the scene with as much interest as everyone else. Tess finally speaks:
"I'll go in half an hour. There's some things I need to do first."
"Fine," says Arrabella.
They both claim it as a victory but it is something of a watershed.

On her arrival home she is greeted by an enormous bunch of flowers. Which makes a change from being greeted by an enormous pregnant lady. They are from Garry. The card simply says 'thank you'.
Tess puts the flowers in the bin. She knows that Hannah will have gone home as she didn't have any other options. She hasn't returned out of love for Garry (she is willing to concede that there is love for the boys) but she also knows that this will be spun in Hannah's favour. That she couldn't live without Garry, that time apart made their love stronger. That they couldn't live without each other. She prepares herself for a Christmas present of a giant canvas of them snogging.

She goes in to her empty flat and puts the kettle on. Then she starts to clean and scrubs away every trace of Hannah.

Chapter 50

After nights and nights of sitting in silence, eating in silence and then going to bed separately, and yes in silence, Daisy and Simon are trying to talk. And to not have that talk descend in to a row. Simon is still monumentally pissed off and Daisy, sick of being cast as the bad one, has joined him in the strop. They are both aware that this needs to come to an end. They just don't know what the end is yet.

Daisy finally speaks, "Sometimes I feel very, very alone. I got married so I didn't have to be alone."
Simon looks like he's just been told that Father Christmas isn't real. "You married me so you didn't have to be alone?"
Daisy sighs, nothing she says comes out right. "I married you because I couldn't imagine doing anything else with my life. Because I was wildly and passionately in love with you and I was so proud to be your wife and I couldn't imagine that changing. But it has. I always thought single people were lying when they said they were happy on their own, I thought they were fooling themselves but now I don't see how it could be any worse than being lonely with someone."
"I'm sorry if I've made you feel like that. If it's any comfort I love you as much today, if not more than I did on our wedding day, and I didn't think that was possible." Simon is sincere.
Daisy's eyes fill with tears. But Simon continues, "But it's not my job to make you happy all the time. The only options aren't happy and unhappy. No one is either of those 100% of the time. And you're not the only one in this relationship that matters. Have you given any thought to how this has affected me? If I have to make you happy, don't you have to make me happy?"
Daisy tries to explain, "You always seemed so content. That you had no more ambitions for us. That we just were. And I know, I

know, you'll say 'why didn't I say something'. Well I think I was stuck in there too and then Kyle came along and I used him as a catalyst to shake things up. I was wrong and I am sorry. You have to believe me, there is nothing between Kyle and me. Whatever it was was only in my head and I treated you badly and I am sorry."

"You keep saying that." Simon isn't going to let it be that easy.

"I mean it. But I'm not going to keep saying it. You have to forgive me or we have to make a decision. Either this is worth saving or it's not but I can't keep being punished for this and we can't live in this mess. We sort it out or we decide it can't be fixed."

"Seems very drastic for something that didn't even happen." Simon reasons.

"Well I'm pleased you accept my point but it's fairly symptomatic don't you think? I think we've been taking each other for granted for too long. We need to decide whether we're together because we're married or if we're together because we want to be. Either way we need to sort it out." Daisy has tears streaming down her cheeks but her voice is steady. "I love you Simon. But I'm not going to stay like this. I'm with you because I want to be with you, I don't want anyone else. But if you don't want me then I value myself enough to leave."

Simon doesn't respond. Then he looks up. "I love you. And I've never stopped. Perhaps I've been a bit slack lately. Getting my head around how this all translates in to all this... well it's going to take some doing. But we've got a good thing and I think we need to work on it a bit more."

He holds his arms out and Daisy walks in to them and they enjoy an incredibly awkward hug. The old rhythms of their marriage gone. Neither sure of the boundaries and neither sure what is next. But both clinging on to each other for dear life.

Chapter 51

Will gasps in horror. He tries to smother it but Tess clearly hears him gasp out loud.

"You have to help me," says the oompa loompa previously know as Tess.

"What happened?" he asks.

"I got a fake tan at this place that Gillian at work recommended. And I'm orange. Not bronzed. Orange. She said it would develop over time and I fell asleep and I woke up and I'm tangoed. Tilly's going to kill me."

"What's the green slime?" Will is confused, Tess is completed naked, bar a shower cap. This should be strangely erotic but she is tangerine and looks like something out of Ghostbusters.

"Fairy liquid. You know, when you dye your hair and it goes wrong if you wash it with Fairy liquid then it strips some of the colour." Tess explains.

"Are you bleeding?" Will questions.

"I got a bit carried away with scrubbing."

Will laughs. After a moment so does Tess but there is a slight air of hysteria.

"I'm going to have to call Tilly and warn her." She says.

She does and within an hour Daisy and Tilly are round with moisturising bath products and exfoliators. Every hour on the hour she showers and scrubs and then is moisturised to within an inch of her life.

"This is certainly one way to take my mind off the stress of an imminent wedding," says Tilly.

"I'm going to go," says Will. "I know I am in touch with my feminine side but this is ridiculous." He kisses the girls goodbye and says he's looking forward to seeing them in all their glory on the wedding day. Then he kisses the tangerine dream goodbye and says he'll think of her every time he looks at a belisha beacon. She kicks him up the arse.

Chapter 52

"I got twenty four hours to go, I got twenty four hours to go. I got something la la la and I'm wearing a big bra I've got twenty four hours before I have to go," Tilly sings whilst doing some slightly strange hand moves.

"What are you doing?" Daisy questions.

"Hang on." Tess is muttering the words to herself, then suddenly high fives Tilly. "So Solid crew! I got twenty-four hours to go. " She joins in the singing with Tilly. Daisy looks like she wants to die. It is 7-30 on the day before the wedding and the girls are up bright and early. They have a lot to achieve before Tilly becomes a Mrs. The first step was to shower Tess and exfoliate her quite severely this morning. She is still quite a peculiar shade and now has a few red scratches on her where Tilly got carried away with the body puff. Their day will be one of picking things up (including the wedding dress – Tess is not allowed anywhere near it), beautifying themselves and making sure Tilly has everything she needs.

Daisy is unsure that her hair is right. They had had hair trials weeks ago where their hair was twisted in to complicated arrangements on top of their heads and secured with a plethora of hair pins. At this trial Daisy had become convinced that her face was unnaturally long and she looked like a horse. Despite everyone telling her she was being ridiculous she had gone to the hairdressers and had a fringe cut in. She had been right, it suited her and it did look lovely when her hair was put up. Now three weeks later it has grown and is grazing her eyes, she constantly pushes it back which means it divides in the middle and has changed the look of her hair. The girls have told her to go and have a fringe trim but she's never found the time and now it's the day before the wedding. She's hoping that she'll find a break in today somewhere to nip in and get it done.

Tilly is remarkably calm. She has reached the point where she knows there is nothing more she can really do. She's not quite sure how everything will work tomorrow but everyone seems confident it will all come together on the day. Besides how wrong can it go? All she really wants to do is marry Simon. If the flowers don't turn up then they won't have flowers, if the best man's speech is awful then they'll have a memory. She and the bridesmaids are staying at the venue tonight so there won't be any getting to the church on time dramas. Not least because there's not a church. The only slight fly in the ointment is her dad, for reasons she can't quite remember she caved and he is walking her down the aisle. Quite why he is doing this is beyond her. He buggered off when she was three and hasn't been around since, why he thinks that one walk of ten metres is more of a fatherly duty than actually raising her she's not sure but she can spend 30 seconds pretending to like him. She's vetoed him doing a speech on the grounds that he'd have to make most of it up.

The day goes swimmingly. Tess fades a little and they are sure that a couple more washes will mean people won't mistake her for Pedro Orange. After lunch they head to the manicurist where they all have their nails shaped and polished. Daisy is done first and when she's finished she says she is going to nip to the loo. Tilly and Tess, deeply engrossed in OK magazine, simply nod their agreements. Tess is done next and it's only when she is finished that she realises Daisy hasn't come back. As Tilly settles herself in to the chair Tess tells her she's going to check on Daisy.

"Daisy?" Tess can hear sobbing. "Daisy what's wrong? Has Simon called?"

The lock on the cubicle is drawn back. Tess stares directly in to the eyes of a simpleton. It takes her a second to realise that it's Daisy.

"What have you done?" Tess gasps and then starts to giggle. Daisy continues to cry and Tess hugs her whilst trying to get her laughter under control.

Daisy has cut her fringe. It is now about an inch and a half long and hits exactly mid forehead. Apart from the few random bits which are vertical.

"My fringe kept annoying me when I was getting my nails done and I couldn't push it back because my nails were wet. I knew we wouldn't have time to go to a hairdressers then I saw the scissors on the side so I thought I'd trim it myself. But it was really bouncy so I thought I'd wet it, then I pulled it down to cut it."

"You pulled it down?" Tess' eyes widen in horror.

Daisy nods sadly. "Then as it dried it sprung back up and now it's this!" Daisy gestures to her head. Due to the high nature of her fringe she looks constantly surprised. The surprised top half of her head is in direct contrast to the desolate lower half.

"Tilly's going to kill me."

"She is." Tess agrees "Lets try damping it down again."

Ten minutes later they emerge to face the wrath of Tilly. Holding Daisy under the hand drier whilst Tess held her fringe taught has had some effect but the look is still slightly Peggy from Hi-de-Hi. They walk down the stairs ready for Tilly to kill Daisy.

Tilly takes one look at Daisy and starts to laugh, and she can't stop.

"What have you done? Oh Daisy, you look....insane," she gasps.

"I'm sorry." Daisy apologises.

"I bet you are! So tomorrow I have one oompa loompa and Jim Carey in dumb and dumber assisting me in my duties. Where did you get the scissors?" Tilly asks.

"I found them on the side." Daisy replies.

"You used my scissors?" The manicurist, who up until now has been gushing over Tilly and the girls suddenly turns on Daisy. "Why did you take my scissors? Do you have any idea how much they cost? They're not for cutting hair."
"Sorry... I... didn't think. Can they be sterilised?"
"Of course they can be, I do between every treatment, what kind of place do you think I'm running here. They are not for hair cutting, you've probably blunted them. You're paying for them." The manicurist says angrily.
"Oh don't be ridiculous, I won't have blunted them after one hair cut."

Daisy is not going to pay for this haircut.

"Daisy I don't think you've got a leg to stand on, you took her scissors without asking." Tilly tries to calm the situation.
"I am not paying." Daisy says.
Tess, ever the peace keeper tries to intervene. "Fine I'll pay. Then can we go?"
"You're not paying either." Says Daisy.
The manicurist squares up to Daisy. "You're a bitch."
This has descended quite rapidly. They hardly know what is happening when the manicurist shoves Daisy, Daisy is about to swing for her when Tilly grabs her round the waist and bundles her out the shop. Tess reaches in to her bag and leaves a handful of notes on the side then joins the others where they run for a couple of streets until they think they are safe.
"Well that went well," says Tilly.

Chapter 53

They have regressed. With the dramas of the day firmly behind them they can finally relax. Three women (they'll call themselves girls but are well aware that that ship has sailed). Women with jobs, mortgages and responsibilities. Modern women, women in control of their lives and destinies in a very Oprah Winfrey way. Put them in a hotel room with a big white dress in the corner and they turn in to thirteen year olds at a sleepover. Tess is still slightly more glowing than usual but one more shower should fix that. Daisy has a pair of tights on her forehead. Flattening her fringe. They hope the hairdresser can sort it out tomorrow. They are in pyjamas, the carpet is littered with the remains of the picnic they had for dinner. They'll clear it away at some point but they've not quite finished picking yet. Tilly is doubled over laughing. Tears streaming down her face, Daisy is laughing; partly at the situation but mainly at Tilly's reaction to it. Tess is pretending to be offended but she keeps breaking in to a broad giggling grin which ruins the effect somewhat.

"Say it again, say it again." Tilly begs.
Tess obliges. All the etiquette books say that everyone should do what the bride wants.
"Bullonj."
The three of them dissolve in to giggles again. Daisy attempts to be helpful.
"Say blanc." She requests.
"Blanc." Tess obliges.
"Say mange." Daisy coaches.
"Mange."
"Blancmange."
"Bullonj." Tess stutters out

All three collapses in hysterics.

"How have I known you for this long and never known you were so special?" asks Daisy.

"One word! I can't say one word! It's not like it comes up a lot. At least I never thought that Swaziland was a made up place like Timbuktu. Both places Daisy." Says Tess pointedly.

"We're lucky you know." Daisy suddenly gets profound.

"We are," Tilly happily agrees. Tilly is in love with the world right now.

"I mean how long have we known each other? And look at what we've been through and we're always there for one another. Not many people have that."

"We are. I love you both." Unusually it's Tess who says this and it is her declaration that pushes them all over the edge. They hug and sob and then laugh at themselves. They all fall asleep in the same bed. Ready for the day ahead.

Chapter 54

As predicted the day is beautiful. Tilly has never looked more stunning. Daisy and Tess look great, Stuart looks dashing and the ceremony is touching, intimate and beautiful. They all pose for photos and not a single smile is forced, they are all on a high of this beautiful occasion.

At the reception the meal is sumptuous, the speeches witty and mercifully short and the wine free flowing. Nothing can bring them down.

"The problem with you single girls is that you keep expecting a handsome prince on a dashing white horse to come sweeping over the horizon and solve all your problems. It doesn't work like that. It's give and take. Sometimes you have to settle. "

"Is that what you did?" Oh Tess knows it's not big and it's not clever but she is sick of being given life advice by people with lives less desirable than her own. She's trapped next to some old woman who is giving Tess the benefit of her experience.

"Me and Alan? Oh no we were a love match and no mistake." Luckily Tess seems to be sitting next to a woman who is oblivious not only to social niceties but also insults. "But it doesn't always work like that. Me and Alan were twenty. That was nearly forty five years ago now and he still makes my heart beat faster. But you don't always get that. Especially not at your age dear, babies are better when you're young."

"Well there you go." Tess says.

Oh and still she carries on. "You think time is on your side but it's not you know. I had both of mine by 25." The woman says.

"Lovely."

"And now I'm a Grandmother. Rachel's got two and my Alison's got three!"

"And what do they do?" Tess asks.

"Who?" The woman is thrown.

"Alison and Rachel."

"Well they're mothers. Hardest job in the world."

Tess looks around for Tilly. This mad bat is clearly related to her in one way or another, therefore she owes it to Tess to get her away from her before the woman is launched head first in to the cake.

"Well I'm very pleased that they're happy with their choices. Just as I am happy with mine." Tess says. Trying to draw the conversation to a close.

"You say that now."

"I do. I do say that now."

"You'll change your mind."

"And perhaps Alison and Rachel will change theirs."

Finally the mad woman understands. She fixes Tess with a piercing gaze. She plays the trump card.

"There's no love in the world like the love of a mother. You don't know love until you have a child."

"I bet Rose West said the same thing. Well it was lovely to meet you," lies Tess.

Tess stands up and walks off to go to the loos but is interrupted by Will who diverts her to the bar where she leans heavily against one of the ornate pillars.

Will passes her a glass of champagne. Tess is looking good. She never normally puts her hair up as she insists it makes her look like Bet Lynch. Tonight it is arranged on her head in a manner which would suggest it was achieved effortlessly but Will knew it had taken around three quarters of an hour. To compensate for the complexity of the hair her bridesmaid dress is stunningly simply. She looks elegant and beautiful. As does Daisy. Tilly allowing them to chose their own dresses had meant they had both played to their strengths and both looked breath taking.

"What's happened?" he asks. Tess was normally in her element at things like this. She could chat to strangers about any kind of rubbish and was fine talking to random old family relatives. So far today she'd been a top class bridesmaid, simultaneously calming Tilly down, chivvying Daisy (who was convinced her dress was too low cut, it wasn't, she looked fantastic) and complimenting Stuart's mother on her 'jazzy' earrings. Now however the darling socialite was replaced with the Sultan of Doom.

"That bitch over there." Tess gestured with her champagne glass. Will looked. All he could see was a rather sweet old lady attempting to eat a satay prawn without impaling herself on the wooden skewer.

"Her?" he asks.

"Yeah, don't be fooled by the cuddly exterior. She's an utter cow. She thinks I'm a barren old whore incapable of love."

"Wow you covered some ground. How long were you talking to her for?" Will questions.

"Too long. What is it about strangers that they think they've got a right to comment on my life."

"Don't we spend our lives commenting on other people's lives?"

"That's different." Tess disagrees.

It seems to Tess that every time she disagrees with Will or says she doesn't want to do anything then he blames it on the depression. The speeches have just finished and they've been asked to vacate the ballroom whilst the staff turn it around for the evening part of the reception. Will and Tess are sat outside on some steps making the most of the lull in bridesmaids' duties.

"Yeah?" Will says. This is obviously a conclusion to something rather than a random interjection.

"Sorry?" she asks.

"I was saying this is a great venue for a wedding. So much space and although there's other stuff going on you don't feel over looked. And it must be nice when there are not events on too. You could easily bring the kids here. You can imagine us having a picnic by the lake whilst they play in the woods."

"Do we know these children or are you suggesting some sort of Hindley/Brady situation?" Tess asks.

"Our children."

"Will." Tess is weary, she's not sure she can have this conversation again.

"Oh I know, I know. But I'm talking about way down the line, when you're better, we know where we're going and the tablets have worked their magic"

"I don't want children. I am taking the tablets to be me again not to turn me in to some automaton who agrees with everything you say." Tess says.

"I just think when you're happier you might see things a bit more normally." Will presses.

"I think the problem is that you think I need to be cured."

"I want you to be happy." Will says.

"No. You want me to be different. I'm still going to be me after all this. All the things that were there before are still going to be there. I'm not going to change."

"I just think"... Will starts to explain but Tess interrupts.

"I want you to take a pill to make you not want kids."

"Now you're being ridiculous." Will sighs.

"Would you take it?" Tess isn't going to let it drop.

"No." he says indignantly.

"Why not?" she asks.

"I want children and..."

"And?" Tess prompts.

"Nothing."

"Say it."

"People are looking."

"No they're not. Say it."

"It'll come out wrong." Will doesn't want to end the sentence so Tess does it for him.

"Wanting them is more valid than not wanting them."

"I didn't say that." Will is confident that that he hasn't said anything incriminating. Tess however can see that this is the end game so decides to keep going.

"You think it." She says.

Will gives in "You make it sound like a crime. Look around you Tess. Child. Child. Child. Pregnant lady. Couple. We're at a wedding Tess, this is perfectly normal. Stop judging them for wanting what they want. Stop making me out to be the weirdo. We're a society we have to procreate to survive. It's biological."

"So I'm the weirdo. Thanks. You know I feel like that every day. I didn't think you thought it about me too." Tess sulks.

"Sorry am I meant to feel sorry for you?" Will has now joined Tess on recognising that this is the end. There's no way back from this so they may as well state their cases as well as they can. "Either you think they've got a point or you don't. If you think they are not normal then you don't care what they think. Maybe you care because they've hit a nerve?"

"Or maybe I respect their decisions and would like a bit of the same respect." Tess says.

It's a blessed relief when a relative of Tilly's comes to speak to them. Sadly it's the mad old woman from earlier. Tess assumes that they actually have a huge amount in common so mutters something about checking on Tilly and wanders away.

She has a look for Tilly and sees her in a quiet corner with Stuart. They are gazing in to each other's eyes, oblivious to everyone else and murmuring sweet nothings to one another. Despite Tess having shoved Tilly's boobs in to a strapless bra this morning and helped her to the toilet several times over the course of the day (big dress) this is strangely the most intimate thing Tess has seen at this wedding. It's such a private, tender, meaningful moment that she blushes and turns away.

Walking through the venue she sees Daisy and Simon sat under a tree talking. Their body language reflects the fact that they are two people who have known and loved one another for a long time but have lost their way slightly. Although they clearly have a long way to go Tess knows that they will find their way back. She thinks about her friends and their relationships and her stomach turns over. She realises that it's not jealousy but hope. "That," she thinks. "I'll settle for that and nothing less."

She figures she has about half an hour before any one notices she's gone. Now she needs to be somewhere where no one will find her. She disregards all the usual haunts, the loos, the conservatory and that is why Matt finds her climbing a tree in a bridesmaid dress.

The first Tess knows about his presence is when she feels two firm hands on her bum pushing her in to a tree. She turns round in shock but finds herself propelled towards the lower branches. She settles herself and despite wanting to be alone isn't put out at all when Matt clambers on next to her.

Inevitably, he reaches in to his pocket for his ever-present packet of cigarettes and lights up. She had forgotten he was going to be here for the evening do. But before she can start with the pleasantries, Matt begins to speak.

"You need to stop trying to please everyone Tess," says Matt. "Hannah, Will, Daisy, Tess, your parents."

Tess and Matt watch as Tilly and Stuart mingle on the other side of the lake. People constantly come up and congratulate them and hug them

Matt continues, "Even Arrabella."

Tess snorts.

"You can laugh," continues Matt. "But it's true. You dance around that lunatic. Anyone who thought anything of themselves would have told her where to go years ago."

"It's my job." She protests.

"No, no it's not. And it's not your job to pander to her. Or keep your parents happy. Or do what other people think you should do. The only person you have to please is yourself and you're

the one person you're failing."
Tess looks at him. He's completely right. She even tries to please people she doesn't know. Living the kind of life she 'should'.
"Aren't you tired Tess." He asks.

Tess doesn't answer but continues to look out across the lake.
"I envy them," Tess says eventually
"Really? Never thought you were the Princess for a day type. Will has changed you young lady." Matt says.
"Oh shut up. I don't want that... I'd like to make a choice that people celebrate and are delighted by. Not question and are convinced I'm lying about."
"Oh boo freaking hoo. Your life is fine. The only person who's got a problem with it is you. I hate to break it to you but people don't really think about you all that much." Matt passes Tess his cigarette and she takes a drag and exhales slowly.
"I'm a twenty eight year old bridesmaid sat in a tree, hiding from my boyfriend who wants to marry me, smoking whilst taking pills to stop me losing it."
"If I haven't said so before: you're a catch." Matt comments.
Tess smiles and takes another drag.
"OK." Matt removes the cigarette from Tess' hand, as she shows no sign of sharing nicely. He takes a drag himself. "Grief woman are you incapable of smoking without butt licking the stupid fag." He pauses, then continues, "I heard it. Anyway. Picture the scene, actually you don't have to. We have a perfect example for us right here, how convenient. Look at this scene." He gestures to the wedding unfolding across the lake. "But it's you in the white dress or whatever you choose to wear. But the point is this: you've just committed to someone for the rest of your life. You're now a Mrs."
Tess shivers. It's barely perceptible but Matt picks up on it.
"See. This isn't for you. What's your problem?"

"I don't want this. But it would be nice to not have to constantly defend not wanting this and have people feel sorry for you. I want to be celebrated. I want to matter." Tess says.

"You matter." Matt confirms. His voice is certain.

"Really? Because I feel like a massive failure. Like I'm wired wrongly. Like I don't fit in."

"Is this what dating Will is all about?"

"No. I like him, I just..."

"Don't want to be in a relationship," Matt concludes. "So don't be. No one's a winner in this situation. You're not happy and I hate to break it to you but if you don't want to be in it then you're not being fair to Will. He adores you and he's willing to put up a great deal of shit for you. Which would be fine if you were willing to do that for him but you're not. You're using him and you shouldn't."

"I love him. It's just not enough. If I can't be happy with him then it's not going to work with anyone." Tess protests.

"My point exactly." Matt says.

"Why am I not normal? Why don't I dream like everybody else. Everyone else is singing the same tune and I'm crashing away on a cymbal in the corner. "

"Maybe you're dreaming the harmonies." Matt replies.

Tess looks at him in astonishment. She's never heard anything so unlike Matt. "Which Disney book did you get that from?"

"Listen to me. Normal is only normal if there's a contrast. That's what you're doing."

"So I get to make everyone else's lives look better. Brilliant. How kind of me. Why me?" she asks.

"Why not you? Now. Are you going to get on with it? Or are you going to join everyone else and be unhappy." Matt asks.

"Not really a choice is it?" she replies.

"Not really." Matt is upbeat. "So where do you go from here?"

"Well let's see. One boss hates me and I think I am on the verge of a disciplinary for not getting her a coffee and I'm shagging the other one and am about to dump him. So I'd imagine there's a new job on the horizon."

"Well done."

"I thank you. But that's all for another day. Today I am going to enjoy my friend's wedding and my last night in a relationship and at some point apologise to Tilly for dating her wedding photos when they were only taken two hours ago." Tess lays out her plan with confidence.

"See even though you don't understand their choices you're supporting them, you're a beacon of hope and tolerance. One day you'll gain the same respect yourself." Matt says.

Tess swings out of the tree. "Just adding a bit of contrast to the bigger picture."

"And you're OK with that?" Matt jumps down next to her.

"I will be. Everyone else can sort themselves out."

Thanks

Thank you to all my friends and family who have supported me through writing this book.
Huge thanks to Jane Fallon for mentoring me and being an amazing sounding board and support.
Thanks to Marie Claire magazine for matching us up!
Thanks to Emily Sleep for proof reading and pointing out wild inconsistencies.
Thanks to Chloe Dymott for the amazing cover art.

Huge thanks to my Mum and Dad and family for everything.

And finally thanks to the 'Ladies'.

Printed in Great Britain
by Amazon